# MOBILE WAS A CATHOLIC TOWN

## A Novel

Bruce Colbert

Mobile Was a Catholic Town
Copyright ©2020 Bruce Colbert

ISBN- 978-1-7333822-5-0

Published by:

Blue Jade Press, LLC

Blue Jade Press, LLC
Vineland, NJ 08360
www.bluejadepress.com

"God is foolish at times, but at least He's a gentleman."

*Sanctuary*, William Faulkner

# Chapter 1

I was raised by my parents in a run-down frame house in a coal town in northern Pennsylvania. They were poor and my father was a callous man who spent his time drinking and creating trepidation in the home.

As an infant, I would lie quietly in my crib amidst milk-scented blankets at night dreading my father's unwelcome footsteps indicating his impending arrival. His incessant teasing was drunken and macabre, and his laugh harsh and hurtful, troubling my small and unformed brain. I would listen for his hard boots on the wooden floor, always fearful of his appearance. The floorboards seemed to creak with a sense of doom with each step. I don't think I ever smiled at him, even after I had started to walk.

By the time I could stand upright in the hand-me-down crib in the back bedroom, I was able to embrace a rather strange solace. I didn't know who they were, but it was a sort of life reprieve, brought to me by others. It was a generous gift, actually.

Who came to me then? It wasn't my mother or even my saintly grandmother, or the others who would periodically stop by to see the first grandchild in the family. No, those who came to me at night, gave me hope as they stood around my white crib in darkness. They used wonderful comforting words when they spoke and occasionally touched my flushed child's face with affection.

I remember them very well. They would stand clustered in a semi-circle at the crib wrapping around it as though protecting me. They would laugh and murmur among themselves and make those same sounds of cooing that children do before they learn a language.

Hours would pass during those darkest of nights with them, and sometimes as they whispered, I could hear my father's drunken snoring. When he was really knocked-down drunk, it was the loudest, shaking the narrow hallway with its

1

reverberations.  With little success, I would try to cover my ears with my small hands to keep the noise out.

I considered my nocturnal visitors as my friends before I knew what the word meant.  I never knew what to call them or what they called themselves.  I don't mean to say that they didn't have any names. They probably did, however they were unknown to me. I can't remember one of them ever speaking to the other using any name, or even some other familiar term of endearment like my mother often did with me.

My first year of life, I slept with the protection of my friends. I never knew what to call those indescribable beings: human, near human, apparitions, or possibly spirits, all who came to me from some unknown existence to visit, and offer succor. Sometimes I would sit straight up in the bed and talk to them. It came out more as babbling since I had yet to learn how to use proper words, however, with their understanding of infinity they would instinctively know what I was trying to convey. I think now that I'm a grown man, it was an inexplicable intervention from a part of the universe that I may never know, or understand for its mysterious origin, and that they simply reached down to a frightened child.

Many years later, before the final physical washed me out of naval flight school at Pensacola, I encountered them once again. During one of the clearest of afternoons in the Florida winter skies, I'd gone up in one of the trainer jets as the lone man in the cockpit. I was free to fly for an hour or two and could climb as high as I cared to, or as fast as I might push the sleek metal airplane. I lived to fly, and was a natural at the controls.

I had climbed to the far edge of the recommended altitude, but then pushed those heights even farther. I don't recall what the exact altitude reading was on the instrument panel, but the needle had rapidly moved into the red zone, and was now clearly approaching dangerous territory.

Gradually, I began to steer the fighter ever higher into sparkling blue skies and it brought a smile to my face as the speed of ascent quickly increased. I watched with a wary eye as the altimeter registered its ever changing needle readings, as the plane moved into the flimsy and transparent cumulus clouds, but that wasn't enough for me. I still needed more. I thought only of the mind boggling magnitude of the whole universe surrounding me, and how I was but an infinitesimal pin prick with little real significance.

The altitude had already exceeded fifty thousand feet and undaunted, I drove it higher to sixty thousand feet, then finally seventy thousand. At last we were on the outskirts of space, and I slowly aborted the steep climb then straightened out the aircraft.

Here in the anonymous silent stratosphere, there was a feeling that overcame me of ultimate clarity and vision instead of the lightheadedness that was to be expected. Cruising at seventy thousand feet, I had broken the fine line between the sky and outer space, and perhaps even the very constraints of time. All bets were off and anything was suddenly possible. Never before had my thoughts been so completely focused, my senses so keen, and a wave of serenity overtook me.

What seemed to be minutes, was merely an instant, as I prepared for a rapid descent. I took a last look at the scene before me and happened to see the reflection of someone sitting in the otherwise vacant navigator seat behind me. I could tell that he was a dark-haired man and was smiling at me. My first thought was how could he possibly get inside the aircraft, and why? My brain finally started registering what I was seeing and the shock jarred me acutely awake, while fright crept in at what was now happening to me.

I looked again and I recognized him immediately. His was the same familiar face from my distant childhood who was once savior to me. He was one of the kind and reassuring people who had surrounded my infant's crib, and had protected me. This very same man, who now nodded his head slightly toward me as tacit affirmation, quickly held up his hand to tell me there was no need for me to speak as all was well in this world of ours and perhaps the next.

He spoke softly to my conscious mind in a voice that I recognized from so long ago. He spoke of the time that I was a child, of how he had watched me as a baby in the crib, and what marvelous evenings we had passed together.

"We would come to watch you, and you were so aware. You would give us your child's smile, and we talked of many things," he said. "Do you remember the pony print on the wall? We brought it for you."

I told him that I did, and in the morning when they weren't around to cheer me, I'd look at it and laugh. It gave me great joy.

Our conversation lasted but a few seconds, and soon he was silent though continued to smile from the navigator's chair as he looked out the cockpit window into the openness of the heavens.

"I will come again, if ever you desire. You need only to wish it, or you can come to us. We are only out there, waiting." He motioned to the heavens outside the aircraft.

"Where?" I asked him.

"Past your imagination."

He told me of a place far beyond what I might understand of human consciousness and longing. It was another dimension with an immeasurable vastness of total understanding. He whispered its very name, but it was spoken in a language of which I had no knowledge and had never heard spoken. He talked of how all moments were the same, how they never came or went, though they existed in this interpretation of some separate forever.

There was so much I couldn't fathom, yet it seemed what he said would somehow be revealed.

As I looked at the instrument panel again, he put a hand on my shoulder with the same gentle touch you would expect from a friend, but as I turned in my seat, he had vanished. The only thing that remained was the confusion of my own crowded thoughts.

Quickly I adjusted the jet's position downward into a normal descent pattern, and as I broke through the scattered cloud cover, I spotted the asphalt runways of the naval station airfield directly below me. I heard the resonant voice of the tower air traffic controller who slowly noted my reentry into the Pensacola air corridor.

A gravelly voice abruptly came through my earphones.

"We had you on the radar and then you disappeared. Poof! Where the hell did you go? Outer space?" There was a loud belly laugh following his apparently amusing comment.

Weeks later, I was talking to an older carrier squadron commander over drinks late on a rainy evening while we were impatiently waiting for a hurricane to make landfall. He had guffawed at the seeming absurdity of what I told him about that flight. I had only mentioned seeing the strange apparition in the airplane's second seat, not that it was a face I knew from my infancy or that we had talked openly, but he had nodded his head knowingly.

"Yeah," he said with a serious look on his chiseled face, "you sometimes see things at high altitudes. Things you can't explain. I know I have. Look, I've seen the face of God." After he said that, he laughed nervously, and I didn't quite know whether to believe him or not.

For a moment he stared blankly at his watery drink. Then he glanced up at me ready to say more though he didn't, but looked at me with what looked like a subdued smile. He didn't say anything more about the unexplained experience he had in the air, and the conversation moved to more familiar subjects about service life.

In another forty minutes Hurricane Isabel finally touched down a hundred miles farther south and caused much destruction.

# Chapter 2

Mobile was always a Catholic town. In a sense, it's a creole cousin to the French influence brought to the New World. Though truthfully in my mind, it wasn't really that at all.

There was a village on its outskirts, called Eight Mile, which at one point was no more than a dozen houses built right before the Civil War. An enclave, really. By some royal Vatican decree, or a simple fiat of the Alabama diocese, it was the nearest point from the downtown Roman Catholic Cathedral where a Protestant church might be found outside the old port city. Canon law of a sort.

Keep your ecumenical distance was the obvious inference from the Jesuit princes of the church. Those papist natives in Mobile celebrated their welcomed Lenten season with the same medieval gusto born of successful mass confessions, say of a Rheims, or Chartres cathedral, or even sybaritic Bologna. They christened it Mardi Gras, and New Orleans soon copied these frolics of the universal faith. Mobile, however, was the first to honor the feast of Fat Tuesday.

It wasn't Selma either, or even big city industrial Birmingham. It was more cultured, and in its own way nicely subdued, particularly when you ventured across the causeway to nearby windy Point Clear. The setback white frame houses on the Eastern Shore seem to remark, "We're really quite nice." St. Matthew's Episcopal Church at Point Clear might easily fit without much notice into Charlottesville's grassy horse-dotted hills but with a beach.

The Episcopal rector, a squat and affable man, who was long divorced, had been a chaplain at Yale. He had studied there and then became an associate at St. John the Divine Cathedral in Manhattan before he returned South.

He was a quite an accomplished seascape painter too, and several of his small oil canvases were set into gilded frames displayed in the church commons room. They reminded me of J.M.W. Turner's painting because of his portrayals of frightening ocean storms.

You could almost imagine the wet-faced, smooth-shaven and jowly Father John Burdette strapped with his chafing starched round collar to the crucifix shaped mast aboard the wooden ship as a typhoon blew him toward Dauphin Island and into the open sea. He was committed to his religion certainly, but also to his art.

In Mobile, you would see the old black ornate iron trellising on the second stories of the buildings that lined Government Street as you drove from the abandoned and forlorn docks that dotted the shore line. The whole place seemed alien to me and had a feeling of otherness to it when I first visited. It was a town that had once embraced the slave trade, in which I'm sure they had always willingly participated. That's what I believed the sunny day I arrived.

I went to Mobile to meet Etta's parents for the first time. She was the willowy, dark-haired daughter of a well-respected doctor and the oldest of five gangly, yet intelligent, children. They were all comfortably housed in one of the columned homes in elegant Spring Hill that was probably built in the twenties.

Etta's father grew up in New Orleans, in the Garden District. While he finished his medical training there, he met her mother at some cotillion party or other. Soon after, he hightailed it out of town to distant Mobile. His final rebellious gesture toward his own physician father who was a tyrant. Etta's paternal grandfather had been a famous surgeon in New Orleans and likewise taught at Tulane, so the medical attraction must have been passed on through the genes.

Her mother was the eldest of two sisters and her grandmother was still living, though now widowed. Her great uncle, who was much younger than her grandmother and once a government lawyer in Washington, had married a local girl and also resided in the Garden District.

7

I met Etta at Mardi Gras, as part of a group of would-be naval aviators from Pensacola who had come over for a weekend. We were a bunch of young, attractive men, and about to be commissioned as naval officers and pilots. I introduced myself to her: Tom Davis from Pennsylvania and she seemed interested in me as both a Navy pilot and a Northerner. Maybe I was just a Yankee to her, something exotic perhaps.

"You're a Yankee, but you're the most handsome one I've ever met, Lieutenant," Etta said to me as I asked her to dance for the first time. My face turned a crimson color, and I thanked her, albeit with some awkwardness.

"You dance well for a flyer," she said as we swung around the room. "Those that I've met before always step on my feet as if they were pedals on an airplane."

I just shook my head at her absurd conversation on the dance floor while my hand was on her small taut waist as we moved in a half circle.

"They do have pedals in the cockpit, don't they?" she asked, still persistent but already knowing the answer.

Finally, I said, "They do have pedals on those airplanes at the carnival. I've flown them." She smiled at me and put her head on my shoulder as the music slowed.

I slogged through much of the flight training without a hitch. I loved flying jets, and qualified on the new F14 fighters that were just delivered to the naval air force. Unfortunately, I had developed a genetic tremor that sometimes forced my hand to shake uncontrollably, so the doctors removed me from flight school because of it. They figured they would avoid having me crash into a carrier deck, or worse. The assistant flight school commandant had pleaded my case with Washington, though to no avail, as it simply flew in the face of Navy regulations.

I remained in the Navy as an ensign. They later transferred me to far less glamorous tasks while my former pilot companions joined the carrier fleets. I shuffled papers at the naval flight school, first as an adjutant to the commander. I spent more and more time in Mobile simply because Pensacola was a dull service town and I had wanted to escape what I thought was my own failure.

After our dance was over, I asked Etta if she wanted to join me for some punch as it was good, spiked with enough bourbon to give it character.

"That's why I come to these ridiculous soirees," she whispered to me, putting her white-gloved arm inside mine.

"Lead on Macduff," Etta announced, and we moved as a couple toward the crowd of revelers who stood around the punch bowl laughing.

Etta had attended Tulane, as had both her parents. She tried to live in the city afterward, but the cloying family tug was far too great, so she had come back to Mobile. What I didn't learn until later was that she had quit Tulane in her sophomore year, and was hiding out somewhere in the French Quarter when the word came back to her parents. They subsequently sent the dean of the Saint Louis Cathedral along with one of his young priests to find her. They were to persuade her to return to Mobile to her parents and then return to school the following year.

The truth was she had been living with a street musician that she had met somewhere on Bourbon Street. They were drinking heavily each night and smoking the occasional joint, according to the report from a local girlfriend.

She came home from New Orleans for a while and then abruptly one night just left. Mercifully for the family, she went to her Aunt's home who lived on a large Mississippi plantation an hour outside of Memphis in Tunica. She stayed there quietly for two months. Afterward she moved into Memphis itself and roomed with a girlfriend who had also left Tulane. She worked in the upscale Overton Square neighborhood with restaurants and bars, which had recently opened, as a hostess and later a cocktail waitress. From what I

9

had heard, she had quite liked slinging burgers and beers. It wasn't the French Quarter, but it was lively for the otherwise Baptist and sleepy Memphis.

Etta loved horses and was a fine equestrian. As a young woman she had joined several of her girlfriends from female Bishop Toolen high school at the polo matches over in Point Clear. She would occasionally water tired horses and muck stalls, and enjoyed getting sweaty. She wore tight blue jeans and a shirt tied in a knot at the midriff with black shiny riding boots. Her long coal black hair hung down her shapely back in a loose ponytail.

So Etta readily found her way into the horsey circles in Memphis. She had started hanging out at the polo fields when she wasn't working in the bars. She was quick on the muscular ponies and often exercised them for Jack Halloran who owned the Germantown fields where the local matches were held. He had a jealous and broadening middle-aged wife, and he shamelessly lusted after a young Etta until she distanced herself from him.

Etta told me she eventually complied with her parent's wishes and completed her degree at Tuscaloosa before returning home to Mobile.

When I met her, Etta was always in a summer print sundress with her thick hair loose, down her back. She had beautiful black eyes that would welcome you and then tell you to go away all at once. It was uncanny. Her own mother wasn't beautiful; handsome may have been the right word, or even stately.

Yet Etta had a straighter nose and smoother arms from somewhere. She moved across the room like a ballet dancer while her mother, Minerva, looked as if she belonged on the golf course where she spent a great deal of time, while leaving the rearing of the children to several black women who had worked for the family for twenty years.

Her father was rather serious, more than even most doctors, and perhaps he had never laughed. He was also an author. He would spend his hours outside of Mercy Hospital writing civil war novels and lyric verse that he never published. He preferred to be alone as odd as it might seem for a man with a wife and five children. The man could easily be a ghost or a shadow in that large house. He would lock himself in his paneled study after the family dinner, which had all five children spread out at a mahogany table, and didn't emerge until he went to bed. Her mother would say goodnight to the children while he had great things to write and ponder.

He did have one slim poetry volume published. A friend of his was a literature professor at the University of Alabama, and he had leaned on the university press to release the book. It was a stream of consciousness narrative of dream sequences of a man who believes he had been a Confederate soldier. It was a present day character who re-lives all the former battles in his dream state, which her father clearly did.

Since I also wrote, he told me one evening while the two of us were drinking on the back terrace, about his most recent recollections of battle. There was the screaming, the smoke and rifle fire, and finally the haunting stony look of the dead. I finally read his poetry book, and it wasn't bad. At that time, I had been shocked that something so introspective had come out of this man next to me whom I could only describe as mildly tedious.

The doctor was raised as a part of the segregated South. He was a soft-spoken man, and I had never heard him use the word nigger as long as I knew him. His obvious breeding and intellectual superiority didn't require it. He treated Mobile and everyone around him benignly. The man lived much of his life hidden inside his own head.

For most of his immediate social interactions with the medical profession, the country club, the downtown cathedral, and his wide circle of friends, he simply imitated them. He was a mime who spoke, but he wasn't really like them at all; the doctor lived half his life in a parallel silence of his own thoughts.

Sometimes he talked to Etta about race, and spoke of the inevitability of their way of life disappearing. He told her things in Mobile and the rest of the South will change, it's coming. "It's already in the air, I can smell it."

Etta had no idea why he was telling her these things, and what she was supposed to do with that knowledge. It confused her.

"It won't happen in my lifetime. Negroes will still be the lower class," he said to her once when they would go into his dark office and den to have their serious father-daughter talks, maybe every six months. "Mark what I tell you now."

She typically did tell him what she thought and listened carefully to what he told her while slightly nodding in her acknowledgement of his sober words.

"Your brother may become a doctor, but you're still the smartest one in this family, a lot smarter than I am. You've got true wisdom, and yet you're only a girl," he pronounced slowly hanging on every other word. Then he touched his temple with his index finger tapping it once or twice.

During one of these conversations they had together, he had talked about war and how the Civil War had been so devastating to the South and later all the other wars.

"We are patriots," he told her though she was uncertain of his meaning, but then during the beginning of the Vietnam War, he acted rashly.

It was the beginning of 1967 after the US had been in Vietnam for a couple of years when he summarily announced to his wife that he was leaving his practice, her and the children, most of whom were small and clearly dependent, for six to eight months to serve as a combat surgeon in the jungle. He said it had come to him in a dream, like an urgent summons and that perhaps the call came from God. He didn't know, nor did he question the source, yet he would heed the call.

He wasn't a religious man, in fact, he rarely read the Bible, or paid attention to the Catholic mass as he sat with the

12

family in a Cathedral pew. Usually he closed his eyes sitting there on Sunday morning projecting himself elsewhere, so his decision came as quite the surprise.

Of course he didn't have to do it. He didn't even like the army. It wasn't from exaggerated patriotism either, because he had never spoken about the rightness of the cause in Southeast Asia. He had no politics.

Regardless, her father left one Tuesday morning and flew out of a military airfield in Texas with six other physicians, most of whom were half his age. They all would attempt to save the young boy soldiers who fought this unpopular war. Of the six surgeons sitting beside him on the C-130 cargo plane, one would be dead within two months, pulverized inside a bombed out field hospital and another burned badly by a mortar explosion.

The money to keep Etta's large family going would arrive every month from the government, although they also had ample investments in several Mobile banks. Her mother angrily accepted the unsavory decision of this man she hardly understood.

Etta was the oldest child and the one who had the clearest memory of her father leaving the house in a green army uniform; his grey hair longish under the leather band of an army beret, with his eyeglasses sliding down his ample nose as they usually did. She remembered touching the two silver bars of his captain's insignia, and hugging him goodbye. Etta was an already grown woman, well, nearly grown, and she cried when he got into the army van and drove away.

He hadn't told her to take care of her brother and sisters. He had just waved to the family assembled under the white porch columns, and soon he was gone.

She did remember her mother saying under her breath as he drove away, "What the hell's wrong with him? I have no idea." Then she lit a cigarette and disappeared into the house. Etta stood on the porch alone.

Etta watched the brown army van pass underneath the leafy oaks on her street, and could see her father sitting in the back seat by himself. The doctor seemed to have a smile on his face as he passed his neighbors' substantial homes.

He wasn't like any of the other fathers she knew. When he passed Judge Holt's house four doors down, the doctor seemed to turn his head slightly and press his narrow face to the window with curiosity although the lawn was empty of people. Even though it was a Saturday, the judge was elsewhere, probably on the golf course where he and his wife often joined her own mother. The doctor didn't play golf, and often told his wife that he required his solitude to write. With hidden irritation, she had reluctantly agreed because she was a Southern woman of an earlier generation who didn't dare complain. Everything emotional was suppressed, as that was what polite people did, at least in Mobile in those years.

The doctor was sent to Hawaii, and for two months he worked in a surgery for the worst of the wounded American soldiers coming out of the war. One day, however, he told his commander, a brigadier general, that he wanted to serve as a surgeon in Vietnam itself and was sent without fanfare to a small coastal city in the northern region of the fledgling southern democratic republic. It was the nearest enclave to the dividing line between both enemy armies, on the road to Hanoi.

He got off the transport plane at Hue. The doctor was driven away from the tarmac by an overly cautious young medic who kept looking down at the roadside as the jeep drove over what could be considered more of a dirt trail than an actual road.

Curious, the doctor asked the driver why he was looking down every ten seconds along the brushy side of the road. The young soldier confessed that two days earlier another medic with a jeep filled with airlifted medicines had been demolished by a land mine as it hugged the road shoulder avoiding the ruts deepened by the pounding monsoon rains.

The doctor had not responded one way or the other to the medic's comment though he had shaken his head slightly in acknowledgement. He simply looked out into the distant verdant countryside. Consequently, there was no further conversation between the two men.

Once there, he labored in a field surgery under a large tent canopy. The doctor patched up, and sometimes saved the lives of boys, mostly teenagers from farm and factory towns, and sometimes the big cities. They were the human fodder for this awful war. Yet, he never commented on the conflict.

In those eight months Etta's father had been away in Vietnam, he had written her mother two letters: one on the day of his arrival in the country and the other the day he left on an outbound Air America flight. Odd behavior for a writer. Occasionally on Saturday afternoons, there would be patched telephone calls from the States to the officers and men of the medical unit, however, he never bothered to request that the laborious connection be done to reach Mobile.

This was the same man I sat across from on the terrace of Etta's spacious family home with an iced bourbon and water she had made for each of us. For the first five minutes of our pained conversation, there were awkward jumps and starts, sometimes talking about the military, though mostly about the Gulf Coast. I started to discuss the war, but he didn't respond, so I dropped it. He never mentioned a word to me as long as I knew him about his experiences in Southeast Asia during that war. Etta told me he had said nothing to her or her mother either. I thought this unmitigated silence was rather strange at the time. It was the mark of a self-contained man.

I tried to sense an opening where I might get his attention, some familiar subject, but I continued to flounder after the first few moments of a new topic. He never encouraged me with a glance, or his demeanor. His face was unreadable.

Hurricanes became a subject I desperately appropriated. The doctor seemed to be comfortable describing the storms of the past thirty years. He named the ten worst turbulent landfalls and floods, and carefully earmarked the awful damage they had wrought. He particularly remembered those from his boyhood, and could easily name them, as well as the extent of the storm's wrath.

Until the ladies joined us, the subject of weather occupied our interest, or I should say, his. I cared little about the velocity of gale force winds when Hurricane Isaac made landfall in Galveston, and then moved eastwardly.

That summer evening as the sun had started to set, the doctor asked me if I had an interest in birds. I told him I found them a real joy in our natural world but confessed I knew only a few species of common birds like cardinals and sparrows from my boyhood in the coal town woods. That response brought a smile to his face, and he paused to reflect.

He asked me if I had looked at the master Audubon's precise drawings and watercolors of fauna, and added that his father had once owned a portfolio of the original drawings that he had purchased sometime in the thirties. It now rested in the collection of the New Orleans art museum he informed me with candor.

He showed no resentment that these same treasures hadn't been passed down to him to grace the walls of their otherwise lovely colonial home. It occurred to me at the time that the value of the original Audubon watercolors must be in the hundreds of thousands today which was a veritable fortune.

"I sometimes listen to bird songs, and their language becomes quite clear," her father offered.

Still he made no attempt to ask me about myself, or about my deepening relationship with his eldest daughter.

To break the proverbial ice, I took the initiative and talked about the wonderful evening when Etta and I had met at Mardi Gras. I told him how beautiful and vivacious his daughter was, the perfect Southern woman to my otherwise hungry eyes.

As I was speaking, he stared at me below a shock of wavy grey hair showing little interest, or even engagement. He only gave me the most perfunctory smile as if like some inquisitive schoolboy I had given him the right answer. He tapped his ample nose with two elegant fingers.

We came to a small period of silence when he rose and slowly turned to me. "Would you like me to refresh your drink?" he asked. I cautiously answered no.

Etta's mother came onto the terrace, and called out, "Are you boys having a good visit?" followed by her girlish giggle, a mannerism her daughter had inherited. "Oh yes," I volunteered, and the doctor smiled in accord.

Her mother liked to command the conversation and that was understandable considering her taciturn husband. Gradually during the warm night, her conversation went from the heat of the summer to sailing on the bay and ended with loose plans for a party of some sort for Etta's friends in the next day or two.

She would assemble their friends, the parents of Etta's school chums from the Catholic girl's school, and sorority sisters from Tuscaloosa who lived nearby. It would be a small festive gathering with no more than fifty at the very most. She started to verbally list the guests for her husband's approval, though he appeared to have little interest in whether they came to a garden party or not.

Because it was sultry in the summer on the Gulf, the guests wouldn't arrive for drinks and a light dinner until after eight when the sun had already set. She continued on with detailing the party plans for tomorrow evening as Etta sat next to me.

Etta put her arm on my leg and gave me a gentle pat in the midst of a quick eye-roll which seemed to mean, "You'll get through it, I promise." Etta held my hand only for an instant, so the intention we had with one another was clear to her parents.

"Mother can be a little too forceful sometimes, but she means well," Etta explained. "She grew up as the one in charge, and you'll see why when you meet her sister. Crazy as they come, but ever so sweet."

Minerva was a striking woman. She was a fashionable buxom lady with pageboy grey hair and so tall that she stood about two inches taller than her husband. The woman had the most winning of smiles and was loquacious to a fault, particularly on the topics that interested her which were mostly of family, the small society she followed around Mobile, and its rigid hierarchy.

One of her closest friends, Diana Kirby, was a direct descendent of the famous Confederate General Kirby Smith, who had been one of the more valiant warriors of the Civil War. Later, Diana's grandfather had been a longtime mayor of Mobile, holding office for almost a decade during the twenties and early thirties. Her husband Charles, who always could be found with a bourbon in his fist, had attended Harvard Law School and served as the managing partner of the family law firm.

Although the doctor's family had included surgeons and lawyers in its own illustrious New Orleans history, there had been a notable gap of those who commanded the glorious butternut clad troops against the unprincipled foe.

His people were a race of wily cotton merchants, and there might have even been a Sephardic Jew among them during those years that nobody claimed. They prospered with both sides of the conflict it seemed, and never left the comfort of their rambling Garden District home.

There had been unfounded rumors that they had entertained the commanding Union generals during the city's occupation though that was considered to have been only malicious gossip.

Diana Kirby was a singular fixture in Etta's home, and together with her mother ran charity programs for The Woman's Exchange. She also served on the board of the best Catholic schools, McGill and Bishop Toolen, where the sexes were divided according to the best traditional European academies.

Mobile, like New Orleans, boasted a unique Catholic elite unlike most of the South where the Episcopalians held sway with their Civil War era schools that had educated Jeb Stuart and Robert E. Lee, and all their women for generations. Those people sent their boys to Virginia or maybe north to Princeton, which was popular with Southerners, and the girls went to Mary Washington in the Tidewater, even from the Middle South. The children of those who had the land and political power on the Gulf did otherwise, and in New Orleans it meant Tulane.

For the same reasons, Etta's mother expected her to behave in a civilized fashion as most young women did in this segregated South. She did until the years in New Orleans had offered her its excesses, and jumped at the bait but that was over now, or so everyone believed. The next step would be the permanence of family, and right here where she should and would settle.

Her mother smiled coyly at me across the flagstones as Etta leaned affectionately on my shoulder. I could see Minerva clearly expected me to stay right here in Mobile, and write, or go into business, or maybe even get a law degree. We'd continue to join them on this same terrace on weekends, so assumptions were made and I hadn't pushed back.

"Do you like Mobile?" her mother asked me knowing that I would answer that I did. "It can be a very elegant place to live, don't you think?"

"Yes, it's a marvelous town. I'm drawn to it and to your daughter who makes me want to live anywhere, even on the moon."

"Stop it, silly!" Etta said laughingly and gently slapped my shoulder.

"Mother, don't put him in a position where he has to always agree with y'all," she told Minerva who only gave her a half smile in return.

"He can say what he wants." Minerva told her daughter, ending the banter.

But Mobile was a fine place. The family also had a cottage on the bay at Point Clear across the causeway, located a mile or two from the sleepy village of Fairhope. It was surrounded on two sides by large screened porches, and filled with ceiling fans. There were four small bedrooms for the five children divided neatly by age and sex.

Etta and her siblings were born in separate clusters. Etta was the oldest followed by her brother eighteen months later then her sister Mary Agnes. There was a hiatus for a few years and then her younger sisters Clara and Maggie were born.

Her brother was currently a student at the University of Alabama, and Mary Agnes was in her last year of high school, or had just started college, I can't recall. The younger girls were still in middle school.

That weekend I stayed with them as a guest, and the whole family drove over the causeway and spent a night in the beach house. It was pleasant enough. The house had a magnificent view of the bay. There were small sailboats to use, and a dock with a swim ladder where you could lower yourself down three small steps into the brown water that was colored by seven rivers that emptied into the bay.

Etta's mother had never swum in the bay as far back as Etta could remember. You would see her in a wide brimmed hat with a colored sundress and espadrilles, sitting in the shade watching the children with a cold drink in hand. That was Minerva.

If she wasn't there, she would be in the small kitchen making potato salad, or a light dinner like locally caught fish.

Etta's taciturn father sat in the living room in shorts and a Hawaiian shirt and read history books, or classical poets like Longfellow, or even Walt Whitman.

As peculiar as he seemed, if he wanted to, he could talk about almost any subject. He would bring to the conversation some piece of relevant knowledge about the place, or its people, or the past. The doctor knew all the forms of Gulf Coast wildlife, although he wasn't a fisherman anymore.

As a boy, he had fished most of the bayous in the entire Mississippi River Delta region as well as the outlying barrier islands with his young friends.

Horn Island was his favorite refuge which was eight miles off the mainland. He had camped there once or twice with the family many years ago but it was too remote and wild for Minerva, and there had been poisonous snakes. A water moccasin had been found in one of the children's tents, and the outdoor camping trips had abruptly ended.

One of his boyhood friends whom he still stayed in contact with, had become editor of the Times Picayune. On his visits, I would listen to tales of the city's legendary vice, and his own obsession with Huey Long who his own father before him had vigorously opposed. They had a personal history of animosity over many years with all the Longs. Russell Long, Huey's son was a seated U.S. Senator, and a familiar target for the editor's bile in both casual conversation and often in print.

The editor had been one of those friends from the doctor's Horn Island youth, and together they had published a book on the Brown Pelican that had its rookery on the island. The doctor supplied the book's photographs during the first five or six years that he had been married. He made about fifteen trips out to the island in those years to collect all the photos he would need for the book. He had a German Leica camera, which had belonged to his father who used it to photograph diseased organs as a resident in pathology.

Like his editor friend, Etta's father wasn't particularly fond of the Longs either. But in polite conversation, the doctor was always apolitical and ventured no opinions of any sort. But it was an incestuous past nevertheless. Another family friend, who was also a physician, had been the misguided and crazed man who drove to the Baton Rouge state house and had shot Huey Long to death.

Huey had just finished his last term as Louisiana governor and had won his recent senate seat. He had returned to Baton Rouge to instruct the new governor, whom he helped elect, on the nuances of that office, and was gunned down before occupying his Washington seat. That was the storied New Orleans of his remembrance.

On the beach Etta and I took one of the Sunfish sailboats out on the water and we had enough wind to make it interesting. We had tacked back and forth for almost two hours before we found a gust to let us sail back to the house. I had learned to sail in Pensacola, small boats at first, and then the larger yachts, so I didn't appear like a complete fool on the water in front of her parents whom I hoped to impress, but Etta wanted to be at the helm so I let her steer.

We caught a strong breeze and I realized that this winsome young woman could sail as well and even better than I could. We moved fast on the little craft, heeling dangerously with me holding onto the opposite rail to stay out of the bay as she aimed it straight for the dock. I was almost in the water, awkward and holding on desperately. Like a shot we headed for the grey wooden boards and around twenty yards in front of the small dock she shoved the rudder to the opposite side, coming about quickly and neatly. The rapid motion forced me backwards into the water.

It was an embarrassing dump overboard, and unexpected. I swallowed more of the fecund surf than I cared to but I could stand upright in the shallows. I kept coughing all along as I trudged to the small beach while she slid onto the sand, pulling up the keel with ease. I was on the beach dripping wet, but still managed a forlorn smile.

"I didn't know you could sail so well," I half shouted to her as she pulled the Sunfish up on a shell-covered sand dune. "Yep," she said to me smilingly.

"You get a lot of good things in this package," Etta threw out as she ran up to the house to get us two cold beers. As she ran, her body twisted and her figure looked like a painting in the fading sunset that cast a rich magenta color across the sky.

While I busied myself on the dock, I noticed her talking to her mother who seemed to be chastising her about the lack of lady-like behavior. Etta quickly threw her long dark hair around in an arc reaching into the cooler half buried in the sand for two bluish Busch beer cans then purposely marched down toward me on the beach.

Her younger sister, Mary Agnes, appeared with some young man who looked similar to most of the young men I had seen in Mobile of a certain class: rather clean cut, fit, and outfitted with an obvious set of fine casual manners. He introduced himself as Aaron while giving me a manly handshake with too much of a grip. After our introductions, he ran into the water for a shallow dive. In a moment he surfaced and beckoned Mary Agnes who dropped her shorts to reveal a bikini bottom then rushed out to meet him in the waist high water.

"Her current love interest," Etta said to me. "He's Jewish and goes to Tulane. His father has the big furniture store downtown." That was all the preamble I got as she sat in the warm water with her legs spread out.

"Mother doesn't like him because he's not one of her crowd. But it seems like a passing thing, so there's little to be said on the subject."
I simply smiled in response while nodding my head with acknowledgement.

23

"I've talked to him a couple of times. He's nice," she added, "and Mary Agnes says he's a great lover when he takes her on little jaunts over to New Orleans."

"Oh good," I said with some sarcasm she didn't miss.

As life would have it, she did marry him. They had a seemingly happy marriage that included very few arguments although before long, their world started to implode with a gale force.

Etta and I had been at his funeral. I could see his squat white-haired father stare every so often out of the side of his forward looking eyes at her mother wearing a black veil. He seemed to do this three or four times with his ever-hardening mouth during the service. It was no one's fault really. These things never are.

Perhaps everyone is complicit and yet nobody knew. The Jewish family had been a part of Mobile life since 1892. They had moved there from Brooklyn where they lived with their extended family. Within a few years of living down here, they had one of the finest modern furniture stores in the lower South, even rivaling Atlanta.

His parents had been against the marriage with Mary Agnes, though they were quite passive about the whole thing. I didn't realize they opposed the union until Aaron himself told me over cocktails one evening as the two of us sat on Etta's breezy terrace waiting for the rest of the family to join us.

Aaron dismissed what his father said to him as Yiddish melodrama, and told me he was tired of their desperate efforts to hold onto some vanished culture that they themselves had never actually followed. He didn't even have a damn Bar Mitzvah, Aaron joked to me.

"And if they ever have a Seder, they'd better find some real Jews to invite." He laughed at what he'd said, and shook his head from side-to-side with its absurdity.

That was as much as he ever uttered on any Jewish subject, and soon after he had said it that evening, everyone descended on the terrace and the topic was closed.

I liked Aaron. He was intelligent but perhaps I was biased in some way because he was a journalist, and we found common interests. Etta's own brother, Jackson, was a medical doctor, and though reasonably well rounded from his privileged family upbringing, he either talked about college sports or medicine and maybe the added conversation about Mardi Gras.

Jackson had an annoying habit of looking away as he invited you to continue in conversation. His attention span was painfully short, and maybe it was a habit of abruptly moving on to the next patient, I don't know.

Aaron was different, and I appreciated the rough and honest edge he had. He was a garrulous and self-deprecating man mostly, which her brother clearly wasn't. Aaron could take being the butt of almost any joke, and laugh the loudest. Jackson would never tell a funny story, as it wasn't in his nature, and bristled at any criticism.

After Tulane, Aaron worked for the Times-Picayune newspaper covering city politics and had been friendly with the Lawson family, who for a decade or more were the 'go-to' people in New Orleans for most anything. He knew the elder Lawson best, and later his son Maurice, or Rees, who were both popular Crescent city mayors.

During those first years he and Mary Agnes lived there, he had also rubbed shoulders with Carlos Marotta, and his unsavory people. Truthfully, Aaron wasn't comfortable with the friendship or marriage of convenience they seemed to have with the Lawsons and the mayor's office. At one point, Aaron had written a story on one of the questionable deals that reeked of collusion between the elder Lawson and Marotta but then there was an incident that he never quite explained, or even commented upon, and things changed for them in New Orleans seemingly for the better.

25

They had moved into a large handsome 1910 white frame house on Milan Street in the Garden District that Mary Agnes loved. Aaron had somehow found the hefty down payment, and they moved in during the early fall of the first year in the city. Since he was making around fifteen thousand dollars a year as a reporter, she assumed that his father had lent him the money.

Aaron said little, if anything about their family finances, and Mary Agnes had never broached the subject since life seemed fine as a traditional Southern girl imagined it should be. Shortly after they moved in, their daughter Rachel was born.

One day, Aaron was asked to meet with one of Marotta's capos and the mayor's events coordinator in some French Quarter bar. He had listened patiently to their plan to develop the seedy section at the end of Canal Street for a new National Football League stadium, which had yet to issue its stadium bond offering.

Four or five blocks of rundown businesses and three flat dwellings were being purchased after being included in a widespread condemnation of properties that failed to live up to the more restrictive city codes. The mayor's office had issued the order two months earlier. The evictions by police were beginning and none of the residents or commercial business owners had successfully protested the action. They were mostly pawn shops, ma and pa taverns and liquor stores, and the occasional convenience store.

The mayor's mouthpiece had said that widespread public knowledge of the eviction action was not to be expected, nor encouraged, and the editors of both the morning and afternoon daily newspapers were seemingly unaware of what was going on. Since this was essentially the beat where Aaron worked, the two men across the table expected no undue attention from him, or his pen, on this. It all came out in the form of a subtle threat, but since the mayor's man did all the talking, it didn't sound quite like one to his ears. Undoubtedly it clearly was.

One of Marotta's real estate companies had bought substantial properties in the forgotten neighborhood after receiving inside information on the NFL stadium location announcement. They were buying them for a nickel on a dollar, and expected to make eighty million dollars by the final groundbreaking ceremony for the lavish Superdome. In the end, they made a hundred million.

Everyone was satisfied with the progress of the football league expansion. The professional team would give New Orleans greatly increased national attention and bring in untold revenues from visitors and residents alike. They named the football team, the Saints, and used the ancient French flower symbol as their athletic brand. Even the Catholic diocese seemed to approve.

The mayor was suggesting that Aaron could help New Orleans by making certain no unpleasant or muckraking articles appear in print; certainly nothing about the behind-the-scenes purchases that would make a handful of men wealthy including the Lawson family and their closest associates, of which he was now included which was what the mayor's representative told him in carefully couched terms while playing the civic responsibility card.

Aaron listened closely and slowly sipped his bourbon. When they had finished, the men got up from the table. As Aaron attempted to rise with them, Marotta's man told him to finish his drink and stay put. The others were leaving, not him. It sounded like an order in a matter-of-fact tone. The mayor's top man shook his head in agreement.

Standing at the scarred table, Marotta's lieutenant reached into his vest pocket and pulled out an overstuffed white envelope. He placed it in front of Aaron.

"That's the first installment," he said with a crooked smile, "and there will be more."

"But I didn't agree to anything with your people," Aaron threw out at the Marotta messenger.

"I'm not the one you need to talk to. You need to tell the boss that and see what he says," and the man laughed. "He eats people like you for breakfast."

"Wait a damn minute," Aaron said, his anger mounting.

Marotta's man just held up his palm for Aaron to stop. "You came here because you knew what was going down, and now you're in," the husky suited man announced. "There's your money," he said motioning toward the envelope with his free hand.

With that, he turned and walked out of the bar without saying anything more, trailed by the Mayor's man who looked uncomfortable in his role as emissary.

Piecing together what he suspected had happened, Aaron reached across the damp tabletop and grabbed the white envelope, peering inside. There were twenty crisp five hundred dollar bills, ten thousand dollars in cash, shining and seemingly new from the bank.

It was perfectly clear to him what they wanted, but why him? He was so far down the chain of authority at the newspaper, though they had selected him as their point man for some obscure reason. They expected him to make certain nothing came out publicly about the hidden transactions, at least not until after the stadium municipal bond issue was launched and its construction started.

He sat there for another five minutes alone at the table as people started to parade inside and call for drinks at the bar. He stared at the envelope with the money.

What should he do? He could take this to the editor, or the managing editor who ran the paper and lay out to him what had occurred. Show him the money that they were trying to bribe him with because they gave it to him for his silence. They wanted to neutralize this thing before any attempt to dig into their activity was ever uncovered. Ballsy on their part, he reckoned, as he sat there with the now watery drink. They bet that he would take the money and help them. How much were they willing to pay? They didn't say, but this was the first indication of the generosity they would show him.

Marotta would make a fortune from the deal, and they could easily afford fifty thousand, or even a hundred. That would change his entire life and make it so much easier and comfortable for them to live in the expensive and exciting city. They could get out of that lousy walkup apartment where they were living and move into a vintage home. Mary Agnes would love having a sweet Garden District address a block off St. Charles.

That day Carlos Marotta had become his modern day Lucifer, and he was the willing Faust. Though after Aaron took the third installment from these criminals, a manila folder with twenty thousand dollars in it, he knew there was no going back. He was too deeply involved. Aaron had taken the bribes, and willingly. He had become a criminal and a part of their sordid underworld.

Within a month, it seemed to Etta's parents that he was spending money lavishly and had assumed that his father had let him have some of his inheritance early. It was an odd kind of tradition that the Jews had that Minerva didn't quite understand and considered it yet another example of the great differences between the two families. In her mind, she tolerated the boy.

Aaron told Mary Agnes he had gotten a huge raise from the Times Picayune. The editor had encouraged friends at the city's top lender, Citizen's Bank, to carry the house mortgage, guaranteeing it through his own honorable word as some sort of latter day gentleman's agreement.

Though Mary Agnes had earned a liberal arts degree from Spring Hill College, and had actually done well there, she believed his dubious story without question, mostly because she wanted to. This fairy tale aspect she had of the so-called striving husband appealed unabashedly to her Southern woman's vanity. After all, she had grown up in a household where, to her eyes, her father had made all the right things happen. There had never been an argument, or even a heated discussion, about money or the lack of it, coming from her parents.

In fact, if her father was displeased about something uttered at the dinner table, or out on the terrace with her mother, he would simply excuse himself. He would retreat to his den, and once inside, lock the door. The doctor detested the raising of anyone's voice in the house. Certainly no one ever shouted, or screamed hysterically in a fit of anger. None of the children had ever done that, and her mother would insist that all of them behave like civilized little ladies and gentlemen.

It was her favorite complaint with the youngest sister Maggie. Minerva would say it to her smallest daughter sometimes rather harshly while shaking her long index figure in warning if the girl somehow became unladylike.

The other word Minerva repeated a lot was Hush! It was a habit Etta had inherited which I actually liked. It sounded better than the jarring 'shut up' I had heard too often in New York, or even in the coal towns of Pennsylvania from women I had known over the years. My own mother and sister used it routinely in their dinner conversation, or sitting in the crowded living room watching television on a warm summer night. There was a vulgarity in it to me somehow, and it never entered into my conversations.

Only later did I hear a story about Aaron where supposedly he had been robbed on the street at night in the Quarter, or so he had said. The side of his face was covered with marks that looked as if some experienced fist had put them there.

Had he asked for more money from Marotta? Or was there some other business he had entered into with them beyond the stadium silence that went bad? I didn't know at the time, nor did anyone else until we learned the whole story about some of his past in New Orleans.

It would be almost two years after his death when several telephone calls came from the FBI who were still investigating these criminal activities. They had found and interrogated some of the participants in buying up the stadium parcels for a song and getting immensely wealthy overnight. There was talk of an indictment.

Of course, nothing was ever proven that implicated Carlos Marotta himself. It was deemed simply a prudent investment by one of his many companies that predicted the depressed area would be eventually developed. They had acted upon it much sooner than anyone else.

This was the seemingly untraceable source of Lawson's wealth from their involvement in the crooked schemes and included the receipt of enormous consulting fees. They were spread around among four or five family members who had various shell companies and had possessed no direct involvement with the football stadium beyond being vocal civic supporters. The trail of tainted money was serpentine and virtually no one could find a single thread to connect these payoffs to the mayor's family.

They had perfected an ingenious money laundering setup early in their careers and rather successfully as had mayors before them. The New Orleans police might on occasion bring in some low-level Marotta thug who had been accused of running prostitution rings for tourists, or conducting illegal gambling operations.

He would receive a five-year prison term in Angola for his part in the criminal schemes, and nothing would ever harken them back to Marotta: not a word, any paper or electronic trail, or bank account entries. Even the wholesale fish and vegetable trade supplying grocery chains and restaurants that found their way into the city from surrounding truck farms, or trawlers was owned in part by Marotta. Earlier competition had been discouraged, or eliminated by brute force.

Again, these activities had the smell of an organized crime ring. It was another tentacle of the Mafia with Carlos Marotta at the head.

Whatever trouble Aaron had gotten himself into in New Orleans, it was deadly serious and dangerous. His life changed radically after the antique pieces began to fill the living room of their splendid Victorian house on the street of magnolias and blossoming orange trees.

There was a formal garden in back of the house that was situated on a deep lot with a gazebo where Mary Agnes and their daughter Rachel could have tea. They invited us to come over one weekend once the intense summer heat began to dissipate and we all sat there during the warm starry evening with the crickets chattering. It was such a lovely spot with rows of sixty-year-old pink azaleas and two flame red crepe myrtles flanking the wooden gazebo.

Mary Agnes loved the Garden District house, and when we were first invited, she had a cold chicken supper for us already spread in the gazebo.

"Etta, isn't this marvelous? The plants and the garden?" she sang to her sister. "I have the best gardener. Our neighbor across the street uses him. He is a wonderful old black man. He must be seventy but oh so good with flowers. He's a regular Johnny Appleseed," she said with a laugh.

We walked with our white wine around the blooming garden as Mary Agnes told us of her plans for the future, eventually adding on a solarium at the back of the house. It was all so very perfect: the lovely house, the fashionable residential neighborhood, the entire Garden District.

"I want to put a Japanese maple over there in that blank spot," Mary Agnes told us, "and maybe later put a small river rock garden around it too."

Her excitement seemed to never end, and as we strolled around the lovely garden, she would hug Etta again and again, showing her happiness.

We had been in the garden for an hour or more before Aaron arrived to join us, as he had been delayed at the newspaper with last minute editorial duties. He proved, once again, to be his affable self and hugged us both in greeting.

"Aaron, how are you?" I said to him as I came through the side street door into the garden.

"Exhausted, I'm afraid. Too much work," he answered, but then smiled.

As we sat there talking together, for some reason Aaron remained almost mute, or maybe distracted, which was unusual for him. He savored an audience around for his non-stop string of stories and was a great spinner of yarns. The smallest occurrence during his day was enough for him to embellish it with his florid speech. Aaron spewed out these anecdotes as if when he spoke, he was writing a novel, which maybe he was. He was a vibrant, creative and dear man, and he became a valued friend.

That night I reminded Aaron again that he always talked about starting a novel, and looking around me, I suggested that now was the perfect time.
He laughed loudly in the sultry air.

"Why not you?" he countered to me, "You write well." To that, I only laughed, shaking my head no.

I said, "You're a creative writer. What I do is piece things together like a jigsaw puzzle, and some television news editor gives his announcer a paragraph of mine that he rewrites to read on the ten o'clock news. Hemingway, I'm not."

"Indeed," Aaron uttered in a dramatic voice, and laughed. He claimed that he would become the real Jewish novelist for the South because there were so few.

"There are what, maybe five hundred Jews in Mobile? What do you think? Is that about right? Out of what, three hundred thousand?"

I didn't know quite what to say. Finally, I answered, "Ok, five hundred."

"That's my point," he added, "think of the opportunity for me."

In fact, there were perhaps no more than five thousand of his self-proclaimed Maccabee tribe in the whole state, and that counted all the cities. New Orleans was far more Jewish and had been for many years.
Aaron said that he would have to return to Mobile for any cache as a writer. Mary Agnes only smiled contentedly to that. Though she loved the elegant Garden District house and the exotic feel of New Orleans itself, she'd gladly return home to friends and family. Go ahead, let us move back home, she must have thought at that moment.

It was a familiar trek for many southerners, particularly from Mobile, who found themselves marginally happy in New York's concrete caverns, or in sprawling Dallas, or even hilly San Francisco for some years. They longed to return home to the muddy bay.

At some point within the next year, Aaron's level of anxiety from the Marotta money had become almost unbearable. Even after the stadium municipal bond issue sailed through the city council unopposed, he felt troubled, and a little frightened with what he had done. Aaron already had eighty thousand dollars of Carlos Marotta's money, most of it spent, and his silence was probably not the only thing he would be asked for from the mobster.

Marotta called himself a hard-nosed businessman, though of course, people knew better. The man was a monster. Everyone in New Orleans knew that troubling fact, and he was not to be refused anything. He was feared.

# Chapter 3

Etta and I got married the following summer. It was the most traditional of southern weddings for that time. Her parents insisted on having the reception in their spacious and elegant home. They erected a large tent in the back garden if rain showers came that evening as they often did without warning.

Etta wore a wedding gown that had belonged to her grandmother who was married in the Mobile cathedral during the summer of 1917. The event had gotten half the society page when the city had one of its more prominent citizens to read about.

I had met the current society editor, Linda Lee Jones, at a party Etta had invited me to in the ballroom of the former Masonic Lodge. The old building was a pyramid-looking structure with a sphinx head adorning the entrance right off Dauphin Street in downtown. Etta introduced me as her gallant Navy officer, and she whispered about our marriage plans to the eager society page reporter.

The next day a photograph of Etta in her gown dancing with me dressed in my formal Navy dress blues, which she insisted I wear to the ball, appeared in the local newspaper. Underneath the photograph, the caption was worded: 'Debutante Announces Engagement' noted in bold. The news was read eagerly by people who had an interest in these sorts of things.

"It's for the texture, that's all, darling," she told me when I baulked at the suggestion of wearing my dress uniform on a weekend visit. "We're at war after all, you know, in Vietnam. You're defending us."

"Etta, that's pushing things," I had uttered.

Unhappy at the prospect, I shook my head in consternation at her point of view. In fact, I usually gave Etta her way because these were such small sacrifices to make, and they pleased her so much. I told her I would wear it to the ball.

She was ecstatic, and I could hear her shouting the news up the staircase to her mother who was on her way down. I overheard her say how dashing she thought it would look among the other young men outfitted in those boring tuxedos. They both were so excited. Etta literally shrieked with joy.

Her grandmother's dress required several visits to the dressmaker, and it took two weeks to make it into the appropriate wedding gown. I remember visiting the dressmaker. He was a tall effeminate ginger-haired man at a formal atelier where he fitted Etta. We were served steaming mint tea and scones by his assistant, a young dark haired man half his age with a fawning manner. He smilingly offered us more sugar or pastries every two minutes even as I took a bite of a single cookie prodded on by Etta, and later a sip of the tea.

There was a painting of Etta's grandmother in that same gown hung in the hallway near her parent's bedroom upstairs. The gracious woman was probably the same age, or slightly younger than Etta was then. She had a remarkable likeness to her granddaughter. There was an identical gentle upward tuft in the eyebrows that Etta possessed, and the same silky raven hair.

I found myself readily agreeing with everyone as we prepared for the wedding. Whatever I was asked, I did. Her mother inquired if I had a white dinner jacket and tux pants for the garden parties we would be invited to by family friends. I informed her I didn't but would get outfitted with one within the next week. She gave me the address and phone number of her husband's tailor who also had a men's clothing store downtown.

He was a masterful Syrian man, she said, making even the most unattractive man look elegant, obliquely referring to her otherwise rumpled husband's weekend wear.

Minerva was a demonstrative woman. She and Etta argued over trifles every day it seemed, with her mother insisting that she be more gracious with people and less like those few young women in Mobile's small upper crust who pushed back against tradition.

Minerva had her own headstrong streak that tended to overwhelm Etta, and the overbearing dominance made Etta feel she couldn't do anything right according to the proscribed beliefs of her mother. Her mother was a manipulator. She was formidable though; it couldn't be mistaken for anything else.

I always kept her at a safe distance when I sensed she was becoming uncomfortable, or seemed irritated with the direction or subject of a conversation. I was wary of her though there was much I liked about the woman.

There was a family story that was much told, and it was legend. When Minerva was ten and her sister Kathryn eight, her father died and the only way her mother could deal with her grief was to send the girls away for a month to her much younger brother. He was a newly-married lawyer working for the State Department in Washington and after some family arm-twisting, he reluctantly agreed to her plan with the two young girls.

Oddly enough, at least to my reckoning of events, he housed the girls for maybe a week and a half, or two weeks. At that point, Minerva announced in her ten-year-old manner that her mother said she and her sister could go to the World's Fair alone and that her mother had given Minerva two hundred and fifty dollars with which to do it. The whole thing, therefore, was settled, and so the journey somehow began.

What was incredible to me, is that this thirty-eight-year-old lawyer who had a responsible State Department position would actually allow the children to do it. He bought train tickets for the girls, and saw them off at the downtown train terminal in Washington.

They went off to New York City where they knew no one, had no hotel reservations, or had any earthly idea of where they would stay on their hasty visit. But off these two young girls went anyway, sitting in a narrow railcar compartment and waving out the window at their uncle and his wife.

How could this happen? It remains unfathomable to most people even today but a generation ago? The uncle must not have called his sister and asked her about this obviously dubious scheme. I can't understand why he didn't; somehow believing it was all right with their mother, though how could it be?

After traveling the entire day on the train the two young girls arrived in the early evening at Grand Central station with their leather suitcases. In another minute, they were outside on the New York City street without a clue as to where exactly they were, or where they should go.

According to the tale, Minerva hailed a yellow cab, and they both piled in dragging their bags. The curious cabbie asked them where they wanted to go, and Minerva had simply said, "A hotel." And when the cabbie asked, "Which hotel?" she quickly answered, "I don't know, a good one."

At that juncture, the cabbie, who fortunately was a married man with a large family, had turned around and looked at the two kids. "Where are your parents?"

Minerva told him that their mother was in Mobile where she always was, and that they had come to New York to see the World's Fair. Little Kathryn had merely nodded her head in acknowledgement, and continued to look out the window at the tall buildings. The man listened to the incredulous tale, and remained dubious.

"We're going to the World's Fair," little Kathryn told the driver.

The concerned cabbie took them to the Roosevelt Hotel which was near the train terminal in midtown. He dropped the two girls at the hotel front door as the bell cap carried their bags inside. Minerva had asked him how much for the fare then took out several bills with which to pay him, counting them slowly to be certain she was accurate. She also gave him an extra dollar which she had seen her own mother do when someone did something nice for her, like carrying her grocery bags or trimming the boxwoods.

The cabbie wrote down his phone number on the business card the company provided. He told them he would come here tomorrow and take them personally to the fairgrounds. He said his wife might even join him since he was so concerned about their welfare.

At the reception desk, Minerva acted very grown up. She asked for a nice room for herself and her sister for two days and paid the clerk in advance from a stack of cash. Kathryn followed her sister, and looked around the hotel lobby which was much larger than the Battle House hotel in Mobile, and very crowded on this Friday evening. They ate at the fine downstairs restaurant later that evening, then returned to their room and prepared for their next day at the World's Fair.

They both were exhausted from the long train trip and slept soundly in the room's twin beds. They received no telephone calls concerning their safety or enjoyment, or why they were there in the first place from either their uncle in Washington or their mother in Mobile.

The following day Minerva had the bellman call the same cabbie. He promptly arrived with his cheerful rotund Italian wife who didn't believe his story until she saw the two children with her own eyes. He had told her the tale over dinner, and she became upset.

Once they arrived at the fairgrounds, the girls left the taxi and paid the nominal admission for children. They entered the park with its towering edifices unlike anything in Mobile, and snacked on chicken and ice cream as they drifted from country pavilion to pavilion. It was such great fun.

They loved the Japanese pavilion the most where they were given kimonos to wear by a painted Geisha. She served them hot tea and strange triangular hard biscuits. Minerva learned to say thank you in Japanese, and felt very mature and confident of herself. She told her little sister that she simply loved New York!

Finally, around 4pm they called the cabbie again when they were ready to leave the fair. He returned without his wife but with his oldest boy along in the front seat who was perhaps sixteen, and took them safely back to the Roosevelt.

Once up in the room, the mammoth city surrounding them had finally unnerved Minerva. She called her mother in Mobile to tell her where they were. Well, with that, all hell broke loose. Her mother was on the telephone in a few minutes tracking down her errant lawyer brother. She called him an idiot and a bloody fool, using unpleasant and scurrilous words that probably had never passed her lips ever before, excoriating him to high heaven for his neglect.

"What fool would let two little girls go to New York on their own?" she shouted furiously into the black cradle receiver in the hallway of her fine home. "Tell me? And you advise the Secretary of State. Goddamn you!" It went on and on, and of course, he had to listen because he had allowed this insane thing to happen.

That evening the mother called the girls again and boarded the overnight train, which would take a full day and half to get to New York. She was a nervous wreck and overcome with fearful anxiety. It was a large city full of sinful, perverse men. She shuddered to herself. She called the Roosevelt hotel manager, and told him to put a detective on watch at night for the children. Hearing her bizarre story, he reluctantly agreed.

The girls didn't want to sit around the hotel room the next day, so Minerva called the same cabbie again. She asked him to take them to a museum, one her younger sister might enjoy. The affable man promptly returned to the hotel and picked them up before noon.

He had selected the Natural History Museum with hallways of stuffed animals, dinosaur bones, and man-eating plants for them. Kathryn simply loved it. To celebrate the occasion, she bought an illustrated book on dinosaurs in its gift shop.

By ten that night, their mother arrived at the hotel. The rest of the story wasn't nearly as interesting. She brought them back to Mobile by train and by-passing any visit to her embarrassed brother at the Capitol. Etta said almost a year passed before her grandmother would speak to him again.

That irrepressible childhood confidence filled the rest of Minerva's life. When she met the then handsome, soft-spoken doctor at a cotillion ball, she set out to marry him, making up her mind that very night among the Confederate jasmine, and doing whatever it took. She was a woman of singular purpose. Her fierce nature, and dominance sucked some of the confidence from her first-born daughter and replaced it with an innate fear of disappointing her. Minerva always had the last word in Etta's life.

That hadn't changed much well into her twenties when most young women begin to find themselves and forge ahead on their own. Later, Etta changed in ways that I believe the unresolved feelings towards Minerva contributed much to. That change came sooner than later in our lives.

Etta's father was kind, and benign for all the years I knew him. He rarely pushed back or challenged his difficult wife. Oddly enough too, the doctor seemed disinterested in children, his own included. His life was pretty much focused on what he did on the operating table. That was his métier, and he was an excellent, even a brilliant, surgeon. He loved saving lives but did not involve himself in the lives of his family and left the running of it to his wife.

\* \* \* \* \* \*

A small wedding rehearsal dinner was planned for us and fifty other people, with the women in gowns and the men in black tie. It would be at the Grand Hotel ballroom in Point Clear with a tent outside for drinks and soft music after the dinner. Her mother had vetoed the Battle House where most Mobile daughters she knew had their dinner before the wedding as she wanted the spaciousness the seaside Grand offered, as well as its elegance.

It was pricey in my mind. Etta had already told me early on as we talked about the eventual coupling that her parents would insist on what they wanted, and would pay for it since my family, or even I, had little in the bank anyway. A Navy junior officer's salary in those days was almost laughable, and could only serve a bachelor.

The planning went ahead, and through it all I smiled without rancor. Minerva was a whirlwind. She had talked with their closest friends and arranged a full week of garden parties in celebration of the wedding at the homes of her friends.

One of the more adventuresome of these husbands, who had been a carrier pilot during the Korean War and was now a local attorney, insisted on hosting a luncheon for me and a handful of Navy pilot friends from Pensacola at the Fairhope Yacht Club.

The day would commence at nine in the morning, and we would all board his forty-foot yacht for a three-hour sail around the Bay. The gruff-talking attorney had hired a black first mate and bartender who would be charged with making Bloody Marys or Mimosas for the morning sail.

A little after high noon we would dock and have a buffet lunch inside the club's dining room overlooking the water. At that point we would possibly down more toasts with plenty of wine and beer.

Since I loved to sail anyway, this was a golden opportunity to test the murky brown waters of Mobile Bay and perhaps even further endear myself with my captain host for whom I might crew during the racing season.

He was a superb ocean racer at the yacht club. He had won a first place trophy at least once over the years in the Dauphin Island Regatta that had been held for fifty years. His boat was a solid Sable craft which surprised me, initially because it's a Maine-built sloop made mostly for the stormy north Atlantic, and not particularly roomy down below for a wife and children.

During the particular brief voyage, I learned that he indeed had a wife, but one who had never set foot on his boat, and three girls now grown who had followed their mother's disdain of the sea. I laughed as he told me the misogynist laden tale.

The ex-pilot wasn't native to Mobile either. Instead, he had grown up in Connecticut and gone to college at Princeton. Later, during his naval flight training at Pensacola and not unlike me, he had met his wife at one of the Mardi Gras parties that had traditionally welcomed young naval pilots too. They were married following his military service in Korea, and spent about five or six years in Westport, Connecticut, then moved back South where his wife wanted to live.

The day was overcast and gusty and he gripped the boat wheel with his meaty hand. He told me he had flown the P-51 Corsairs in Korea. In those days, our pilots had started to encounter Russian MIGs, which could easily outmaneuver the American carrier planes in dog fights.

This was the start of the deadly conflict that was the Korean War. It was almost a year before the UN could get comparable jets into the skies in order to tip the balance.

Blair was an interesting man and I liked him. He had an honest and direct way of speaking while looking you straight in the eye. His conversation was devoid of the more flowery speech patterns I heard from many of his coastal contemporaries.

When speaking, they generally overcrowded their speech with far too many colorful metaphors as though left over from fifty years earlier. But I learned to embrace that subtle difference, though much later, I confess that I liked that as well. In fact, I preferred it to the coarse daily bread references I had grown up with that consisted of Sunday morning beer breath and hard pews of the First Baptist church.

The self-righteous speeches that I grew up hearing came from the same gaunt and pious miners who would later turn out my cousin Hadyn from the pulpit because he wanted a more diverse world. It all came to a head after his service as a wartime chaplain with the First Marine Division in Vietnam for a year and a half. He had been wounded for his front line efforts. The new testament bible he carried with him was stained with his own blood.

His sin, for which his congregation deemed him unworthy, had been to stand on some dusty and abandoned forty-year-old hymnals and a hardbound bible from the church basement because unfortunately he was a rather short squat man.

He needed a bit more height to see the small congregation over the wooden church lectern. It was absurd, you would think, as any rational man would.

Hadyn had written several inspirational books, and his loyal wife Joan served as a missionary in Patagonia for several years. She was the church organist as well, though that wasn't nearly enough to make amends for what he had done that snowy Sunday nor did it slow his indictment either.

One ominous clear and cold morning, several of the parish men had waited for him at the church front door to attack his heretic behavior. A sinful act, really? This was the same man who had prayed with dying Marines who were mere boys. He had somehow endured all of that horror of violent death and its sadness while bringing them whatever succor he could.

After that disturbing incident, my visits to the coal town diminished, but with Etta along we became duly bound to rush off on a given Sunday either for the Greek Orthodox Catholic Church, or St. Ann's, the Irish and Italian parish. All the Catholicism was naturally perplexing to my mother.

Before we married, I cheerfully became a Catholic supplicant to please Etta and of course, Minerva. Whether it was a Christian religion, or any other religion, it was all the same to me. I was a believer and I found I could safely pray in anyone's church.

We agreed I would go to catechism classes taught by the dean of the cathedral who himself was an erudite man, although he had the brazen certainty of rightness more than any Jesuit I had ever met before him. On two Saturday afternoons for a month, I would drive over to the cathedral and we would meet in his study.

Initially as these classes began, there was another young man who joined us, but he only attended one of the sessions as he moved out of the area subsequently deserting his papist bride. I never asked Father John why, but he really didn't seem to care either. He only enjoyed debating with me, trying desperately to defrock the fundamentalist Baptist liturgy I had come to embrace as a boy.

It was theology for doubters, Catholicism, and in all the time I had coffee with him we spent much of our time dissecting the epiphany of Thomas Merton and Saint Paul. He readily dismissed anything C. S. Lewis had ever written, who I had read in college, and refuted any arguments I had against present-day Catholicism point by point. The Jesuit priest was not merciful toward The Reformation. The Society of Jesus Christ produced scholar-warriors for the cross.

The dean had been educated at Notre Dame, and for a time he was an assistant to Chicago Cardinal Bernstand. After that rewarding stint, he had been sent to the Vatican as one of a handful of the most intellectual of the young American priests, groomed for increased authority and perhaps on a track to Cardinal.

He had turned fifty while our talks were going on. The dean had been named as a replacement bishop for the South Alabama diocese, with his headquarters at the Cathedral, and that investiture would take place by the next Christmas season.

Father John was a frequent guest at dinners with Etta's parents. They were often joined by a few other loyal and prosperous local Catholics. On several of these occasions, and during my indoctrination into the church, I was included among the dinner guests.

The Jesuit president of Spring Hill College was a regular. He was tall, gaunt and elegant, and had the face of an apostle if Hollywood had ever cast an epic Last Supper film.

Being the oldest on the verge of marriage with her warrior fiancé next to her at the table, Etta was the only sibling invited. Her brother was somehow excused, and was always off doing something or other in Tuscaloosa. I guessed maybe he was getting drunk at fraternity parties, though he was studious, and planned on medicine. He had more or less eschewed the family life in Mobile.

What started out as a pleasant dinner conversation soon found its way into the more esoteric investigation of Christ's transmogrification, plus original sin and worse, for which I had only the most marginal interest. Etta seemed to have none either, yet Minerva's eyes demanded her eldest daughter ask penetrating and complex questions of the Jesuit patricians across the table from her.

I was the single Protestant who had to distinguish myself as a Catholic aspirant, that Minerva expected to perhaps say the same erudite things that had made British Novelist Graham Greene a willing and vocal Roman.

I tried desperately to please everyone. It was a painful role I didn't particularly relish. Etta was of little help. Instead, she moved the conversation from subjects that I would have liked to further amplify, to what I might disagree with, and focused an inordinate amount of time on birth control. I was charged with how I felt about abortion and a woman's right to choose. This had not as of yet divided the Catholics. Both Jesuits wanted my capitulation to their staunch position. The act was murder to them.

I was presented the pointed question by the Spring Hill president. "How do you feel about abortion?" he asked in a stern and accusing manner then crossed his arms at the table with his stare fixed on me, awaiting my answer.

"To be honest, I have mixed feelings," I answered.

"You do? I don't see how that is possible." the priest continued.

I gave him a rather disjointed answer that was closer to the Catholic Church Pro-Life position, but expressed some doubts. I confessed that it had taken on political pressures, and that confused people. Little of my answer pleased anyone around the table, yet they refrained from taking me to task. The Catholic college president simply shook his head, only acknowledging what I had tried to express.

My conversation wavered and moved to other safer subjects. I told them of the unfair treatment of Haydn which was greeted with stony faces from the two Jesuits, and a false cough from Minerva. Etta beamed at me as she often did. That made me feel a part of the uncomfortable inquisition. But even with her serenity, I imagined difficulties in the future with us, though I couldn't exactly recognize them at the time.

The classes continued with the Cathedral dean. We were always friendly and shared interests on a great many things beyond religion. Those were the days of a confirmation to the faith that would allow my once heathen knee beyond the so-called rail of the sacristy. I could now enter into the ritual of sanctified marriage.

This was important to Etta, even more so to Minerva, and my opinion on religion was simply that faith and charity transcended the rigid rules of the church. Etta could wear her mantilla veil to Mass, and we would share the holy ritual of communion, as no doubt so would our children. She wanted the same large family as her own, but sadly, circumstances, hers as well as mine, prevented that from happening.

The last Cathedral class finished and my confirmation as a Catholic moved us rapidly toward the calendar dates chosen for the wedding. It would be the twentieth of June. It was a Saturday and a day that traditionally escaped the midsummer heat of July or August, with warm nights of bearable humidity and no rain.

Etta was ecstatic at my confirmation itself with a beatific look on her pretty face. Father John had remained benevolent considering the last class conversation on abortion had taken a rather acrimonious and unplanned turn. I had simply tired of agreeing with everyone in our tight little circle as an accommodation to Etta and her family. My words had been sharper than I had wished.

Yet the Dauphin Square rector was a man of untold substance and wide experience. Certainly he had obviously encountered these same arguments several hundred times, or even more. I regretted that heated moment with him, apologizing before I even left his study, but he had wanly smiled, and waved me on, quickly congratulating me on the path I had taken for a happier marriage and bright future strengthened by faith.

Perhaps I should have questioned him further, since I had achieved some kind of faith earlier. I thought my Protestant church years counted for something with its surety too. Instead, I said nothing and waved goodbye, turning first to the altar on my way out of the church and making the sign of the cross with my hand. This lone act of compliance obviously pleased him, and he called out, "See you soon, my son."

He would perform the marriage ceremony, and that pleased Minerva immensely and with that, Etta would be happy.

My own mother would never understand my conversion, but we were distant as mother and son. Any disapproval might be a mild irritant voiced the few times we would be together. She would never show her contempt toward Etta. Etta's parents' lofty station in life was far better than hers, and this would buy her eternal silence. It would never be mentioned in their presence.

Once, as we sat alone in the kitchen of my grandfather's house that she had inherited she voiced her annoyance. "Your religion wasn't good enough for her, was it?"

I took a deep breath, stuffed my own mounting anger and remembered her long painful life with my father. I forced a smile, and said something like, "Well, you know, it's easier for her."

With my forced utterance, there came a downturned mouth as she looked off into space but it was short-lived. Her anger was gone in another instant. It, of course, would never be forgotten, only revisited among her long list of regrets she nursed in her thoughts each day.

The irony to all the rumination on religion was that my father had been born into a French Catholic family with an Irish mother. Eventually they all had ceased to think about attending mass, any mass, even the requisite Christmas or Easter services.

It was similar to the Jews I had known during my brief days in New York, and later in Chicago, who still had some distant pull to their faith. At the very most, they might drag the family to a synagogue during the High Holy days though that accommodation had pretty much vanished among many contemporary Jews. They supported Israel, and it ended there.

One options trader I had known for years in Chicago had a Jewish wife, and she had insisted on the Bat Mitzvahs for their daughters, which had cost him plenty. They ended up becoming these lavish, expensive parties for her private school girlfriends, he had later told me once when the subject of mixed marriages came up.

He said it was a small price to pay for happiness though I'm not sure I entirely believed him. His wife worked as a corporate attorney and had been making more than he did for some years. He was not so subtly reminded of that painful fact when they had harsh words.

When my mother attended our wedding at the cathedral, she sat there entranced, staring wildly around her every few seconds during the ceremony at the gold and silks of the high church ritual.

Her own miner's congregation made the scant effort to put additional candles on the altar at Christmas and maybe two potted Lilies at Easter that bookended the dark-suited pastor.

Over the years, the most prominent Catholics I've known have always surrounded themselves with priests at social events. A church the size of the cathedral usually had at least four priests assigned to it, and on several occasions the dean might bring another to dinner. They celebrate these princes of the universal church, often at dinners or summer parties. Minerva was no different.

The Jesuits were the intellectual saviors of the Catholic Church to her. They were black-cassocked men whose fierceness and vast knowledge of this world and the next somehow protected her and represented the last bastion for whatever morality she believed. To Minerva, they weren't simple clergymen but men who sat next to the Holy Father himself. They were confident and well-appointed, perhaps clutching the single key to the vast wealth of this church in their pocket should they ever need it.

Of the several who came to those dinners or garden parties, I liked Harold Jelinek who was a second generation Pole from Milwaukee who found his way South to Vanderbilt University, and was chosen for the priesthood by Tennessee Bishop O'Reilly. Harold had been sent to the seminary attached to Fordham in the Bronx and afterward he had served on the staff of the Cardinal in Manhattan as an aide.

Father Jelinek was a sophisticated and worldly young man of thirty-four, a jazz pianist of some talent, and a first-rate tennis player. He was the bellwether of a new and more relevant Catholicism, or so it had seemed. The man was handsome, smooth, and erudite too. He fit like a suede glove into all of the better Catholic society of Mobile: the doctors, lawyers, and real estate developers. The Jesuits employed him as the advance party with these families.

Father Jelinek ran an affable interference on any fundraising or political initiative that came out of the Alabama diocese. He did it effortlessly clearing the path for the cathedral dean.

Groomed for greater things in New York, vicious gossip had circulated about his supposed involvement with the Cardinal's young female Puerto Rican housekeeper Alma who was maybe twenty at the time. She had ostensibly confessed to some wrongdoing. Perhaps a nascent affair, but who knows? I didn't learn anything because the Cardinal quashed it in the telling. He had termed it the unfortunate behavior of a misguided and hysterical woman at the time, and had saved the young Jelinek.

However, this was a transgression from which you're never quite freed. The young Jesuit represented the finest in the future of American priests but had been branded with the faith's own stigmata. He would never recover.

Alma had told the Cardinal that she had physical relations with the young Jelinek. She couldn't bring herself to say the word sex in front of his Eminence, but the message to him was clear. That act alone should have been sufficient grounds for dismissal from the holy order as it certainly had been in the past, and of course it was the venial sin of being all too human.

The frightened girl had wept on her knees during her sinful confession, and asked for the Cardinal's forgiveness.

He had answered her as a man of his cleric wisdom indeed would, "My child, only God can forgive you. And as his servant, I will hear your confession this very moment."

So Alma told the Cardinal that she and Father Jelinek had been intimate for almost three months, sharing their embraces within his very rectory.

"But we made love in my apartment. That was the only place," she told the Cardinal in tears. "Father Jelinek said it was sinful, but his love for me was too great, and his flesh was weak."

"How often did he do this?" the Cardinal asked the woman, who had to look away from his face because of her mortification.

"We slept together on Friday nights, your Eminence, when he had no church duties," she said in an almost whisper. "I tempted him. I brought him to this. It was my fault," Alma burst out. He had told her no several times, but his passion for the beautiful young woman had undone his Jesuit resolve.

As the Cardinal heard the sordid details of his priest's affair, he thought of the saints who had died on the rack before abandoning their vows, and his mouth hardened toward his favorite young priest.

He whispered inaudibly to himself as she continued speaking head bowed, "How could he have been such a fool? He had so much before him."

At last, the young woman finished her painful confession, and the Cardinal blessed her, giving her a simple penance to follow in atonement. His thoughts had left her and rested on this betrayal by the young priest. The Cardinal himself had grown up in a hard-scrabble South Bronx Irish neighborhood, and his father was a drunken and abusive day laborer on the railroad. He understood human imperfection, and was perhaps among the most liberal in that way of Rome's royalty.

"Tell me of your life, my child," he advised the distraught young woman, and she began to tell him a tale not wholly dissimilar to his own. The father was rarely at home, and kept the small household of four children in abject poverty with his alcoholism.

The prelate remembered as a boy of ten cleaning up the kitchen after his father who slept in his own vomit one winter night at the table. Even at seventy, those memories had never left him. It was all so clear to him as the young woman told him of her own trials in a soft accented voice. He had followed his own father's violent ways on the mean streets and at fourteen had become a Golden Gloves boxer, winning five straight matches with knockouts.

At his last fight for the championship, something had happened to him in the ring that he didn't understand. He was faster than his opponent and his punches were harder, yet this time he didn't seek a knockout because he wanted to spare his opponent that pain. He had simply outpointed the other boy when he could have knocked him to the canvas early in the fight. He won on points of course, but his trainer saw that the earlier violence that had characterized the Cardinal's fights had disappeared.

He had feelings of unmistakable gentleness that had crept into his very character, and an overwhelming feeling of compassion for his fellow man. Soon after the champion bout, the young Irish teenager, who would become a prince of the church, left the world of fists and their punishment to heed a different calling. At sixteen, he had asked his parish priest to recommend him for entry to a Jesuit seminary because he sought the holy orders. God had come to him in the ring with a subtle whisper of purpose, and the prelate had never wavered on that path.

The young Puerto Rican housekeeper talked on to the prelate, of the abuse she received from her uncle, the frequent unwanted sexual advances from him as she entered young womanhood, and how she had kept silent. He had forced himself upon her, taking her virtue and she could tell no one, not even in the confessional, as she was too embarrassed.

The Cardinal said to her, "God forgives the sinner, and the victims of those who commit these sins are the innocent, beloved of the father."

She sat before the Cardinal and wept for her shame. He laid his hand on her bowed head, and told her, "You are forgiven of your sins with the priest, as he will be forgiven of his. You are the child of a forgiving God, who has formed the world in his image, who has given his children the burden of choice, seeking right."

"How many times have you had physical relations with Father Jelinek?" the Cardinal inquired of Alma.

She looked up at the Cardinal's beatific face, and her lip began to tremble as she sought the words to answer.

"Tell me, my child," the Cardinal insisted, and the smallest of smiles came to his mouth, encouraging her to complete her confession and seek absolution.

"I slept with him eight times, your Eminence," she uttered the words, fearful of what the clergyman would say in response.

"And you know those acts were wrong, blasphemous outside of the sacrament of holy marriage and far worse with a priest?" the Cardinal asked.

"Yes, your Eminence. It was sinful and I want God to punish me for what I have done," Alma answered.

"God is merciful," the Cardinal told her, "he accepts your confession, and asks you to atone for these sins." That was the end of the interview. Nothing more needed to be said of the unseemly episode.

He added, "Do not tell anyone of our conversation, and end the relationship with the confused priest. But tell him nothing of what we said here. Nothing."

It was best, however, that she leave the Cardinal's residence, and he arranged for her to work in another capacity with Catholic Charities in the city. Unfortunately, Father Jelinek would no longer be considered for the Vatican Council, or as a new faculty star at the prestigious Catholic seminaries like Georgetown, or Notre Dame.

Instead he was exiled to lower Alabama. There he would become a cathedral assistant, saying mass on the days the dean was busy or traveling. He would do the nominal hospital and nursing home visitations in his place. He wasn't a heretic exactly, or one of those inflamed priests who challenged the church orthodoxy as Matthew Fox had done and was now defrocked, but perhaps this young priest was the garden variety of sinner like us all.

Jelinek had lied and pleaded his innocence to the Cardinal. Perhaps once he would have been believed, yet he was blamed for putting himself in familiar and compromising circumstances, when he clearly should have known better. Jelinek's actual fate was that of a very hard hand slapping, which would change his career as a Jesuit. From then on, he would have a checkered past. This would prevent him from becoming one of the center stage priests of the next generation of Catholic thinkers and theologians.

\* \* \* \* \* \*

The day came for the marriage ceremony and despite the obvious nervousness of Minerva and Etta, the event unfolded. There were two hundred and fifty guests for the service itself and naturally the dean officiated, assisted by Father Jelinek. They made me kneel with a bowed head as if I were at Westminster among the legendary royals of Great Britain. The service lasted almost three quarters of an hour with half of it in Latin. The ceremony seemed overly long to me, though I was anxious.

We were driven back to the house by her brother in a Lincoln Town car and he joked with us all along the route, nearly hitting a pedestrian on Government Street. When we arrived at the house, a staff of black bartenders were ready to serve inside and on the terrace, and further battalions of waiters prepared to move through the guests with tray after tray of hors d'oeuvres. There was a chocolate fountain inside the house library and the room overflowed with French and creole pastries.

After Etta had at last cut the four-tiered wedding cake and drank champagne from her high-heeled slipper while crying with joy, we quickly changed to casual clothes upstairs. I had rented a Thunderbird convertible and we drove to the beach house at Point Clear. Etta and I decided to postpone any trip to the islands, or Europe until later when we had more time to reflect on where we wanted to go. We spent two days at the beach house, then set off to New Orleans where we stayed at a lovely courtyard suite inside a vintage French Quarter hotel for two nights. That was more than enough revelry for the both of us.

One night, after an elegant evening meal we strolled through the Quarter and ended up at a small wine bar overlooking the Mississippi. As the last customers of the night, we danced fueled by our newly minted ecstasy. Etta hummed and sang different songs as I spun her around and around in her pastel sundress. I asked why didn't she sing or at least hum some Eric Clapton, and she just sputtered with laughter.

Although she had a wide circle of friends in that city, she had told no one of our current visit. She didn't want to interrupt our time with others. It became one of the best memories I had of our time together.

Back in the room as I prepared for bed, Etta had opened a bag she brought with her for the trip, and took out a bottle of Johnnie Walker Red Label scotch. She had said that bar and restaurant drinks were all watered down, and we should enjoy some nightcaps before sleep. Smiling, I agreed. We sat on the balcony and looked out over the courtyard garden. She put her head on my shoulder and was soon drifting off to sleep.

The second night we did pretty much the same, but Etta had one more scotch than I did before bed, and somehow emptied the bottle. Little did I know then how much a part of my life New Orleans would come to play and if I had known, maybe I would have picked a different place for a honeymoon, but I didn't.

Driving back to Mobile, it seemed life couldn't get any better than it was. I had been blessed with a beautiful dark haired woman who seemed to be overflowing with life. We blared the radio for the entire road trip before pulling into her parent's driveway before dinner.

Inside the foyer there were continuous hugs from her family who rushed out with arms extended in a wave of dark curls. It made me breathless to look at the loveliness in front of me, and for a moment my eyes filled with joyful tears. At the time, I secretly wished that I had grown up in this spacious home, with these kind and quirky people. Mine had been so harsh. I had experienced the opposite for most of my young life in that small coal town, but right now I had taken a tremendous leap forward into the normalcy and tradition that I observed under these tall white porticos. In my mind, I whispered to myself that I had finally come home.

Cunning as ever, Minerva had cast her net house-hunting around the Eastern Shore, because I liked the sea. She found us a two-year rental on Nolte Creek in Magnolia Springs. It was the home of a successful Dallas real estate executive who had grown up here and had moved back for five or six years, but he wanted to live in France with his much younger wife who was French.

He had made a stack of money over the years with one of the big hotel chains, in addition to what his Mobile banker father had left him, allowing him to do what he wanted. The dream was simply that he desired a couple of years in Paris to please his young wife, and himself. He said that very thing to Minerva at a cocktail party and the woman worked fast when it was something she wanted.

The rent was surprisingly low for the house, which had been built as one of the Key West style houses on stilts to keep rising bayou water out. It was around three thousand square feet with ceiling fans and screened porches. It had Western art he had collected, including a small bronze sculpture which looked a lot like a Remington to me.

We were doing him a favor, he had said, having friends looking after his house during his grand tour. Being that far away would allow us to get to know each other without the family pressure we might encounter in Mobile itself, socially and otherwise, though as it happened, we were often with everyone at the Point Clear house in the warm weather.

There was a large boathouse on the creek that led to the Magnolia River which eventually took you out into the Gulf. Inside were two powerboats, a massive two-engine Sea King and a smaller Boston Whaler that I recognized immediately. He had told Minerva we could use them, though I felt it better not to invite disaster with an expensive boat that I didn't own, and argued against it. Etta didn't care either way since she spotted two kayaks underneath the house in a storage area that we could amuse ourselves with on the water.

He had the two powerboats on metal lifts, and all around us were neon sculptures of fish. Several deep sea nets hung from the building rafters, though more for décor than for actual ocean fishing. Although he had maybe eight or ten fishing rods under the main house, he had a few here too. They were all covered with patterns of spider webs, and I reckoned they hadn't been used for years.

Kevin had made quite a bit of money over the years, and though quite personable, he had experienced one or two unpleasant marriages which continued to trouble him. There was an artist daughter living in Fairhope, who, although a decent painter who sometimes sold her canvases locally through galleries, was quick to anger. Most of the townspeople gave her a wide berth. They called her eccentric, which was a genteel way of explaining away her rudeness.

On her property was a small garden with flowering plants, particularly camellias. It had been done in an almost mythical tone with storybook creatures. I thought the woman had a vivid imagination and great talent. She lived alone in a small cottage across from seaside Promenade Park, and behind the house was a small studio where she created most of her art. However, they were such a troubled father daughter combination and after talking with her once, I believe they both welcomed his move to France as a relief.

Standing with Etta in the doorway of her small garage studio, she turned down the flame on her plasma torch for a moment. She threw back her hard face mask and laughed when we told her we would be living in the Magnolia Springs house.

"Well, now he can munch on his French tart in peace," she had added, laughing a false shrill laugh, pushing the mask higher on her forehead to uncover a small pretty face encircled with red dust. At her rather pointed words, Etta's long face turned crimson with sudden embarrassment. Daunted a bit, I could only offer a slight smile during the whole uncomfortable episode.

Another daughter, with two young children, lived in the wealthy Highland Park section of Dallas next to SMU. She was married to a burly man from a family in the oil and natural gas business, with its company headquarters in an East Texas community on the Red River called Uncertain. Over the years with the erratic movement of the river, it was uncertain whether most of this tiny town was in Texas or Louisiana.

We enjoyed the Magnolia Springs house. Mary Agnes and Aaron would come up to Point Clear for a summer weekend to escape the New Orleans heat about two weekends a month and during those visits we became close. Aaron and I would sit alone on the porch and talk about politics, the family, or even books. He read two novels each month to keep his hand in the lit world but for me, reading was a more occasional thing.

By this time, the illegal business with Marotta had careened out of control. Aaron had become a nervous wreck during the weekends trying to keep himself distracted from the bribe nightmare, while his wife was oblivious to his pain. I later learned Marotta was ready to make more demands on him, and since Aaron had a hundred thousand dollars of his, this made him a virtual slave. I didn't know what the nature of the requests might have been, yet they involved things that were certainly shady, and probably criminal.

Essentially Aaron, who was thought to be a young ally of the daily newspaper editor, was betraying his trust, monitoring stories that were negative about Marotta. He was even stealing copies off his editor's desk, taking pieces of some muckraking series half in progress. Aaron continued to push any real evidence to back up the charges under the rug. That's as much as I ever knew about that time.

It was at the end of his association with Marotta that Aaron finally bolted and returned to Mobile. He was hired as a general assignment reporter on the Press Register and for the most part, Marotta had left him alone, or so it seemed.

* * * * * *

I requested an early discharge from the Navy since I wasn't an aviator and they had agreed, if I would remain a reservist for several years. I left the Navy after three years' active service, and moved to Magnolia Springs with Etta without effort.

Again, one of Minerva's friends proved useful as their introduction landed me at one of Mobile's oldest advertising agencies as a business director. It proved to be a marvelous experience.

My boss had been a destroyer lieutenant in the Pacific and we bonded over our military service. As we talked, I found that he was an old newspaper reporter who had crossed the street to do advertising. He had been in New York in the early Sixties and worked on Madison Ave for adman legend David Ogilvy.

He was a political animal too. He became involved with gubernatorial politics first in Alabama and across the region. This was the end of the Democrat reign in Congress and the beginning of the Republican majority following Nixon's first term in office. It continued with the GOP winning most elections. He built a fairly large ad agency through political work alone and grew quickly beyond the proliferation of TV commercials for local banks and car dealers. In the years that I worked with him, he slowly led me toward financial independence.

Etta and I became a prosperous and gregarious young Mobile area couple. We threw our share of dinner parties and entertained non-stop during Mardi Gras like all of our close friends. Life was good indeed, and after the second year at Magnolia Springs, the Dallas mogul had decided to sell us the house, again with Minerva's connivance, and we settled into a handful of blissful years.

Everyone expected children to follow soon, as was the path of many of her friends already, however, they didn't come. An earlier abortion, before we had met, and unknown to everyone in Mobile, had scarred Etta's fallopian tubes. It had been difficult for us to conceive, and so we both started to prepare ourselves for a life without children of our own.

That sentence wasn't an absolute certainty though each of us thought it had become truly hopeless. Still, we kept trying and every month brought frustration. Sometimes Etta's blame for her earlier life mistakes and their aftermath pulled her under water in fits of self-punishment and guilt.

One night I brought up the subject of adoption and she uncharacteristically screamed at me. Her voice shattered the stillness of the calm night on the water as we watched the pink sunset sky descend into blackness. It seemed that this particular night marked the increase in her drinking, however, I couldn't be sure because for the most part I kept up with her.

The year had gotten exciting for me as I ran the campaign for Alabama governor candidate, Ward Johnson, an ex-district attorney who seemed to be leading in the polls. I spent that later summer and early fall with him traveling in a Winnebago to Montgomery, Birmingham, and Auburn for local television appearances.

We visited the smaller towns and cities that might have been too folksy, but it worked. He had attended Cornell law school up North, though, he kept that same good ole boy demeanor he inherited from his courthouse lawyer father easily winning the primary.

After that, the statewide race was his to lose, as Democrats had lost favor across most of the South. Not overly confident of the outcome, we canvassed every bayou and country store within the state. I liked him and believed he would make a fine governor and with the rising tide of his political fortunes, I naturally rose with them.

During that three-month period, I was gone a lot. Etta had been substitute teaching at Fairhope High School as an English teacher, filling in for one of her childhood friends who had left on maternity leave for four months. She liked children and she enjoyed teaching them. Adults, stray dogs, and children all seemed to adore her. In earnest, the principal began looking for a budget increase to fit her on the faculty, but she assured him this was only a temporary diversion.

It kept her busy, and that was a blessing because I wasn't there for weeks at a time, particularly in the final month of the general election. For the month of September, I was home only two Saturdays, and came in at eleven at night for one of them.

The candidate won handily, and we had a victory celebration at the Battle House. It had been the first time in more than a decade that someone from Mobile had won the statehouse, or even attempted a run. He draped his arm around my neck when the final announcement of the vote count had been announced and the crowd went wild. Etta was off to the side and when I glanced back at her for a moment, she had a look of sadness on her face but it changed quickly to her familiar smile as she caught my glance.

With his official seating in Montgomery, Ward offered me a job to join his staff as a high level assistant, though the prospect of living in the capital when I had a wonderful bayou house held no attraction.

I had begun to build a profitable niche at the agency with a wave of political advertising.

Word of mouth brought candidates from Mississippi, Tennessee and Georgia to our doorstep. The attorney general for Alabama came to us to handle his US Senate race. The man was a certain winner against some obscure chicken restaurant owner with three stores around the state.

The political game challenged me. I had free rein to conduct the campaigns and create the advertising as I saw fit. Two writers were assigned to me and a separate profit center where I would share revenues. I had a loose business agreement, and went far beyond all the other agency employees in what I earned. I took in twice the paychecks of the two agency vice presidents.

Etta's sojourn as a teacher came to its logical end. She did more volunteer work afterward, taking on the task of raising money for expansion of the children's wing of Catholic St. Joseph Hospital, and they met all their goals. She raised four million dollars for the new construction and renovations within eight months. Everyone liked her wherever she went.

The adoption talk had ended with us, and although we were both barely thirty, we behaved as though we were over fifty with kids out of college. We now entertained more than our friends, or certainly as much, and the spreads we laid out became more and more lavish. Then came the small yacht, and we both took a great interest in maintaining and sailing it on weekends.

We bought a used thirty-eight foot Newport sloop that had been restored nicely. We would sail it on Saturdays and Sundays all spring long as well as in the later summer heat. In the fall, we stayed overnight while moored at a berth alongside the Fairhope Yacht Club, and sometimes barbecued on the warm evenings.

At first we had a coterie of friends who might join us, though one by one they seemed to tire of sailing to Mobile and back or drinking cold beer in the relentless summer heat. Etta was a decent sailor to begin with, but became even better while slowly honing her navigation skills at the helm.

Once or twice when I traveled across the South she took the boat out herself, though that was rare. Usually she would have her sister Mary Agnes go along, and sometimes Aaron who would come up for the weekend. They liked to stay onboard the boat then drive over to the Point Clear or Magnolia Springs house for meals and swimming. The empty sailboat gave them some semblance of independence.

# Chapter 4

Aaron, surprisingly, became a fair sailor considering he was a man who didn't particularly like the water and couldn't swim. He had failed to get into NROTC at Tulane because he couldn't manage a stroke, and two cadets had to pull him out of the university Olympic pool half drowned during the Navy survival test.

The four of us grew closer than anyone else in the family and the sailboat became our common bond. Things were pretty much low-key, although it was surprising when Etta's cousin Jean abruptly left her lawyer husband Charles. She had drifted to Nashville with some musician she had met years before.

Jean wanted a career as a country and western singer. I had heard her play guitar and sing, and she wasn't bad, really. She wasn't true country but had a sort of Linda Ronstadt quality and her songwriting seemed a bit more folk than country. The lyrics were poetic to me but they were filled with far too much about trucks, booze and divorce. She almost finished a master's degree at Emory on the English lake country poets, so that might be partially responsible for the too-classical sound of her lyrics. I don't know.

Aaron once claimed she lacked the scars the popular country singers had: a checkered history of repossessed cars, and beaten-up trailers. Instead, she lived in her husband's large family home right off Government Street for a few years, an impressive antebellum white columned house. After that, she wanted to get out of the city, so they bought a four bedroom Victorian country place on the water in Fairhope. They still kept the 1860s Mobile manor, and rented it to some well-heeled family friend.

Her husband was devastated when she left. They had only been married for a few years, and the poor man had no clue anything was wrong between the two of them. Certainly, the breakup must have been much more than musical ambition, I thought.

They had both been over to the Magnolia Springs house for dinner once and Jean had played her songs for about twenty minutes while sitting cross-legged on the screened porch. She reminded me of a tall Carole King. The husband was equally attractive but had already started a paunch from his weekend indulgences. He was seemingly kind and listened closely to each song she had sung, greeting them with thunderous applause.

Etta had only talked with Jean maybe twice on the telephone when the split occurred, but there was no real explanation as to why. Friends were shocked, and the only thing Etta ever said about the breakup was that he was the wrong man from the beginning. Her mother had pressured her, and it was better this way with no children to worry about.

"Let her chase her music in Nashville," she said, and closed the subject.

I recollect a painter friend who came over to dinner saying, "What does she know about trailer trash living and two months behind with the rent? She's spent her life sitting around the country club pool."

The musician Jean left with had been a fixture around town, usually playing his own music at the local bars and shrimp houses. I heard him at Felix's restaurant once and thought he was an accomplished guitarist. Everyone else in town had called him a bad drunk and that he was divorced with two small children who ran around in rags.

Jean had her parent's money, or at least some of it, and perhaps she would do the heavy lifting before they got a hit on Music Row. Together they cut a first album, and when I heard it I thought Jean found a twang with the lyrics she didn't have before.

Jean became the only one of the women who had ever gone north to school and had attended Smith. She remained a fixture on the college equestrian team as was the custom in the

66

South. Otherwise she behaved like most of the other Smith girls from New York and Boston; drinking and going to mixers at Brown and the Coast Guard Academy.

Her own mother once scolded her, "Jean, you're too uppity with young men here, and they don't like it. You're quoting Chaucer, for heaven's sake."

"Mother, they're all peasants," she had answered, and her poor mother had taken her knitting and vacated the living room. Jean was incorrigible.

She had missed two summers in Mobile during those years, periodically joining her classmates working, drinking, and dating on the Cape, where invariably one of them seemed to have a family cottage.

Jean became somewhat different from the other young women in Minerva's family, though not particularly rebellious. She was just different in personality.

Her own mother had been less dominating than her sister Minerva, and seemed to be a nervous sort while always hanging on her brawny husband who was clearly in charge of everything in their lives. Bo had been an Alabama football star until a broken leg ended his career after which he joined the other young men of his circle in their fathers' businesses.

In his case, it was lucrative Eastern Shore and Gulf real estate sales. His claim to notoriety, which we heard about often, was that after he had been injured on the football field against Auburn, he had been replaced by someone who went on to the NFL as a football great, but I forget the player's name.

Jean was the first in the family to ever date a Jew. He was a young man from Manhattan who was at Dartmouth, and whose father did something important on Wall Street. They were Reformed Jews, whatever that meant.

Again, she clashed with her more traditional mother on her choices and said, "Maybe I'll marry him, and convert. You'd like some grandchildren running around with those yarmulke's, wouldn't you, mother?"

Her mother had answered with exasperation, "Must you be rude, always?"

Jean only laughed at the woman's discomfort. What eventually occurred in the relationship was that the young man became a Buddhist, and went off to some monastery in Tibet in sandals with a shaved head. It happened sometimes in those days.

Two years younger than Etta, Jean had been a childhood confidante, as their mothers stayed close, though during Smith it all changed. In truth, nobody was completely shocked that Jean had left her passive husband, and some people I talked with afterward said they were surprised it had taken so long. Poor Charles was a rather taciturn man trying to manage a headstrong musician and free-spirited woman, and perhaps this was the expected ending to the saga.

I remember one evening when they were over for dinner and we all were seated at the table with another couple. During the dinner, Jean had taken one of her sandals off, and would periodically run her toes up and down my bare leg while smiling at me.

When I glanced at her, it seemed she was silently asking with her eyes, "What are you going to do about that?"

For my thirty-first birthday, which was a surprise party, Jean had cornered me in Minerva's beach house kitchen and whispered, "Don't you think we should have an affair, a little one, for maybe two months?" She quickly kissed me on the mouth and disappeared to join the others on the sand. She had been teasing of course; it was her way, that's all. The Northeast years had inevitably changed her, and parts of her didn't operate the same way as they did with many of her Mobile contemporaries.

After Jean left for Nashville, her husband Charles insisted on coming to family summer outings and out of guilt he was probably invited to the garden and Mardi Gras parties Minerva's friends hosted. He would always be the morose sandy haired man with a small belly next to the bar talking idly to the bartender or at the back of somebody's swimming pool staring out into the darkness.

For a while, most people sympathized with poor Charles, then people, being what they are, simply forgot about him and he disappeared from the social scene. A year later we would see him driving around town in a green convertible with a recent blond Tuscaloosa graduate he had been introduced to. He would hang his arm on the car door and flash a false smile but you couldn't mistake the sadness in his brown eyes.

It seemed that Nashville had worked for Jean. It would be years before we would run into each other again as she had pretty much put her family and Mobile behind her.

Tom Gately, an artist friend who had an exhibit in Nashville sometime later that same year, had seen her at his opening. She had metallic reddish hair and was dressed in a tailored western jacket and jeans. He had said she looked attractive, and they had a nice talk for maybe a five-minute encounter.

\* \* \* \* \* \*

When Etta finally became pregnant, our lives changed overnight. She became ecstatic, depressed, and ecstatic again. It went on that way for the first month, and I was completely disarmed. I didn't know what to say or do, and defensively I thought to surround ourselves with other people and made the attempt to fill the house with people each weekend.

There would be friends, almost-friends, casual acquaintances from work, and people from the larger political scene I found myself drawn toward. Ten people at a time would sit around the table on Saturdays and Sundays, and sometimes we would take them up and down the Magnolia River or out into Weeks Bay.

At the end of the eighth week, Etta had a miscarriage and it was awful for her. She carried the pain, the sorrow, and for reasons known only to us, the lasting abortion clinic scars from New Orleans. For two months after that, she sunk into the deepest of depressions, and fortunately everyone saw why.

We had her father prescribe the mildest doses of antidepressant drugs, Valium or Xanax. It took us through the difficulty of those first three or four weeks, and then one morning, Etta became herself again as if nothing had happened.

I thought she should talk to someone about it, but Minerva said that was completely unnecessary since we all knew the obvious reason for her despondency. She was strong and young, and she would heal like so many women before her in similar straits. Honestly I didn't believe that would occur, and when I talked with Minerva, I finally said that I would call the psychologist myself.

She hissed at me, "Don't you dare. This is a family matter, and no one else needs to be involved." After she had said that, she stared hard at me with her mouth downturned, and stood unblinking for a moment or two. "I will take care of my own daughter. I want you to realize that."

70

# Chapter 5

In rapid dismissal of any feelings I might express on the subject of her daughter, Minerva rose from the table of her dining room where we had been sitting, and started up the stairs. I sat at the large mahogany table alone for another minute or two before I reluctantly walked out the door and drove back to Magnolia Springs.

I'm an accommodating man, I'll admit, and maybe passive-aggressive, however, I thought about the situation as I drove over the causeway. "She can go screw herself, I'll do what I think best," as my hands tightened on the steering wheel in anger. Etta's self-centered mother would sacrifice her daughter for propriety and possible embarrassment.

Fortunately, once home, it appeared that Etta had recovered from the tragedy and her spirits seemed to soar in those few weeks following the hospital visit. We resumed our normal routine. We entertained people, and that spring Etta started to play tennis again, and competitively. Her family had a membership at the Mobile Country Club so she was on the court during the weekdays when she had time, and her game vastly improved.

By the middle of May, she was ready to play women's singles, and won quite a few matches. Encouraged, Etta entered the club's Memorial Day tournament and got all the way to semi-finals before losing to a twenty-year-old woman who played regularly on Auburn's tennis team.

I watched her final match. Etta moved around the court fearlessly hitting the serves hard and keeping her opponent on her heels for most of the game. What finally killed her game were her own silly mistakes that came from not enough time on the courts, but she was impressive nevertheless. There was a strong core within this woman that not many people saw. When she left the tennis court, you saw a strong woman.

Tennis took over her obsessive side not long afterward. She would play around Mobile and enter tournaments that she had started to win, so when the winter championships were held at the spacious country club, she was ready. Etta took her first two opponents down in straight sets until the finals where she met the same local girl from Auburn who had beaten her earlier in the year.

Everyone in the family was in the stands and that last match went back and forth. There were a couple of questionable referee calls, but it was hard fought. During the frantic last few minutes, Etta's serve somehow got stronger and her opponent missed enough of them to lose the match.

After she finally won, I rushed onto the court and gave her a big bear hug though her arms hung limp at her sides. Without a word, she put her head on my shoulder and cried. I thought they were tears of joy though later I knew they weren't. Etta was crying about the past and everything inside her that hurt.

Minerva naturally laid out a lavish victory celebration. Aaron and her sister, who made the trip from New Orleans for the finals, joined us. Her would-be doctor brother had brought his fiancée too, who was an attractive girl from the exclusive Mountain Brook suburb in Birmingham that he had met through some other medical school colleagues. She was blond, slim, and also Catholic from a long time family there. Minerva would welcome the pedigree.

After we left the Mobile house that night to drive back to Magnolia Springs, Etta told me she was through with tennis. When I asked her if she might just take a break from it, she shouted at me. "I'm finished! What the hell don't you understand about finished?"

Her lips had started to tremble and she silently looked blankly out the side window until we got home.
Once inside, she went to our living room where she stormed to the bar and made herself a quick drink. She told me she was going to sit outside at the boathouse for a little while and that she would like to be alone if I didn't mind.

"Go ahead," I said, "You need time to decompress from that pressure cooker. Honestly I don't know how you stood it. I couldn't."

With that, she slipped off her shoes and put on her sandals by the door. She ran down the two steps and along the narrow path to the boathouse.

An hour later, I made myself a second drink and took it to the boathouse. As I approached, I could see her shake her head and she seemed to be saying something aloud to herself. It sounded vaguely like, "I hate her. I can. It's alright to do."

When I stepped inside, Etta turned with the sound of my footsteps with a forlorn smile. She reached her hand out to mine. "I'm sorry about what I said in the car. You know I don't mean any of it. It was childish." I leaned down to kiss the top of her dark hair then sat across from her at the picnic table the original owner had installed for his many guests.

Since both Etta and I enjoyed painting, (she painted flowery watercolors and I painted loose looking landscapes) we began to use the boathouse as our studio. That summer we turned out six or eight canvases with river themes. This was the peak period of our art making.

I liked the bayou feel of some of them with the winding brackish creek. I didn't usually swim in it after I heard several stories from local residents who had bumped into otherwise reclusive alligators half asleep in the reeds. One woman inadvertently dove into a den of baby water moccasins, and although they were only four or five inches long, it was enough to terrify her.

One night when Etta was with girlfriends, or maybe at her mother's, I did venture into the water off the dock. I swam a few strokes for a minute or two until I saw a dark curved shape on top of the murky water. In a fright, I literally scampered up the wooden dock ladder, fearing poisonous snakes. It turned out to be nothing more than a shock of marsh grass that had been bent into an S shape, though it was enough to chasten me. I reckoned it might be foolhardy to challenge the unseen presence of any moccasins, particularly if there had been a nest somewhere in the reeds.

There were alligators around all the bayou country. Etta told me a story of a school kayak trip where she and her girlfriend paddled alongside the shoreline and had surprised one. Though the creature fled into the deeper water, it had been at least six or seven feet long with the sheer jaw power to do them grave bodily harm.

As a rule, alligators flee humans who startle them, having an animal's prepossessed knowledge that they are indeed the ultimate predator. But alas, if you unknowingly come upon either creature nesting, it may prove dangerous. We safely watched the natural world from the dock, which unfortunately wasn't very adventurous.

Etta and I had what I thought was a good marriage. It didn't occur to me how devastating her miscarriage had been. That painful loss piled on top of the dysfunction from the entire Mobile household became a catalyst for misfortune. We started to argue more often, not about important things, but about television programs we would want to watch, or plays we might attend, or whether it was a waste of time to be a symphony subscriber.

Once it was about whether one or both of us should go to law school. It all became incessant and ludicrous after a time and soon I carefully monitored what I said to her to avoid arguments.

The bickering escalated when she drank. I kept up with her on whiskeys and answered her taunts, but usually with a milder temperament and was less frequently drawn into any real fights. One night she stormed out over some criticism that I had made of her mother's interference in our lives.

Etta snapped back at me with a few harsh words and headed out the door. I heard her start the car and slam down the accelerator which caused an arc of sand and sea shells to fly into the air as she spun away from the yard. From the window you could see the cloud of dust. She was absent for about three hours, and when she returned, she acted contrite. We both offered apologies at the same time while talking over one another, then finally hugged each other hard for our stupid excesses.

There were times when I would come home from work ready to make a light dinner, and a cooked meal would be sitting on the stovetop under a linen cloth ready to be eaten. She asked her former family maid and nanny, who at eighty still drove a car, to stop by and make dinner twice a week. This arrangement seemed so strange to me, though I remained silent.
There was certainly something truly southern in it that I couldn't figure out.

There was an affection and trust between them, but to my mind, it was subtly tinged with a servant master-attitude that Etta clearly possessed, yet it wasn't quite that either. It was something far more mysterious to me. I once brought it up to Etta, but she dismissed it simply as my ignorance about the people who lived here.

"We're different than you," she said to me, "and we like being different. It's our uniqueness. At least, that's what I'd like to believe." Then she laughed her lilting laugh which successfully dismissed most uncomfortable subjects then and there.

"Etta, this seems really unnecessary to drag this woman over here for some meal we barely eat anyway." I said and that seemed to set her off.

She answered me a little too forcefully. "Josie was always kind to me. Her kindness saved me from going crazy in that house. I want her here. OK?"

I shrugged my shoulders in acquiescence. Sometimes Etta treated me like a distant alien she heard about whose habits were different from her own, and had nothing to do with this life in front of her. I tried responding with more dignity than Etta did, but to Josie, I really didn't exist at all. I was simply some foreign object taking up room in the house with her precious Etta.

I never quite fathomed why we needed a part-time housekeeper and cook some of the week. I went along with things without complaint. Maybe I was wrong. In my mind, this black woman went home at night and cursed us awful whites that had forced her into domestic subservience and talked to her the way you would to a child.

One time I was taking her back home because her daughter borrowed her car, and when she put her tote bag into the backseat, she slid in next to it. I was nonplussed as to why she still remained in the backseat. I thought perhaps it was to rummage through the bag for something so I waited for her to come up front and join me, but she didn't.

Finally, I asked her to come up front with me, and she flatly said no. I asked why, and she replied that she liked the backseat better. "More room." The front seat made her nervous. It was too close to the road. It seemed a rather bizarre explanation though I accepted it at the time.

When I mentioned the incident to Etta, she didn't respond. I repeated myself and a bit exasperated, she turned to me. "Black women don't like to ride in the front with white men if you want an honest answer. They feel that it compromises them."

"With whom?" I asked, and she shook her head then stood up.

"It's a race thing. People may think they're having some kind of physical relationship," she said sadly.

"What? She's forty-five years older than me. You'd get that from someone riding up front? You can't be serious."

"It's the way things work here, even though she's wearing a white maid's uniform plus the age and all. It's stupid, I realize. But I don't resist. It's pointless, really."

"Well, tell her to get up front with me next time," I said, a little heated.

"That would make her very uncomfortable, and actually hurt her. You don't respect her feelings, her history. Do you want to make Josie our enemy by putting her in that awful position? Well, do you? If you don't, then respect how she feels."

I relented, "OK, ok, I get it, but this is absurd."

Etta replied, "Call it what you want. It's how we live."

It was best to let that rest, I reasoned. It was such a small thing in our life, and I was a stranger in a strange land. I had gotten along with almost everyone, and it was because I became a part of their established order. I felt that the South got blamed by outsiders for far more than they deserved. The circles I traveled inside within business and socially in Mobile rarely saw outright racists, or obscenely bigoted instances, however, one does come to mind.

Etta and I were attending a garden party at her parent's house and Bill Robinson, the estranged husband of one of Minerva's oldest friends from childhood was invited. I had been introduced to him, and even then I could recognize that he seemed a little drunk. He was a rather large man and seemed to be wobbly on his legs. Apparently, he had played football at Alabama to some success, but he was thought of as a troublemaker.

I noticed the doctor look over his glasses as the man put his hand on some woman's lower back as he passed her on the lawn, forcing her to quickly turn around uncomfortably. I learned that the woman was his soon to be ex-wife. She was currently intimately involved with a local veterinarian who was a first-rate polo player and former linebacker at Auburn, and the two men had come to blows one night at the local country club.

Bill leaned over and whispered something to his estranged wife, and she responded in kind, with a tight mouth, and a cutting remark in return. Her veterinarian friend was over at the bar getting them both refills, and when he turned around and saw the Bill whom he loathed, his whole body

77

stiffened. He cautiously and quietly returned to the small circle around the woman and handed her the cool drink then instinctively glanced over his shoulder to watch the movements of the soon to be ex-husband who was now at the bar. In the next moment, the quiet night air was broken with a string of obscenities as Bill shouted at the bartender who wasn't quick enough with his drink.

He moved back a few steps from the bar and shouted so loudly that everyone could hear him.

"Nigger, I'm talking to you," he said. "I want my goddamn drink now. Not when you feel like it. Understand?"

The black man froze with the vulgar tirade and looked across the table aghast. He stepped back from the table, took his apron off, then marched over to where the doctor and Minerva stood.

"Miss Minerva, I don't let any man speak to me that way," he told her in a very quiet voice, "I'm leaving."

"Frank, please forget it. He's just an awful drunk, and everybody knows it. Please stay."

"I don't think I can," Frank said.

At that point, the doctor did the most demonstrative thing I had ever seen him do. He turned to Minerva and said, "I'm going to tell him to leave. I'm going to escort him out the damn door."

He handed his wife his drink as Frank watched and walked over to Bill who was looking around at the assembled little groups who stared back at him in disbelief for how he acted.

Bill stood with his face flushed, either from his drinking or embarrassment, and watched as the doctor approached. When he reached where Bill was standing, the doctor had raised his hand toward Frank and quickly shook his head no. He raised his voice a bit for him, and put his hand on the man's arm to guide him toward the house. Bill wretched his arm free with great force and I saw a dangerous look pass across the face of the veterinarian who was hurrying to where they stood. Something violent was about to happen, I thought to myself, and Etta squeezed my arm in fear.

By the time the veterinarian reached the doctor's side, Bill had already started to walk toward the house, but then turned and made some throwaway cutting remark to the doctor before turning back to the house. Like an experienced European diplomat, the doctor showed no emotion on his face to the scurrilous words then smiled.

At that moment, the tough-looking veterinarian had started walking toward Bill with a clear purpose of pummeling him in public but the adroit doctor rapidly moved in front of him and put his hand on his chest to stop him. "Stop this now," he commanded.

He spoke quietly to the angry man for a moment in order to gradually calm him. Seeking a smile to match his own, he put his arm around the bigger man's shoulders and turned him in the direction of the women.

At last the doctor walked back to the bar with a recalcitrant Frank, pulling several twenties out of his wallet and handing them to him. Frank refused them by shaking his head as though lost for words. The doctor closed Frank's hand over the bills while also putting his arm around the black man with an affectionate squeeze. They both laughed.

Etta turned to me saying, "He's terrible, but mother felt she had no choice but to invite him. Bill usually behaves himself, though the oncoming divorce, and his wife's display of affection for another man drove him over the edge."

"Your parents handled that very well," I noted. "Especially your father. He acted like a prime minister. He knew exactly how to diffuse the situation. I'm truly impressed."

"Daddy has his moments. He just likes his solitude more than most men, and living with mother is, well, pretty challenging, I'm afraid."

"Minerva?" I asked her, and we both started laughing hard. I couldn't swallow my mouthful of whiskey so I accidentally spit it out onto her bare shoulders, and she shrieked.

"You barbarian," she joked.

The balance of the evening was without incident. I spoke pleasantly with those I knew there, kissed the mothers on the cheek as was expected, and met a few new people as well.

When Etta and I returned home that night, we talked about the incident at the party. "Betty can act a little trashy without much prompting. Now that they're both getting divorced, the whole thing has become a scandal."

She added, "Bill tried to sneak in Betty's bedroom window one evening and the veterinarian was already in her bed. He slugged the poor fool as he was coming in the window and knocked him back out into the yard. What a soap opera."

"Your father handled it very well for a man who doesn't like conflict. Though when you're saving people on the operating table, you must have a quiet courage most people miss. He did it smoothly without the anger. It was masterful."

She got up and rummaged through her bag and pulled out a pack of cigarettes then lit one. I had never seen her smoke and watched as she tilted her long slender neck in the moonlight and blew the smoke into the air. Etta looked at me directly not expecting a comment on the new habit.

"It's not a habit, mister perfect. It's an addiction," she added, and gave me a wan half smile.
I remained silent and stared at her as she flicked a small ash into an ashtray that served as a candy dish.

"I've never understood how he can live with my mother and with all the children. It goes way beyond my understanding. I guess he loves her, though I've never heard her be affectionate to him. No caress at the table, in the hallway, nothing."

Etta was mostly an outdoorswoman, healthy and even a little athletic as she had shown when playing tennis. I couldn't hear what she was saying as I watched her smoke. It was so unlike her and it wasn't something that could be unnoticed. I felt that I had to say something.

"Why the smoking now?" I asked her trying to appear nonchalant in my calm manner. I wanted her to think I was more curious than irritated.

"Nervous habit left over from those years at Tulane. It's nothing. Don't worry," she volunteered. "I'll probably quit next week, and who cares?"

I shrugged my shoulders and said, "Fine," and we left it at that as she put out the cigarette, then walked to our small bar.

"A drink?" she asked. She had gotten two glasses before I could respond and filled them with ice at the refrigerator.

"Scotch?" she inquired further, and when I shook my head yes, she smiled back at me. "A man who knows his own mind."

It was the following week that her father had his stroke at only sixty-two. It had come over him without warning as I suppose they all do. He had lost his balance coming out of the hospital after an emergency appendectomy on a ten-year-old girl, who would be fine. It was a difficult operation with some scary breathing issues, but the doctor was always a consummate professional. He had the respect of every doctor on the Gulf Coast. Mention his name, and you would get a nod of approval.

At first everyone, including the doctor himself, had figured it was exhaustion. He had been doing surgery non-stop for over thirty years, but further testing had uncovered some neurological warning signs.

Within two weeks, there had been a change in his speech pattern, a slight slur within conversations, and he recognized what was happening to him. Within another week in the hospital, he had lost some muscle function in his right hand, and by that time he realized his career in surgery was over. On Friday of the second week, he was released, and for two weeks after, he went through a battery of neurological tests that determined that the effects of the stroke were irreversible.

When Etta learned of it over a phone call, she screamed. We were both at home, and I ran to embrace her fearing the worst.

"He's had a stroke, and God, I know it will kill him," she said to me with tears already streaming down her face. "Such a fine man. There never was a finer man than him," she sobbed.

I told her people recover from strokes. I told her what I remembered about blood clots and the possibility of removing them.

"Let's see what happens, and trust he'll get through it," I said. "At least he was at the hospital when it happened, so someone can help him."

"He's probably already dead," she shrieked, and pounded her fists on the wall.

"Etta, we don't know that. Stop it," I uttered, and held her tightly seeking to quell her obvious anxiety. "One step at a time. That's what we do."

We had visited him both at the hospital then at home, and surprisingly, he didn't seem depressed. Minerva's behavior during the whole thing was erratic. It went from nervousness to a depression worse than what her husband might have been suffering, to abject fear and back, then through the same gamut again. Etta and I couldn't do much but we tried to bring some semblance of cheer into the otherwise morbid household. I was particularly sensitive to her needs and the situation.

I could understand that Minerva was fearful for a house of young children and the possibility of having an invalid husband on her hands. There also was the disappearance of a surgeon's sizable income, though perhaps that was only looking at the practical side of things in this case. The emotional cost of a disabled husband and father would obviously be high for her and the family. She had a lot to consider.

It was summer and into the second month of the doctor's convalescence that we were on the terrace one evening. We spoke of his vision for the future, and it was rather clear to him.

"I have a plan for the rest of my life. To do some good for people like me," he had slowly explained since his words were now tentative. "There is no stroke facility here, so I will start one. I had a vision last night in my sleep of what it will be," the doctor sounded like a mystic.

Etta inquired: "Daddy, do you think you really have the strength for this? You're still recovering."

"My recovery is over. The damage is already done. Now to marshal what I have left, Etta. I'm ready right now."

The doctor said that he had made a number of calls to other physicians and hospital administrator friends, and had gotten their wholehearted support for the establishment of a stroke rehabilitation center funded by a consortium of five or six large Mobile and Eastern shore hospitals. He had secured the active participation of Mercy Medical, which would provide facilities and adjunct staff for the center to housed in a satellite building on their campus.

He admitted that his surgeon years were over, though he could still practice medicine and make a difference in people's lives. I was awestruck by his selflessness. He said that he would create a business plan for the venture, and with his notable reputation in the community, he expected it to be a success.

"I've been wanting to get out of surgery anyway," the doctor had said with candor. "It's a young man's game, and I don't particularly like to teach. This is more important anyway."

Minerva sat across from me stone faced, the only way I could describe her reticence. Later, Etta had told me that her mother was very worried about how it all would work out, and even if her father's health would hold up.

My attitude toward her mother softened.
Etta soon became indispensable to the Mobile household. She would run errands but more importantly, she was the only person who would sit with her father and talk at length about these new possibilities while trying her best to bring cheer into this otherwise rapidly changing world. Mary Agnes and her brother, Jackson, were conspicuously absent from these afternoons and evenings.

The work I was doing and the travel around the South also increased. The advertising agency had won favor with some members of the RNC. More trips to Washington were called for. At first it was simply showing the flag though they gradually became something more. Slowly I became noticed in the corridors of power.

We were called upon to help unseat the longtime Democratic senator in Tennessee who had spent so little time in the state that it had become a joke among the voters. He was clearly in our rifle sights. It seemed that he would be particularly vulnerable this election cycle. Senator Albert Gore had developed an anti-war reputation which had become his Achilles heel, and we used it against him.

I would report all this to Etta in evening conversation, and she would get glassy eyed while I was talking. Once, she had asked, "Do you care about anything except winning?"

She hadn't meant it to particularly hurt me but rather to warn me off chasing the brass ring of success as such a young man: Getting a bigger house, increasing our leisure time and privilege in this world. It stung somewhat, though, there might have been some truth in it. Her words did make me think about what I was doing in politics and why. My answer at first was crass even if it was the truth. I had wanted all the spoils, the low hanging fruit, and I thought I deserved it. Maybe not more than another man, but not any less either. The smell of ambition and victory hurled me forth.

On the campaign trail we took a dull and stuttering Chattanooga candy heir with a sing-song speaking manner and got him elected against all the odds. We brought down a man who had actually done something during his long tenure in Congress. But this race, and many of the others, sometimes goes to the fastest if you know the curves in the road like we did.

There was a biting television commercial with embarrassing sound bites that helped us push enough voters toward our side. It was all legitimate, though perhaps not taking the higher moral ground. This was politics, after all, and anything goes.

The television commercial I produced for the candidate won countless awards within the industry. It was mean-spirited and meant to hurt the man, which it had. He did take the higher road, but it was the only road offered to him. Senator Gore came to the half-asleep electorate with too little, too late, and he lost.

Our life didn't change very much with more money.

We did the same things and saw the same people. We became established as a couple of a certain social circle, and that was what Minerva wanted for her daughter and herself. For me, I was simply an interloper from some coal patch though I had adapted well to this way of life, and she thought the life fit me. I imagine it did. I felt satisfied and happy.

In the many political races, I was constantly thrown together with attractive and willing young women, particularly during the heat of campaigns, which were already a form of aphrodisiac anyway. The scent of power became seductive. It was tempting, true enough, though I turned my back on the obvious temptations and instead became a focused worker bee, flying on puddle jumpers from Louisville to Clarksville to Sikeston. Looking around the political environment, including Washington, I didn't want to succumb to what so many men and women around me had. There was an obscenity in the whole dance of American government, the flawed election process at least.

Etta's father recovered to the point where he could assume a role in the new stroke center. He didn't drive because he knew his propensity toward an aneurysm could happen again at any moment, and he didn't want to be responsible for killing an innocent family on the highway. He hired a retired black man to drive him back and forth from the center.

Within six months, word had spread throughout the Alabama medical community, and he started to receive visits from stroke victims in Montgomery, Birmingham, and Huntsville. He hired two young female doctors that had been known to assist him, and the stroke center became his passion. There had never been a facility devoted to stroke rehabilitation alone, and the doctor threw himself into it.

Etta saw the change and enthusiasm within him, and she felt relieved. Minerva grudgingly accepted the inevitable change, but the absence of a hundred thousand dollars each year had put her constantly on edge. After all, they had two young children she needed to provide for in the custom that they had come to embrace.

The doctor's speech was distinctively slurred now but certainly understandable. He had recorded his voice, then studied the changing speech patterns in order to further assist his work with patients. He added a speech pathologist to the center staff and his holistic view of rehabilitation began to find its way into medical journals with its innovation. He added a review of dietary methods and consulted with international experts, some of which were outside the mainstream medical world.

His own eating regimen changed radically. He added organic vegetable juicing as a therapeutic practice and removed the unhealthier parts of his diet. With that, he measured the gradual increase of his own stamina, and began to introduce these findings to his patients. Etta and I tried to follow him occasionally with raw vegetables, but we soon tired of that and went back to the rich diets of the past, though

86

we were moderate eaters. It was tiresome to do the raw juicing since there was so much work in preparation, though we did try.

None of his newfound passion, however, was directed toward his own children, and Minerva developed an awful bitterness. She treated his behavior now as sheer madness and blamed it on the stroke's effect on his brain. She would complain about her difficulties at home since the stroke. There hadn't been much tenderness in the household toward the doctor before it happened, but it had completely disappeared now. It was replaced by resentment, and sometimes harsh words.

This hurt Etta as the oldest child and Minerva's confidante, yet, there was little she could do about it. She would patiently try to make peace between her parents. Her brother treated it all very clinically and with a certain amount of disinterest like any other disease or malady. Earlier he had married the Mountain Brook debutante, and moved to a new Birmingham research hospital. They seemed very happy, or perhaps serene was the right word. They had the advantage of distance.

By this time, Aaron and Mary Agnes had their own set of worries, mostly as the result of his miscues with the Marotta crowd who had become more demanding of him. Aaron turned into a nervous wreck and when they last joined us for dinner, his conversation was vague about everything. None of us would know much about any of it, not even his wife, until it was already too late.

The whole unsolved mystery was that he had enough money. Marotta had given him plenty of cash, and it was inexplicable why he was constantly upset about it. Yet not a single soul in Mobile, other than Aaron, knew this. It was his own secret, and his alone. I think he was just afraid that Marotta would kill him, and maybe Mary Agnes too. That's what worried him.

Mary Agnes was a good woman. Minerva had unfortunately taught her that being clueless as to a family's finances was the prescription for a happier life. Minerva probably considered herself as happy, or perhaps simply normal for that time, and had purposely excluded her daughters from those life lessons. Smile, be attractive, charming and intelligent if you must, but let the man handle everything outside the home. This progression of enviable southern living was apparently a much better way of life.

None of us expected Aaron would, or could, do what he finally did. He died alone in some cheap hotel room in New Orleans from an overdose of sleeping pills. He had been in the hotel room for two days before he was found by one of the housekeepers. It was a painful and horrible saga, and an unfitting end to his troubled young life.

Aaron had been served a court subpoena for a state criminal investigation on New Orleans city corruption charges, and had panicked crazy with fear and worry then took this exit. Yet this was only the tip of the iceberg.

There must have been other things going on as well to push him to the painful solution that really served no one. But to the truly mentally ill, suicide has always been an unfortunate and willing option. But why? There was no evidence that Marotta had any hand in the death except for the intimidation that perhaps drove Aaron to take his own life.

Later, after he had been buried, we learned second hand from friends who had attended the funeral that he had emotional problems as an adolescent. Aaron had once spent two weeks in a convalescent hospital. It was termed a rest home. This was at the end of his freshman year at Tulane and after that, he seemed the perfect model son and hard-working student. The young man had joined a popular fraternity and became a columnist for the daily student newspaper.

What he had done at the Times Picayune later had been more unethical than illegal. It violated the ethics of the entire profession, and it damned him. What did he really do for this mobster? Who wanted Aaron to testify and about exactly what? Perhaps it had involved some statute like the RICO crime laws, and that became a net to cast far and wide in the pursuit of organized crime. There was no doubt that Marotta was a hideous criminal. Even though he served the one or two light month-long jail terms, there was far worse that had not been uncovered. He was somehow always ahead of his so-called pursuers.

There was hardly anything left from his life insurance. Aaron had put all of his money from Marotta into their live-oak fronted home. However, there was the prospect that the residential property would be seized as proceeds from fraud, and it probably wouldn't have a pleasant end for his wife and child. New laws had allowed it. At the very worst, Minerva and the doctor would find the money to bail Mary Agnes out of some of this mess and maybe save the house at least, and pay many of the legal bills. Etta and I could help too.

Naturally, Etta and I talked about the tragedy often the first few weeks after Aaron's death. We both searched ourselves and each other to somehow determine the why's and the two of us could find nothing. None of the conversations we had with him while sitting on the sailboat with a cold beer, splayed out together in the sand at Point Clear, or half-asleep on the dock at Magnolia Springs, had warned us about what would happen to him.

Aaron gave no clues as to his misery and fear. Neither of us had ever probed about his financial good fortune with the fine home in New Orleans. How could he ever afford it? We never asked.

It reminded me of a distant friend that I had in college that had committed suicide. It came as a great shock because on the outside, he was gregarious and popular, especially with young women. I didn't think drugs or even alcohol had played any part in it. He just didn't return to the tree-lined campus one September. It was two months into the winter semester that I had learned he had killed himself, but never why. Those reasons aren't ever completely revealed to us, and why would they be? They're locked away in the troubled mind.

That Aaron wasn't meant for this world was the only conclusion we could come to. He was too sensitive and broken to live the life he felt he must, and it all came unraveled around him. His fear and utter despair and the shame were too much to endure, and he saw no other way out of his dilemma. He had been cursed from the beginning.

"I don't know how he could have lost his way so much," Etta said to me with tears in her eyes. "There had to be a way out. Something."

"Not to him," I answered. I knew that if there had been any other thing, he would have done it to save himself. I believed that.

Etta got up from the couch and poured herself a tall drink, mostly whiskey and a little ice. She drank half of it in two loud gulps. She sat down again, and kept shaking her head back and forth in distress. She took a deep breath.

"Mary Agnes will go on. She's such a positive creature, and if anyone can begin living again it will be her," she said.

I agreed with her. Her sister looked at life in a practical Southern woman's manner: an attitude of guarded optimism with some strength. She would be fine. She was still an attractive woman of good family in a place that honored them, and she would find a man who valued those gifts. I didn't doubt it.

As families go, I imagined that Aaron's Jewish family, who had never wanted the marriage anyway, thought that he had been forced into his despair trying to become what he never was. He had tried to fit into the Catholic aristocracy which was what Minerva wanted and it had killed him. His family went through the ritual of a morose funeral, and looked like the grieving family they obviously were, though you had a sense that both his mother and father wanted to shout, "You drove him to it, with this false life!" But those words were never uttered, and his father spent time patiently speaking with each of Minerva's family.

A New York sister had returned for the funeral, and spent her entire time in a forced silence. With her demitasse teacup, she leaned against the doorframe of Minerva's house and nervously scanned the room with her catlike eyes. She greeted no one, certainly none of Mary Agnes' family, though she would smile when prompted. It was a tight and patently false smile, or half smile, fading quickly from her narrow face.

She was divorced with two half grown children in Queens, and had nothing to do with Mobile or the entire South anymore. She hardly ever visited her parents, or brother. I watched her as she stood in the corner alone.

Finally, she did come over to me, probably having remembered me from some gathering where we had all been together. I wasn't like them, she must have reasoned, since I came from another part of the country. When she reintroduced herself, I told her she had our condolences, and that I had loved Aaron. I had found his presence one of the high points of my life here.

"You're the one with the politicians, right?" she asked, giving me a look that wasn't cold but wasn't welcoming either.

"I work with campaigns, governors and senators. You may have heard that when you talked to Aaron, or maybe your dad," I added quietly trying to make this confrontation less painful for either one of us.

"He was the token Jew," she said with some sarcasm motioning with her head toward the small tight cluster across the room of Minerva and the rest of the family.

"Did he entertain them? Aaron was good at people pleasing. He learned it at home, but I imagine he felt he'd never be enough…for them."

"Everyone adored Aaron," I told her, and she laughed a sinister laugh, and shook her head from side to side.

"The last time I talked to Aaron on the phone, he wasn't right. He called me, and that was strange because we aren't close," she volunteered.

His sister moved nearer to me and I could smell the stink of cigarettes on her breath as she spoke now that her face was next to mine.

"He told me that Mary Agnes, that wonderful wife and mother over there, was killing him, little by little," she said. "He couldn't offer her the life she wanted, and he was so fucking guilty it made him sick. Sick in his body and in the head too."

"I didn't know that," I responded with a calm that I knew was needed for this conversation. I moved a step back from her onslaught to stand my ground.

"He told me that he'd become an addict to booze and pills and that was the only way he could keep working. He said he was dying. All to keep her in that bubble of a life she needed. That bitch right over there, her."

I offered some response to the whys of his demise, but she held up her hand for me to stop talking.

"It was her, that bitch, who killed him," she uttered raising her voice, and people in the room started to look our way. In the next moment, she stormed out the door bumping into an elderly woman who was a friend of Minerva's, nearly knocking her to the floor.

Etta quickly came over to my side and inquired, "What on earth was that about?"

I told her she didn't want to know. It was only the demonstration of someone's pain over Aaron's death. That's all.

My feeling about Aaron was that he kept hidden those demons hidden that caused such absolute hopelessness to make a man want to end his life. His family saw him as functional in the ways they understood: job, marriage, and a man's responsibility. They believed that they need look no further, and so they hadn't.

Etta didn't rebound very quickly from Aaron's death. It seemed to open those places of emotional pain in her own life, particularly with her mother with whom she hadn't really gotten along with for years. She feared Minerva and subsequently obeyed because of that fear.

It didn't seem like the usual mother-daughter relationship but my own family wasn't functional either in any definition of normalcy. Continuous chaos, drunkenness, cruelty, depression and poverty was pretty much the sum of my family legacy.

On most days when I left for the office, Etta would already be awake. We would have coffee together and talk, and she might continue to sit there for hours before stirring. She would look out over the water and if she moved before noon, it was to visit her parents in Mobile. Usually it was just Minerva, though maybe one or two days a week the doctor might stay home and work while managing his continual pain.

If the doctor stayed home, he would be sitting at his desk in the den by ten in the morning after having had breakfast with Minerva. He would work through lunch, stop to make his vegetable juice, and quit at two to nap. Minerva was usually gone visiting friends, or attending meetings for civic and charitable groups, or occasionally shopping. She had the housekeeper do the real grocery shopping, but on the rare occasion might pick up one or two missing items. She might go to the liquor store, but generally she would have one of the men who worked for the store deliver the wine and whiskey in the white company van.

That was her typical day. Once in a while, a friend might come by for an afternoon tea and Minerva would buy pastries in advance from a French baker in the city. The owner claimed he was French though he was probably Cajun if I had to speculate.

Etta might join her teatime guests, but otherwise they would talk while Minerva busied herself with writing out thank you cards, or invitations, or some other task. What they discussed I didn't know. I don't think Etta complained about me, or our marriage. If she had, I think Minerva probably would have told her to suck it up.

Friends would come over for a light dinner and increasingly there would be children in the mix. It was the child-rearing years for all of us in our expansive Mobile circle. With the remoteness of Magnolia Springs, it was generally a weekend visit, so we planned our time around boats, water, and children. The time seemed to stand still during this time of deepening our lives. If it was difficult for Etta, she never let on and she was always open and honest.

Mary Agnes and Rachel stayed with us a lot in those early days after Aaron's death. She had taken her great heartache better than most women. Though not stoic, there was the realistic acceptance of what had happened and a desire to go on. She never complained to me. She never fully understood why Aaron had done all he had or why he never came to her in his hour of darkest need. She didn't dwell on the unanswered why's, as she knew they were unanswerable questions. Rather, she quietly went on with her life, leaning on Etta a lot, but eventually finding her place.

Mary Agnes was still attractive. She had only one small child and came from a notable family which made her marketable. A man from the small social circle would eventually find his way to her door, and one did. He was a childhood friend who was a lawyer, living out in Boulder, and he wanted to return home. He was a well-spoken and a rugged sort of man whose careful manners bespoke where he grew up while obviously intelligent and caring. As a civil rights lawyer, he would have to have some appetite for compassion so it couldn't all be about money, at least that's what I figured. So his friendship with her grew unhurried, and blossomed.

# Chapter 6

After a year had passed, Aaron's family had stopped asking to see their granddaughter. They wanted the distance, though they continued to send holiday cards and presents. They blamed Mary Agnes, and maybe Minerva too, for Aaron's failures.

Unfortunately, this was the way they handled their grief. It seemed cruel for the innocent child, but I imagined there would probably be a stepfather before too long and a progression of other children. It was a rather safe bet, and the forced distance between the families continued.

I had run into Aaron's father after a business lunch on Dauphin Street, and at the time, he had treated me like a complete stranger. He failed to introduce me to the couple he was with, and was awfully short with his answers. His eyes showed me a hatred unsuccessfully hidden by his wide and ingratiating smile and false friendliness. But who could blame him? How can someone recover from that kind of loss? I thought about it as I watched him turn the narrow corner and disappear from sight.

Even during the few luncheons or meetings I had attended around town, I didn't run into him again, and I don't think I saw him but a few times over the following years. The once familiar family quickly vanished from my consciousness, though I'm certain we remained in theirs as a rather painful chapter.

What we learned about Aaron much later, was shocking and none of us could believe it since the story seemed so unreal. It all came out after Carlos Marotta was deported to Italy as an undesirable following several small crimes that amounted to almost nothing. Many of the men associated with their dealings were interrogated and revealed surprising information. Aaron had fooled us all.

As a young boy, Aaron had been interested in aviation. He joined the civil air patrol which was more active than even the Boy Scouts in Mobile in those years since the naval flight school was just an hour away in Pensacola. Every teenage boy in town in the Cold War years dreamt of becoming a Navy fighter pilot and with the consent of his parents, he had learned to fly. He took lessons from a longtime bush pilot who had flown both WWII fighters and later biplane crop dusters. Aaron initially learned to fly in a small Cessna, then gradually worked his way up to a two engine Mooney which he rented out periodically from the airport.

No one thought much of it. It was the passion of a youngster and was never a burden for his parents. In those days it was cheap. He collected the needed flying hours on weekends so for most Saturdays, a sixteen-year-old Aaron had done his ubiquitous touch and goes at the airport. By his eighteenth birthday, he had become a competent pilot of small aircraft. At nineteen, he had easily earned an FAA commercial cargo license.

He was an accomplished pilot and mastered night instrument certification so that he could fly anywhere, anytime. During his first years at Tulane, he had taken fraternity brothers to Cancun, or maybe the Bahamas for a couple weekends in a rented aircraft that could make the several hour journey. It was a wonderful experience for the young men.

The first hold Marotta had on him with the Superdome collusion was the tip of the iceberg. We subsequently learned that he had been enlisted by Marotta to bring cocaine back from as far away as Chile. Aaron was outfitted with a powerful aircraft with enough geographic coverage that it only needed a single stop on the flight before going to Santiago, and then return to the same refueling spot on the way back to the United States. It was rather diabolical.

Aaron had covered his tracks with his wife with the excuse that he had been given additional responsibilities that forced him to do more out-of-town travel. Some of it had become international, and at one time, the Times Picayune did indeed have a Central American bureau of a sort. They had hired a freelance writer out of Panama and later Guatemala. That was during the heyday of the newspaper following the second war when it was perhaps the finest newspaper in the entire South. It was a much better paper than even Atlanta which was a far larger city.

In addition to the cocaine shipments, Marotta had negotiated with some federal government covert operatives in the Central Intelligence Agency to have the pilots he hired transport weapons secretly to the Contras in Nicaragua. They became gun runners.

It's mind-boggling that the United States government would hire a known criminal such as Marotta, then have his Mafia organization transport weapons for the American-backed insurgency forces. How could someone like Marotta negotiate with the federal government for a secret military operation, and handily smuggle illegal drugs into the country as well, all untouched? It was beyond my understanding, but it happened.

The operation was small in the arms dealing world and it never amounted to more than several million for the weapons. The money itself was significant enough along with the government's goodwill. The Mafioso ferried weapons to the scattered Contras and were rewarded by loads of cocaine that Aaron scattered at different drop locations along the Gulf Coast.

There was one experienced pilot who did most of the flying. His name was Barry Sloan, and he had been a CIA pilot in Vietnam in the early days of involvement. Sloan got most of the money for the guns-and-coke transport. Aaron did well too, and far better than the first deal with Marotta. This was really big money now.

Marotta told Aaron after he learned that he could fly, "Look, what you're making now is pocket change. This deal with the feds will make you rich. You want the biggest goddamn house in the Garden District, huh? Okay, in a year you'll have it." And he burst into laughter. He added, "I want people I trust, who won't get greedy or stupid. You're a smart boy. You like money."

That's all it took to make him Marotta's pawn forever. Sure enough, the money came: much more than he could ever have imagined. For each flight, he was paid twenty-five thousand dollars' cash, so in four months, he and Mary Agnes were completely without money worries. She had a ten-thousand-dollar balance in her personal checking account, and never bothered to ask why it was so high.

Aaron had started to fly weekends. Generally, he would do one weekend a month, or sometimes two, and was always careful with detailed explanations for his absence to his wife. He would be gone from New Orleans sometimes three days at a stretch, yet she never suspected anything sinister. After all, why would she? Mary Agnes wasn't made that way. The poor woman wasn't all that inquisitive. None of the women in her family were either.

At the height of these flights, Aaron was bringing in a million dollars' worth of cocaine a trip for distribution. The exotic white powder had really taken off and addiction was soon at every level of American life. It infiltrated the Board of Trade brokers in Chicago, street hustlers in Miami, and part-time dancers and prostitutes in the French Quarter.

There were three main suppliers for the South American cocaine traffic into the United States: two were from Colombia with Pablo Escobar's being the largest. The smallest of the suppliers was based in Chile. The cocaine cache coming into Chile was from Peru.

Aaron would fly into Santiago worry-free since most of the scrutiny was on the Colombians. On the way down, he would fly out of New Orleans to a remote airfield within Guatemala while skirting the Nicaragua border where the Contras were safely hidden, then offload the weapons and fly on to Santiago. Sometimes he might fly to another Chilean airfield, but Santiago was safest for the trade.

The weapons Aaron carried were the result of the secret agreement between the American government and Marotta, which appeared to be more about unrestricted narcotics trafficking, but Reagan didn't ask how his generals and spymasters did their business. It was always on a 'need to know' basis in order to protect those higher up the chain of command.

Aaron and Barry Sloan worked in tandem to supply Marotta's drug trade.

The dollars had become enormous. In addition to a flat twenty-five thousand dollars a flight from Chile, there was an added ten thousand dollars if they dropped gun shipments in Nicaragua. That was at least seventy thousand a month for each of them but Sloan wanted even more, so he upped the number of flights he would make and asked more for each trip.

That didn't please Marotta, though he agreed. It seemed that on one particular flight, there had been an attack as a plane was off-loading weapons on some obscure runway. It was an ambush by Ortega's troops that killed several Contras, and Sloan had been lucky to get off the ground at all in an emergency departure. It was no longer considered safe, but the American government had wanted it to continue and the CIA had said that it would deploy more protection from Contra allies for the gun drops.

There was now so much money involved that Marotta upped the ante for the pilots. Each trip was now worth fifty thousand dollars flat. Aaron was seduced into more flying so that he could become filthy rich within a year, and then he would quit.

I couldn't believe that a man as sophisticated as Aaron could think that he could simply walk away from a murderer like Marotta when he felt like it and not expect repercussions, some of which might be deadly. That was his master plan. Barry Sloan had other ideas. Sloan wanted Aaron out of the drug running equation entirely. He wanted to do all the flights himself, and in truth, he was a more seasoned and better pilot.

Aaron had been brought in because Marotta was new to high stakes drug trafficking, particularly cocaine. Aaron was simply available because he had a hold on his present loyalty. Marotta could let the Sandinistas shoot Aaron, or even have him slaughtered in the States when he felt the time was right. It didn't matter much to him as either solution would work out in his favor.

Escobar had the East Coast Mafia out of New York handling the part of the country from Miami north to Boston. That left Marotta alone with his sources of the cocaine and final distribution. The raw cocoa left from Peru then was processed in Chile, which wasn't on the American drug watch list. It was safe trafficking thus far.

Aaron did two flights a month, no more. Sloan would do at least four. He could handle the pressure and he wanted the money. Aaron was happy with his smaller cash windfall and he wasn't greedy. It was a gift from heaven. Yet, he was a bundle of nerves over the whole operation: the constant lying to Mary Agnes, a plane crash in the jungle, and the risk of arrest.

Aaron had asked to cut back his hours on the Times Picayune, telling his editor that he had a book contract with a looming publisher deadline.

The lie was believed, so he was free to fly. He told Mary Agnes the same thing, and said he had gotten a huge advance but needed to put the time in, particularly the travel for research. The subject had something to do with civil rights.

She had never seen a chapter, and since Aaron was such a good storyteller anyway, he strung her along with the false narrative when he talked about it at all. Her life was perfect anyway and there was nothing to ask of her husband.

One night she had asked him, "Please let me have a peak at the new novel. Just a few pages so I can see what you're writing. Pretty please."

He answered with affection, "That's bad luck in the writing world, to take a look at a book before it's done. None of the greats would allow it. Except for that Alabama girl Zelda Fitzgerald, and she stole Scott's story."

Mary Agnes, who was well-read, and knew the Zelda history quite well, said to him, "You've got that wrong. Scott took her stories. The things she was writing about her family and all that, he used it for his own book while she was writing hers."

She laughed and shook her finger at Aaron in a school headmistress way, and then sat in his lap. "You know *Tender is the Night* was about her nervous breakdown," she continued. "He wrote the main character, Nicole, based on Zelda. Her looks, her mannerisms, the way she said her words, everything."

He caressed her hair while she spoke, "When she saw his novel, she went crazy, maybe crazier because she was already over the top, and she cursed him to high heaven. The story goes that Scott begged her to let him finish it, use her life, because without her, he was empty. He was at the end of his rope."

"That's quite a story," Aaron said, "but for a first time novelist like me, it's bad luck, darling. Honestly. Trust me."

"Zelda did write her book but Scott had used up all the interesting things about their lives: Paris, the secret lovers, or would-be lovers, the opium, the parties, and all of the strange people in Zelda's tribe. They're all crazy in Montgomery I can tell you for certain. I had a Spring Hill roommate who tried to kill herself in our room when I was up in Tuscaloosa for the weekend. She didn't die, but it scared the bejeezus out of me, I can tell you."

Aaron laughed. "You're my wild thing, and in my new book, I'm going to write that you snore almost like a water buffalo."

Mary Agnes sat up with a pouty lip and added: "I think you meant snort, not snore. So get it right." They both burst into raucous laughter.

After that evening, she never mentioned the book again. She assumed that writing was a journey that required solitude and secrecy.

Marotta arranged for some of the cocaine to go through Miami or to possibly stay there, and Sloan had made two flights already to the South Florida metropolis. He was returning from the third flight at night, and usually refueled at Chubb Island, which was a small atoll with an airstrip and facilities not far off Key West and Havana.

The approach looked as it always did. There were two lights to watch for, a green light that meant you were free to land unencumbered, or a red light, which meant you couldn't. But this time as he lowered his plane's altitude for the final approach, he noticed there were no lights. Thinking he had missed them somehow, he made a second approach and as he turned, he spotted two Navy fighter jets coming at him, clearly marking him on the radio and ready to force him down.

He could see into the lit cockpit of one. The pilot was motioning for him to land and had already fired some warning shots with his machine guns. The message was abundantly clear, and Sloane had no choice or they would shoot him down. The drug war was a war to the Americans. Reagan had publicly called upon all the armed services and law enforcement agencies to do what was necessary to stop the offshore drug traffic, and they did, so Sloan landed on the deserted runway. He was caught.

As his plane taxied slowly, several SUVs with armed soldiers came out of the darkness. When he finally stopped, Sloan was surrounded by twenty men ready to shoot him if he made any hasty moves, or decided to try to take off again.

Sloan's plane carried sacks of cocaine which were neatly piled where the passenger seats had once been, and there was nowhere for him to escape. He was flying the commodious Gulfstream twin propeller aircraft, usually dedicated for ferrying around corporate executives.

He was arrested immediately as he deplaned, handcuffed and carted off to the small makeshift terminal for questioning. Within another two hours, a plane landed to take him to the mainland.

Sloan had been arrested once before as a suspected drug trafficker, and authorities were prepared to offer him a deal to help cast out the net further to involve as many of the players in the ring as he could name.

Though, it's true he wasn't ready to denounce Marotta as the mastermind behind the drug operation, he had another strategy. Instead, to give the DEA agents some small piece of the trafficker's pie, he named Aaron as his handler and the man who had organized the transport of the cocaine. Sloane figured it was a betrayal that would cost him nothing, but perhaps with the lie he would buy himself some time before he would play the Contra card.

Sloan would eventually go public with the Contra scheme, and it would create a firestorm in the US. Congress and the public would feel used by the federal government where the authorization for these secret operations led directly to the President. For now, that was his trump card, but he wasn't ready to play it quite yet.

Aaron's name and role became the sharp point of the investigation and Sloan believed that Aaron would quickly give over Marotta out of fear of a long prison sentence. He would be imprisoned for a time, then quickly disappear after being stabbed in the back some night at a urinal by Marotta's paid assassin.

It was difficult to know what would happen to Marotta. He might claim he was doing this as an American patriot, and that the men he hired were the real drug dealers. They had taken it upon themselves to betray his trust. He was completely innocent of drug trafficking.

Besides, Marotta had been working undercover to provide needed weapons to beleaguered Latin freedom fighters. They were men prepared to give up their miserable lives to stop the communist evil taking over the entirety of Central America. Daniel Ortega was already a well-known fiend who must be stopped. There were others too, like Chavez in Venezuela, who were all ready to exploit their own people for absolute power. Sloan was his most trusted and experienced freedom-fighter pilot willing to fly into merciless fire with the needed weapons for the anti-communist insurgents. That took courage.

To some degree Sloan's plan was successful. The DEA had wanted more than simple couriers. Along with Aaron, he could turn over the names and details of the whole Chilean connection, which in turn, would lead the authorities into the Peruvian jungle to find the cocaine factories and those criminals who ran them. It was a war. He was no more than a simple freedom fighter.

He accused Aaron of creating this entire Chilean connection, and maybe that might be believable to someone who was ignorant of the facts, however, it still sounded far-fetched. How could a thirty-four-year-old journalist from New Orleans accomplish all this on his own? With Aaron in federal custody, it would only be a matter of time before he led them to Marotta's door and who would the Mafioso believe betrayed him? Some scared kid, right?

The plan played over and over in Barry Sloan's mind as he sat in a holding cell in a federal lockup on the outskirts of Miami. He was convinced that the plan would work, and a smile came to his still boyish face. He had been decorated as a combat helicopter pilot in Vietnam with over sixty missions under fire. He had flown Air America charters into the same incendiary land for two years afterward, and army general upon general had praised his courage. For Christ's sake, he held a Distinguished Flying Cross, had been an army captain, and later was given a Bronze Star as an afterthought.

One night on the Cambodian border under the heaviest enemy fire imaginable, he had gone in and picked up half of a stranded Ranger company. Later, he counted a dozen bullet holes around the cockpit window. There wasn't a better pilot on the American side. There was a lot of truth in that.

He was a trafficker during those later years too. How else could he afford the huge bayou house and his place on the beach in the Bahamas? He had gotten a taste for moving large quantities of illegal drugs, and the opium trade in Laos had made him a small fortune too, but he wanted more. He was bored and he needed that adrenalin rush, twisted as it was.

Sloan also liked all the beautiful women that the drug money bought him in Asia, and in the States too, because he was a high roller at heart. Sometimes, he figured he should have just stayed put in Bangkok. He had a swank high-rise apartment there with enough money and all the female company he ever wanted, but he missed the States. Underneath it all, he was still a loyal Cajun kid.

In a short time, Sloan was recognized in several government secretive circles. As his name and incarceration became known throughout the covert network, his knowledge of illegal weapons transport served to make him a person of interest at the highest government levels.

"Be careful with Sloan," warned a four-star general at the Pentagon, who knew these things.

In less than two weeks, Sloan had been granted bail. He was given his freedom for five thousand dollars, which was a rather small amount of money considering the charges. Someone upstairs was concerned about the fallout from the weapons transport operation, and the Contra involvement might save him for a time.

His girlfriend came to the downtown Miami courthouse with a lawyer she knew and handed the authorities five thousand dollars in cash stuffed inside an envelope. Two hours later, Barry was released and free to leave Miami. He had been granted the option to return to Louisiana, however, he couldn't leave that state until the whole mess had come to a hearing, or maybe dismissal. There was no talk of a criminal indictment. None.

Sloan took his time leaving, as was his nature. He spent the weekend with the girlfriend at her apartment in South Beach, and also had dinner with a few questionable Latin friends. For some reason, Sloan seemed unconcerned that the threat of prison would go anywhere. He suspected that they would slap his hand with a far lesser criminal charge, maybe as an accessory to drug trafficking if anything. At worst, he would spend a month in some municipal lockup in Baton Rouge.

Barry and his attorney had plea-bargained for government information, and he had agreed to spend a nominal amount of time behind bars. He got thirty-eight days, just as he expected.

Aaron was picked up for questioning by federal agents one afternoon in New Orleans, right after he had left the newspaper office downtown and was getting on the streetcar to go into the Garden District. They escorted him off the St. Charles streetcar and took him to a nearby café where they talked. The agent who did most of the talking asked him mostly about his flights to Nicaragua with the weapons.

Initially, Aaron had denied everything but when they mentioned that his underling Sloan had told them everything already, he knew he was already on shaky ground. They said that Sloan was out on bail and if he contacted Aaron, they wanted to know about it, what was said, and why. They didn't expect Sloan to flee the country, but they wanted Aaron to realize that he was part of this investigation. He was implicated in serious criminal activities.

They asked him about the cocaine trafficking, and he lied as Sloan had initially done, though Aaron didn't know that. He explained to them that he was simply a backup pilot with less experience than Sloan, hired for offshore flights. He claimed he didn't know anything about the cargo he had been transporting and that his job was to simply fly the plane.

Aaron said he didn't realize anything illegal was going on and after the brief meeting with the agents, he knew they didn't believe any of what he had told them. Aaron had no choice now but to dance to whatever tune they played, and the government probably wanted him to land the far bigger fish, Carlos Marotta.

The fact that he wasn't arrested and jailed amazed him. Aaron tried to follow the strategy of the undercover men from whatever agency they came from, other than the DEA, or the New Orleans police. At first he thought they were FBI agents. They had flashed their identification so quickly he didn't really notice then grabbed him by the arms and helped him off the streetcar. They said he would hear from them soon, and would be required to answer further questions, then left him sitting at the cafe.

Aaron slowly walked the three blocks home uncertain of whether Sloan had been caught with either the drugs or the guns. Later he sat on the back terrace of his Garden District home listening to Mary Agnes tell him about some young mother's luncheon, but not really hearing a word. She didn't even notice the distraction in his vacant eyes, as he would shake his head once in a while to whatever she was telling him.

That night, unable to sleep, he had finally called Sloan who had picked up the second number that was designated for instructions, and asked him what happened. The story that Sloan fabricated was half-truth, but Aaron did manage to learn that authorities had confiscated a planeload of cocaine. It wasn't him who was caught with the telltale kilos, so Aaron felt that it came down to his word against Sloan's and they already had evidence of Sloan's guilt.

Sloan warned him to keep quiet, saying the Feds were less interested in the drugs than the illegal guns they had been supplying to the Nicaragua insurgents, but Aaron didn't believe him. He thought that somehow he would be pulled into this mess, and Sloan would escape a prison term.

Aaron had asked Sloan point blank, "Does Carlos know what happened?" There was a long pause on the other end of the phone before an answer came.

"No," Sloan said, "I haven't talked to him, but he'll know soon enough. I expect I'll be hearing from him soon. Nothing escapes him."

"What do we do then?" Aaron inquired.

Sloan laughed and said, "Well, I don't know, do I, amigo? Maybe nothing. But if I were you, I wouldn't be throwing around his name when they chat you up again. You know they're not finished with you, right?"

There came this loud bellow over the telephone as Sloan had found something humorous in Aaron's obvious terror. Sloane hung up the phone without another word, or a goodbye as Aaron sat there speechless and afraid. He looked into the darkness on the back screened-in porch as his wife and daughter slept soundly in their beds.

Still, Aaron kept it all from Mary Agnes and continued going through the motions of false normalcy. Four days later he received a call from the same man who had done all the talking at the cafe. He told Aaron that he would pick him up in front of the same café and that they would be taking a ride for a few hours.

"Be there, Aaron, because if you're not, we'll arrest you in front of your wife and daughter. We'll throw you in the lock-up until we get this sorted out," he said matter-of-factly. "Am I clear on this?"

Aaron swallowed hard, and he said, "Yes, I'll be there."

"Good," said the other deep voice, and Aaron heard a hard click.

They picked Aaron up in front of the Red Lion Cafe on St. Charles and motioned him into the backseat of a sedan where another man sat. The man who was in charge only said he was pleased that Aaron had decided to cooperate with them, and it would be in his best interest. He added nothing else to the brief conversation.

It was an overcast day and it threatened rain. The New Orleans industrial landscape started to depress Aaron as they drove less traveled back streets. They had driven down by the Mississippi River past the Dixie brewery into a seedy industrial park before stopping at a metal Butler building. They exited the vehicle and entered the oblong building that housed a modern office with three or four large computer monitors surrounded by a warren of rooms.

Aaron was led into one of the rooms that had five chairs and a table. The man in charge directed him to sit down. A grey-haired and lanky middle aged man entered then shut the door behind him. He nodded to the men present and seated himself next to Aaron.
He let out a deep sigh, and a knowing smile crossed his face before he spoke.

"You know why you're here?" he summarily asked.

Aaron was silent for a moment, then uttered, "I think so, but you have the wrong person."

"The wrong person," the older man repeated and turned to one of the others and added, "Can that be?"

He answered his own question with a tinge of irritation, "I don't think so. You see, we have been following your activities rather closely. Your friend Mr. Sloan has been kind enough to fill in some of the blanks," he reported, pleased with himself.

"I have nothing to do with any of this. Whatever you think it is," Aaron told them unconvincingly, and he felt his hands get clammy with the tension he was experiencing that moment.

"Look, I met Sloan once when I was doing a story and he told me a bunch of things he'd supposedly done. Probably all made up. That's my connection with him, period."

His eyes said he wasn't telling the truth. "He was some ex-Vietnam pilot. That's all."

The man smiled and looked distractedly at his open hand then suddenly at Aaron. His smile seemed to linger on his face for longer than was normal.

"Aaron," he said in a calm voice, "We know all there is to know about Sloan, and you're right, some of it isn't good. And like you, he's been running drugs for some mysterious someone. I want to know who that someone is."

"I'm not involved with him, or any of this. I'm a reporter for The Times Picayune. I track down news stories. That's all I do."

Two men in the room laughed in response to what Aaron said. "We don't believe you," the man continued. "You have a pilot's license and you've filed bogus flight plans for some time now. That's on the record."

"What?" exclaimed an uncomfortable Aaron.

One of the other men sitting next to the man who was questioning Aaron, handed him a manila folder. The man opened it, and shuffled through the pile of papers then threw a small stack of papers which looked like official forms on the table. The papers slid toward Aaron and splayed in front of him.

The man moved several of the sheets closer toward Aaron who momentarily looked down at them. Aaron took in a fast breath, held it, and exhaled quickly.

"Take a look at them," the man suggested, "and tell me if that's your handwriting and signature." He pointed to a line on the bottom of the page. "Right there," he said.

The other men in the narrow room said nothing during the exchange and simply looked across the table at Aaron. The talkative one who had first met with him in the café, now cleared his throat but added nothing.

"We have men who saw you fill out these forms, and talked to you from the tower for takeoff clearance," the man answered. "Better tell us the truth, don't you think?"

The interrogators looked unconcerned, and they believed that their case against Aaron's involvement was already established. There was little he could say in denial. He was clearly a guilty man. Finally, after a prolonged silence the older man uttered, "Well?"

Aaron thought that the safest thing he could do was to admit to the transport of the illegal guns into Nicaragua, since it was political, and clandestinely sponsored by someone in the American government. Even the White House had come out publicly for the Contra insurgents calling for their support in the press.

"OK," Aaron said nervously, gathering his thoughts. "I've flown weapons for someone in the American government into Nicaragua for the insurgents. I've made those flights. Done it as a patriot. To fight the communists."

"Tell us," one of the other men at the table suggested, and shook his head with a smile now on his taut face.

"Who told you to make those flights?" the older man now went on. "Tell us who organized all this. We'd like to know some names."

"It was all done through Sloan. He was the experienced pilot. He'd flown in Vietnam. He talked me into it to help my country."

"So you did this for Mr. Sloan, right?" the older man asked. "Sloan," someone else in the room echoed.

"Yeah," Aaron added, "He told me the CIA had wanted this done. Came from the highest levels."

The older man leaned over toward one of the others at the table whispering for a few seconds. The man, he spoke to, acknowledged the comment with an affirmative nod of his head.

"Isn't what you did against the law?" the older man probed. Not waiting for an answer, he continued with his interrogation. "You broke the law by moving firearms out of this country without a license, or any authorization. You supplied them to illegal combats, men fighting against an established government, sanctioned by the United Nations. Is what I'm saying correct?"

"Not quite," Aaron uttered, and found the words difficult to form.

The men at the table looked from one to the other with confidence, all ready to pounce on the unlikely suspect.

Aaron sighed at the persistent line of questioning, and he said, "I assumed that all this was legal. I was simply a pilot for the government. That's what Sloan told me."

"You were paid for the flights of course?" the man asked. "Exactly how much, and by whom?"

"Sloan took care of it all," Aaron said shaky in his response. "He gave me some money. That's it."

"We can look at your bank deposits if you'd like, and you can tell us about each transaction. That would take a telephone call."

At this point, Aaron thought he'd better tell them at least some of the story. He cleared his throat hurriedly as if that was a precursor to telling the truth.

"This work for the government was risky, and I could've been shot down, or ambushed on the ground anytime. We were paid well to put our lives on the line, and that's what we did."

"How much?" the unknown agency man persisted.

"A fair amount. I don't know the exact number," Aaron responded.

"You were working for the CIA. They were responsible for all this. Every flight that you made, and they paid you, right?"

"I got the money for each trip. It would be deposited into my New Orleans bank account by somebody. I don't know who did that, but it would get done."

The man got a little testy now, and he said, more heatedly, "Let's get serious here. You're a drug runner. You and Sloan were bringing hundreds of kilos of cocaine into the

United States each trip, and you were working with someone higher up who had the money. That's the truth, isn't it?"

"I brought guns to freedom fighters, OK. I'm guilty of that," Aaron threw out, and thought that with some luck he would escape the narcotics charges on the table.

He would hang the blame on Sloan, a known international drug smuggler for some years and began to calculate his strategy mentally. After all, for five years Sloan had smuggled heroin from Laos and Cambodia. A lot of people knew that. He had lived in Bangkok then.

If Aaron mentioned Marotta's name to these men, it would be an eventual death sentence for him. Aaron was convinced Marotta would murder him, anywhere he could hide. Whether it was inside federal prison walls, or even with a new identity as part of some witness protection scheme.

Sloan was a small time criminal. He was already known to these men. He had been in prison once or twice anyway, and hanging the blame on Sloan's shoulders would be Aaron's only path out of here. Marotta would understand. This happened sometimes in that unsettled world, and he would continue to trust Aaron for not involving him or giving him over to the authorities. At least that's what Aaron believed as he sat across from his unsmiling accusers. He touched his face several times to calm his nerves.

The grey haired man, who was called Wunderlich, had Aaron stuck in an uncomfortable corner. They had confiscated a planeload of cocaine from Sloan who had implicated him. It had seemed that the responsibilities for the trafficking were presented in an odd form of reversal by Sloan's confession. Some-body was going to take the fall here.

Within the next forty-eight hours, Marotta would learn of Sloan's capture, his cocaine cargo loss, and the pick-up and questioning of Aaron. His intelligence sources had already passed this information on to him in New Orleans, and he hadn't acted as of yet. It wasn't time.

113

The questioning continued for another two hours but Aaron held steady and didn't break. His only chance to escape would be to let the government explain away the illegal gun transport. He figured his best odds would be if the federal government decided to stonewall, and they pressured investigators to drop the whole incident. They could easily drop it into some circuitous unending investigation. Who was about to charge the federal government with illegal arms dealing anyway?

Sloan fashioned his final bargaining deal for the drugs by passing on his Chilean suppliers, and random details about collusion with Chilean and Peruvian police and foreign government officials. That revelation came as no surprise to anyone familiar with the drug traffickers.

Aaron finally was able to leave the Butler building on the river, but he wasn't free. He would be tied to these jailers until they had what they wanted from him however long it took them to get it. In fact, he was pulled in for questioning on two more occasions by other unnamed federal officials, but he stayed with his earlier alibi. He put all the blame on Sloan as the flight trafficking organizer. That made the most sense to the investigators. Sloan calling Aaron a criminal mastermind of the network made absolutely no sense to anyone. The investigators laughed at the mere suggestion, and it was forgotten.

It would take almost eight months for the bargaining deal to be completed, and Sloan continued doing his normal small-time illegal deals.

Between the next two meetings Aaron had with the investigators, Marotta met him once inside a parked car near St. Charles. Marotta's lieutenant waited for him to step off the streetcar then escorted Aaron three or four cars down the crowded sidewalk to the tinted window Cadillac where the boss sat in the backseat. The boss had a wry smile on his face.

Inside, the mobster was naturally composed and did most of the talking. He reviewed everything that had occurred and what he thought should be done next. He told Aaron that he was pleased with his testimony under federal questioning, and that Aaron had acted the way he expected his friends to, by keeping Marotta's name out of any so-called involvement. Sloan hadn't mentioned Marotta either in the subsequent interrogations. He indicated to Aaron that Sloan couldn't be trusted anymore, and he would be dealt with accordingly.

Marotta informed Aaron that he would have one of his lawyers represent him if this continued, or if the investigation deepened, but to remain calm.

"You talk to no one," he said to Aaron dismissing him as his man opened the car door. "You understand."

Aaron nodded his head in agreement. As he walked home, Marotta's words echoed in his troubled mind. Could he simply have someone kill Aaron with a word? Of course, he could, but would he want to? For now, Aaron appeared safe, though for how long?

Aaron told Mary Agnes he had been working with shady anonymous sources for a corruption story that the paper would run within two months. It involved state and New Orleans officials so therefore he had been a little secretive around her lately. He apologized for it. She lovingly said she understood, and was proud of the important work he did. Was she that gullible? His past as an investigative reporter made it seem quite real. He told her little outside of what was necessary for the harmony they enjoyed in their lives.

The problem came later. Marotta wasn't finished with him. I think that he expected that Aaron would cave in, either within himself and his own guilt, or to outside pressure from investigators. Aaron would never walk away.

Aaron made something like four hundred thousand dollars with cocaine trafficking. He had hidden it in four or five accounts with the largest amount of money in a Cayman bank. The advice had come from Marotta himself and he didn't want Aaron to become obvious with lavish spending.

The Mafia boss told Aaron to parcel out the cash, and under no circumstances buy luxury cars or beachside condos.

"You keep a low profile, you hear?" he warned Aaron, "Very low."

Coming from Marotta this made Aaron fearful about the illegal money he had accumulated. When they bought the house, Mary Agnes started to put some period antiques inside. Aaron claimed his magazine freelance writing paid for it since he wrote on southern topics for one or two national magazines.

One evening, I recall, he threw about names like the Saturday Evening Post, the Atlantic, and Harper's. They were his magazine clients, and they loved his stuff in New York.

Aaron was an intelligent and self-effacing man. During his years of journalism, he had perfected a style that was mainstream in its mass appeal, particularly with past and present racial themes taken through his unique Alabama prism. He was southern, and those editors weren't. It was quite an accomplishment, really.

His prose was fluid, and it often had the sophistication and the same kind of smoothness you would come to expect from longtime facile writers in New York and Boston. There was even a feature article on vintage homes in Mobile that had appeared in Southern Living that he had written. The family bragged on it and Etta kept a copy of the magazine issue on top of the two or three coffee table photography books on a side table in the Magnolia Springs living room.

Aaron sometimes also taught journalism at Tulane, and occasionally at Loyola as an adjunct professor. There, he had met Walker Percy, the novelist, who had once stopped by the Spring Hill house for drinks on his way to the Georgia Sea Islands. That particular evening was rather important to Minerva who had invited some of her more bookish friends. There was a lively discussion about the state of Southern letters among the assembled guests.

116

How had Aaron pulled his criminality off? It was mind-boggling. No one had any idea he had this secret life and had crawled so far out on the limb.

In the end, whatever Marotta did finished him. We wouldn't learn the account of events for months and even then, it came only in dregs. It was never the whole story but rather a piece that might find its way into the more knowledgeable mouths that was sometimes repeated in a whisper or occasionally in print.

The federal government didn't indict Marotta for any drug dealing but instead they found some obscure part of the RICO act for leverage, and decided to deport him as an undesirable. They would send him back to his childhood roots on some stony hillside in Sicily where he died three years later of a heart attack while leaving certainly dozens, or maybe even hundreds, of dead bodies in his wake.

He didn't have to kill Aaron to keep him quiet. Marotta only needed to frighten him enough with the slaughter of his family, and Aaron believed he would kill them. Late night calls made by people claiming to be from their neighborhood said suspicious things known only to Aaron.

There was no question the Mafia don could kill them all, maybe singly, or burn down the Garden District house in the middle of a winter's night. Maybe he would have some black thug rape and murder Mary Agnes on her way back from the grocery store. The list of possibilities was macabre and seemed endless.

To save everyone somehow, Aaron swallowed a bottle of sleeping pills then chased it all down his throat with a bottle of vodka on the top floor of some rundown Canal Street transient hotel. He was so very desperate, and abandoned.

Marotta was forever silent about his arrangement with the Central Intelligence Agency to supply the unsanctioned and renegade Contra army. The weapons smuggling continued without him, but was run by other secretive men. He was trusted by the feds to do it for the money and they would turn a blind eye to his narcotics trafficking. That was the deal. In fact, Marotta did the United States government a big favor. He held up his part of the bargain until someone outside of their circle nailed the drug smuggler Sloan who had never attempted to cover his tracks. He could hide in the Vietnam maelstrom but he couldn't hide here.

Sloan finally pleaded guilty to something marginal that found its way to some back court docket. When his jail time finally came, he languished in near luxury for nearly two months inside a Fort Worth white-collar holding facility mostly filled with crooked investment bankers. It was easy time to do, however, he wanted to continue trafficking without Marotta, and that was his mistake. Barry Sloan was gunned down in his Baton Rouge home driveway. Two Chileans might have pulled the trigger but someone else had clearly put the whole murder into motion.

The day before the hit happened, Aaron got an anonymous message that something terrible was about to happen to the so-called 'rats,' and the caller told him to watch Sloan because he would be next. It was frightening. The Sloan killing drove him into absolute madness and utter despair, and prepared him for the suicide. Why wouldn't Marotta kill him along with his family now? The Mafia don was removed from the situation, supposedly sitting complacently and unconnected in an Italian villa thousands of miles away apparently innocent.

After we learned about everything, Etta and I would sit around most nights for weeks afterward, thinking how we could've stopped it, or at least seen the warning signs that Aaron was careening out of control. Why did we believe they could afford to live the life they did in New Orleans? It didn't add up. His furniture merchant father wasn't all that successful to unload that much money on his son's family. The steep house price alone should have drawn our skepticism, though it didn't. We ignored all the signs, and never suspected anything untoward in all this.

Of course, not long afterward in Washington, the whole incident about secret American money supporting rebel insurgents was never proven and disappeared under a blanket of subterfuge. It also didn't explain how Marotta could escape prison for this in addition to everything else he had done including murder. Somehow, he had developed the necessary friends in high enough places. His government sponsors had to let him flee.

I don't remember who finally ended up telling Mary Agnes the whole sordid truth about Aaron. She disappeared inside herself with what she learned, and it changed her entire life. She would always be slightly broken.

Etta had let what we discovered go and as an extended family, we circled the wagons and spent as much time as we could with Mary Agnes. She would sleep over on weekends, sometimes twice a month, with us. She didn't want to live in New Orleans with the memories any longer and the house was put on the market. It was a lovely Garden District residence and sold quickly. This provided enough cushion for Mary Agnes. Later on, the bank accounts Aaron had set up in the Caymans were seized by the authorities.

Etta helped her organize moving and found a small frame house in Fairhope on a quiet street a block from the bay for her. That way Etta figured she could check on her sister and niece regularly, yet they would have some semblance of independence. That was the better solution than having Mary Agnes near the cloying tentacles of her mother in Mobile. As usual, her father remained relatively silent about the whole thing, which was his way.

In Fairhope, Mary Agnes would join other young mothers who were either married or divorced with similar age children. They would carve out a pleasant life. It was a lovely and progressive town with a mixture of the artsy and the forever eccentric, including the spawn of Alabama and Auburn fraternities. Within this diverse mix of people, we both believed she would find some degree of comfort.

There was a depression that had followed her from New Orleans, and I think that it ran through the entire Mobile family gene pool. Etta certainly suffered from occasional bouts that I would pull her out from when I could, but not always.

Naturally we had a few small dinner parties where we would invite people we knew beyond the Mobile crowd that had known Aaron, and it worked. By the end of the third month in the Fairhope house, the cloud that hung over her following Aaron's untimely death somehow lifted a little. Mary Agnes smiled, and there were moments when she seemed like that young woman I first met on the terrace, garrulous and full of enthusiasm. In six months, she broke out of the despondency completely. Her conversation moved back to that of her former Alabama girlish self. It was the same old smile again which could light up a room as she entered.

Right after things had become at least tolerable for her, another tragedy struck the family. The doctor died. He had a deadly final stroke at his rehabilitation center and died without regaining consciousness the next day. He knew his days were numbered. The doctor felt it physically happening to him and calmly accepted the consequences of his death. He never complained once to anyone. His new work had been widely lauded both by other doctors and patients as a selfless act. He inhabited that special place until the end.

The doctor had always been a fine man, and I had liked him from the first evening we had met. With Minerva, I couldn't say quite the same. She exuded her overbearing and hurtful dominance that had long ago turned into a debilitating control she had held over her daughters that wasn't healthy or normal.

Minerva was a closet drinker. By the time Etta and I had married, her drinking had accelerated beyond the social. I'm sure her husband had recognized her excessive drinking too. Whether he had attempted to moderate it, I'll never know. Often, when we would go over there in the early evening, she would have a drink melting in a glass on the counter. With the doctor's death, it slowly got out of control.

There was a cruel side to Minerva that surfaced long ago with her daughters, but eventually it showed itself in a putative and horrible judgment of how they lived. As with everything, time passed and it made its inexorable trek forward.

It wasn't long before Mary Agnes got involved with a divorced real estate speculator in the city that she had met. The man was narcissistic and rough. Whenever he was in Minerva's presence, she started to blink uncontrollably in what was her nervous response.

His crude speech announced who he was, and though he was handsome in a rugged sort of way, the unfortunate man had a propensity for saying the wrong things in mixed company. At least for this particular woman of a certain society and place. He was all wrong as Aaron's replacement. He put his drinks on her Civil War antique parlor table without a coaster and on one visit, his glass had warped the wood fueling Minerva's inherent distaste for him even further. She only spoke of him in hushed tones, if asked.

His name was Wade. The man was the product of a family on pine scrub land ten miles outside of Foley. He had spent six years as an Army ranger and returned home to a string of jobs, starting with selling insurance and eventually finding real estate and small time farmstead sales lucrative. His first marriage of thirteen years had produced four children, all with learning disabilities and a wife who had moved from one local fundamentalist cult to the other all while homeschooling the children. He hardly contributed any child support, seeming to rather spend the money on a new late model muscle car.

He could be charming, and initially he treated Mary Agnes like a princess with lavish restaurant dinners and sunset cruises out of Gulf Shores. Then it ceased, and he reverted to his more narcissistic behaviors, confident he held her emotions safely in his hand.

I tried to like him as Etta had, but there was little to recommend him. Even when they joined us as a couple without Minerva, it was tense. Etta would be too familiar with him, asking about his work, or his children, yet it was still all forced somehow. Mostly I remained silent, unless we would share something about a common military experience, or his business.

His oldest daughter had turned twelve, and she still couldn't tell time. Once or twice he brought her to Magnolia Springs and both Etta and I felt sorry for her. The parents had given her so little, no start in life, that we were afraid that it would become the same irreversible sentence to a life of poverty and dysfunction.

He told us of his concerns, and that he had tried to get the children into public school, but a judge had told him to mind his own business, or he would be charged with harassment. Even if that were true, it seemed that all his efforts toward his young family were half-hearted and far less important than his tailgating weekends at Tuscaloosa, or whitewater rafting with some ex-army buddy on a North Georgia river.

Though all of Etta's siblings attended top-flight tuition schools as had Minerva, she was sensitive to Wade's school dilemma, and she would offer plausible suggestions. His girls didn't all have to go to Bishop Toolen.

Naturally after several months, he wanted to move into Mary Agnes' quaint Fairhope home. And to her credit, she told him it was too soon as both she and her daughter needed time to heal from Aaron's death. He had grudgingly agreed, though he clearly didn't like that particular outcome. It was a subject he would bring up with Mary Agnes frequently without bothering to hide his disdain.

The few friends he brought to Magnolia Springs for summer barbecues were worse. They were usually too loud and coarse, and often already half-drunk when they arrived, so we stopped the invitations altogether. After a time, we would invite Mary Agnes herself on a weeknight and go about our own business on the weekends.

During all the back and forth chaos, two properties Wade owned went into foreclosure. He would lose them unless he came up with a backlog of four months' mortgage payments, which he managed to borrow from Mary Agnes. When Etta learned about it, she was furious and called him, berating the man for taking advantage of her fragile sister. He had told her to stay out of his damn life. That more or less ended all contact with him. Even Mary Agnes recognized the whole thing was a disaster, though she claimed she loved him. She had enough force of character left to walk away, but then the loneliness overtook her and she would see him again and again. It went on for maybe six or seven months. Minerva called him white trash and told her daughter never to bring him to the house again.

Etta distanced herself as much as she could from it all, though she was perhaps her sister's only confidante at the time. It was infuriating to her what his obvious manipulations had done to her sister's feelings. I don't think he ever paid back the money, or had any intention to do so. He was that kind of a man, a compulsive liar rolled up into a sometimes charming country boy persona that had served him well thus far.

He finally crossed the line when he had gotten into a shouting match with Mary Agnes at the Fairhope Inn restaurant. In the dining room, one of Minerva's oldest friends heard his spewed obscenities directed at an embarrassed Mary Agnes.

All the next morning, Minerva's telephone had rung off the hook with the dismay and dire warnings from a coterie of old friends, including the outraged wives of two retired surgeons who had been close colleagues of her late husband. One had known the doctor since medical school. It was awful to watch, and she felt she had no choice but to act, but by the time she reached Mary Agnes it was over.

A few conversations shed light on Wade's behavior that made the reasons for the failed marriage and troubled children more understandable. His father came home drunk one night in a rage when Wade was young. He killed his own wife with a single brutal punch to the face and was charged with involuntary manslaughter. It's a horrible experience for any child, or adult for that matter, to witness. He and his younger brother had lived with a relative for the next five years, and the year he graduated from high school, his father was released from the state prison.

To escape this father, Wade enlisted in the army at seventeen and was shipped off immediately to Fort Bragg for basic training then combat school. Soon afterward, he found himself as a combat infantry soldier in Vietnam. There, he was assigned to the 101st Airborne unit with the highest rate of American casualties in the long war. He spent eight or ten months on hour long jeep rides or more outside Hue. It simply amazed me that this man was seemingly normal for the most part. His life had been a gruesome tale from start to finish.

With Wade out of the picture, Mary Agnes dated a rock musician, then a wildlife biologist who worked at the nearby Weeks Bay preserve. Finally, through Minerva, she met the young divorced lawyer son of a distant friend.

He was who Minerva had chosen. The man was nice enough, and good company socially. He had a decent family background. Six years earlier, he had married an Atlanta girl who was more pretty than practical, it seemed. The whole thing had ended after only seven months, and it almost didn't count as a marriage to anyone. He wasn't a Catholic and that might complicate things if the relationship with Mary Agnes blossomed, though Minerva was way ahead of herself on this one. He could convert.

The young woman he had married came from the arts and was thought to be high strung. She danced with the

Atlanta Ballet, and he hadn't understood her strong artistic temperament. They stayed friends, although it hardly mattered since it was a childless union, and he never saw her.

Another thing that endeared him to Minerva's heart was his passion for polo, and he played regularly for the Point Clear team. He had followed polo growing up and even continued playing university matches at law school in Charlottesville. The Mobile team played at the large polo complex outside Point Clear and each year had a big charity fundraiser event during a game. There were auctions in tents and an elegant luncheon that he had invited Minerva and Mary Agnes to attend. That particular invite had sealed the deal, certainly with her mother and probably with Mary Agnes too.

This was 'her' crowd, as Minerva would purr in her most pretentious moments. Their relationship blossomed, and they would marry before too long. In less than a year, Mary Agnes and her daughter would be in a rambling white house on the water.

Etta and I went to the polo games where he played and after winning it by a chucker or two, the lawyer would appear in tall riding boots and sweaty shirt looking every bit the dashing sportsman. In truth, he was kind and thoughtful, and it seemed that fate had indeed given Mary Agnes a good turn.

As I talked with him, he would look over my head making eye contact with more important people than me. Chuckling to myself, I predicted that he would have a career in politics ahead of him. Two years later, he ran unsuccessfully for district attorney of Baldwin County. Within the subsequent four years, he became a state senator. By that time, I had a nose for politically ambitious types.

Before long, I received a job offer for an executive position in Chicago with one of the American advertising giants. I ruminated about the opportunity. We talked about it forever at home it seemed, and the Chicago agency grew tired of my hesitation. Finally, we decided I should accept it, and after a couple years, maybe return South. No one agreed with our decision. But I left that summer and stayed in an agency-owned apartment off Michigan Avenue while Etta remained in Alabama.

Opportunities for advancement there were clear. The work challenged me, as did the fascinating people I rubbed shoulders with, many of whom had already spent time in New York and London. I presumed that it would also be my own journey.

I flew back to Alabama one weekend a month, and the first day there was generally surrounded by the excitement and newness I brought with me. Oddly, Etta's whole attitude abruptly changed. It was remarkable how negative she had become so quickly. I was patient, and one weekend I asked Etta to fly to Chicago for a short visit.

It was a sort of honeymoon experience for a day or two, but by the third day we had started to argue. I had wanted us to get a city apartment, and immerse ourselves in this stimulating world, while Etta found it too dirty, frenetic, and perhaps even frightening. It had been a murder capitol once under Al Capone after all.

A week after she had returned to Mobile, we were talking on the telephone in the evening, and she flatly told me that she wouldn't move to Chicago. She couldn't as it was too painful to leave this place where she had lived forever and wanted to continue to live. To her, or to us, as she told me, my advancement in this so-called business world wasn't all that important. What would the money buy?

It was up to me to choose, she at last confessed. That wasn't any sort of choice, instead it was an ultimatum, or a break-up, which was inconceivable to me. I wasn't prepared to do that. So I resigned from Young and Rubicam after less than three months to the astonishment of their affable upper management, and flew back permanently to Mobile over the Labor Day weekend. I did it with a heavy heart.

What would I possibly do now? I thought to myself on the plane, while looking out the coach window, sipping a cold beer. Where would I work? I couldn't go back to my former employer with hat in hand, and tell him I had made a big mistake. Yet I trusted that things would somehow work out, and the most important thing was the happiness of all concerned. It was a duty I had shouldered willingly.

Etta was ecstatic, and in her heart she knew I would return. She reassured me that everything would fall into place as it always did, and we went on as before.

The first few weeks of idleness didn't much matter, then a month passed, then the middle of the second one. We were drawing down our cash reserves, and it started to concern me. Quickly, I took some outside political planning work, and found myself producing TV commercials for a mayoral candidate and a handful of nonprofits.

It lacked the excitement I found earlier in major league politics, but once Washington came into play, I found my hands were tied. I thought about law school, but getting through three years on the money we had accumulated seemed impossible.

The solution seemed to be to work all over the South in political races, as a sort of hired gun, moving from campaign to campaign. I had made a few contacts in the past who would recommend me, and after making a few telephone calls it all seemed doable.

The first campaign I did was for the governor's race in Tennessee. The candidate was a retired dentist who was also Chairman of the state GOP. The man had decent credentials, important friends in Memphis where he lived, and he could find money. That was always a good start to any political campaign: fund raising.

Within a month of his announcement in the primary, he had collected over two hundred thousand dollars, which was a handsome sum in those years. We were ready to push it to half a million and be front-runners in the horse race. The deal was I would spend two weeks a month in Memphis managing the campaign and return to Alabama for the balance while being able to leave for a short return trip if I were needed. I could do that comfortably, and Etta seemed pleased with the arrangement.

On Election Day, we had gotten thirty-five percent of the primary votes in a crowded field and the nomination was ours. The general election would be easier because the South had been converted to the more conservative GOP opposition party.

An unpopular incumbent governor, who had several messy scandals on his hands, became our shaky opponent. He was a tired and vulnerable candidate. The scandals continued to plague him and his chief state corrections officer had sold prison pardons for cash. He was under a separate criminal indictment. We made honesty in government our campaign centerpiece and hung his malfeasance around his neck.

We easily won the election. With that, more business came my way that went even beyond the political arena, including higher level consulting projects, as well as a few unrelated state contracts. This gave me some breathing room.

Financially, Etta and I were better off than before, and seemingly happy though the constant travel had taken its toll. As a couple, we had gotten thornier with each other in conversation, and oftentimes, too sarcastic.

The drinking sometimes escalated into pointless arguments but life was peaceful for the most part. That is, unless we pushed things too far and dug too deeply into painful subjects. I avoided bringing up anything unpleasant, and found myself going along with much in our Mobile life that I might have otherwise questioned.

# Chapter 7

Etta had decided to go back to school and enrolled at the University of South Alabama. She wanted to do work in social services and public policy, which surprised me, so she started working on a master's degree in clinical social work.

At the same time, the school had arranged for her to work three-quarters of the time for the Mobile welfare department in its case services division. That meant that she would go out in her car three days a week visiting people who received public assistance.

She would verify their eligibility and more importantly see if their needs were being met by the state, which was stingy in this area. It had become a political football, thrown around in each election cycle.

She excelled at it. People liked her and she liked them. She had grown up with black people, albeit in subordinate roles all her life, so Etta was never uncomfortable in most black homes, no matter how modest.

Her supervisors at the Welfare Department loved her as did most, if not all, of her graduate school professors at the university. She had that kind of personality that made whomever was in front of her comfortable, valued, and they instinctively trusted her.

The choice of her particular profession had shocked Minerva a bit, who saw social classes as all within the perfect balance. Though I never heard anything racially demeaning pass her lips, she felt it wasn't a worry within her closely defined world.

Etta was offered a full time case worker position because she was so competent. They wanted to bring her in as a supervisor well before her time, and she had tacitly agreed. Before long, I learned that Etta was lending her welfare clients money. Maybe not much at my reckoning, though she had already fallen into the trap. The lines of what she could or couldn't do for these people, who were all in some kind of dire need, had started to blur.

I finally put my foot down when she had asked me if we could pay the first semester's tuition of a welfare mother's intelligent daughter at Spring Hill, at least until her scholarship payments started. It was four thousand dollars. That was enough and I asked her to please look at her situation realistically. They were all in need, and it was impossible for us to take on these never ending additional burdens. Most of these loans, if not all, would never be repaid.

She smiled in her usual Etta way and said, "I know." Before long, the problem started to go away, though I imagined that she would give people a twenty-dollar bill every so often.

During her stint in social services, she had invited a black female co-worker and her husband for dinner. They came on Friday night in the late spring, and we barbecued and sat in the boathouse for the evening. They had been married a short time, and the wife was shouldering the couple's household expenses while her husband was in dental school in Mobile.

They were a lively and intelligent couple and I liked them. I figured that we could repeat the invitation at another time, but Etta told me they would be more comfortable with this one-time invitation. They would reciprocate themselves with an outdoor barbecue. One. After that, we would continue with our parallel lives.

It wasn't particularly difficult to grasp why, and honestly I didn't give it much more thought. I was a racially neutral person anyway. My concern was Etta and achieving the quality of life I thought we would both want. Any sort of civil rights concerns and social activist behavior wasn't a part of my political world anyway, at least not now.

I had been doing political consulting work for almost ten years and Etta and I were at the far edge of our marriage.

We loved and respected one another, though there was something wrong at the core of it.

Minerva had undermined our marriage for years. The fact that I wasn't native to her world, and the way she treated it with a mild irritation, never helped.

We tolerated each other, though barely, and over the years her softness had turned into bitterness. I believed the death of the doctor contributed to that a lot, but even when he lived, she manipulated everyone around her without reason,

Etta started to show these more frequent emotional breakdowns in our daily life, and had gotten almost porcelain fragile. Anything that I'd say that wasn't total agreement was viewed as criticism of her, and sometimes I admit, I did push back too hard.

I had grown weary of her family trying to rule my life, and often my words were harsh and sometimes unkind. There was nothing I could do to keep Minerva out of my life, or even to temper her interference.

Etta had left the Welfare Department after a few years of casework, and holding out for the director's position in two years wasn't enough to keep her interested. She had wanted to earn a doctorate in psychology but in the meantime, she wanted to have her own private practice, and so she opened her door.

Her clients at first were women friends, and then a few familiar men, all adrift in failing marriages. She tried to bring emotionless clear thinking to their problems, and honestly I think she was successful. Then out of the blue on a warm evening, she asked me how I would fix our own marriage.

It wasn't a far-fetched question but I changed the subject. In the past two years, we had stopped touching and put distance between ourselves except perhaps with conversation. That had become more clinical as it was about work, or friends with obvious marriage issues, and the talk was always about how we might help them get over it. We had put this no-fly zone across the range of our own emotions. It had served us as it prevented stupid arguments, but it hadn't improved our day-to-day lives.

On the road, I started to look at the attractive and younger women in the various campaigns I was involved in, and the excitement of politics drew them like flies.

One night in Louisville, while at a fund-raiser for the seated governor, his pretty director of communications was my dinner companion, and later, we had a couple of drinks together in the hotel bar.

Getting off at the same elevator floor, she had turned and said to me in an almost whisper, "Will you come in, and help me to relax," as her long white fingers went up and down my sport coat sleeves.

I forced a smile and shook my head. I turned toward my door, waving and said "Goodnight."

Inside I felt my heart pounding. I wanted to go back out the door and down the hall to her room and knock, though I didn't. I fell on the bed in my jacket and slacks, and stared at the ceiling for maybe an hour.

Once or twice I turned on my side and looked again at the door, but finally closed my eyes. Certainly I was tempted, though I didn't want to become the sort of man I loathed, and that lingering distaste was enough to keep me on the bed.

The next day I met her at breakfast, and we went over the three-day puddle jumper route we had planned with the governor around the state. She didn't say anything about the night before, but the next evening she was more aggressive in her suggestions. I snapped at her in anger.

From then on, until we parted ways, she kept her distance. We created artificial barriers between us. It was a warning to me that I might easily succumb to the temptation, or the time after that. It would come.

I asked Etta if we could get past our distant behavior and maybe try to return to the place we'd once been with the same affection that had drawn us together. She fought all intimacy now, and I couldn't see how I could break through.

She was drinking more. She had developed a largish counseling practice and was immensely pleased with herself. For that outcome, I was grateful. She saved confessions for the closed-door clients. I asked her if we might talk with someone, even a priest, and she simply laughed. To me, Etta was too afraid of what she might find out about her own feelings toward me, her mother, and the rest of the family.

I badgered her into a parish visit, and the old priest who had known her for her whole life, listened quietly to both of us. He didn't interrupt and asked only a few questions that first meeting together.

Halfway through the second meeting, he had stopped her. He asked her to stop telling him how she should feel, but rather, how she actually felt. She hesitated, and stumbled in her speech, finally standing, and yelled out, "Shit."

With that she started to cry uncontrollably, and the priest held up his hand for me to stop when I rose from the chair to comfort her. She seemed to cry non-stop for the longest time, and slowly stopped saying to him, "I'm sorry."

He nodded, saying, "There's an absence of anything spiritual in your lives. Etta, this can't continue, or you'll be doomed as a couple." With that, I had attempted to answer, and he raised his soft compassionate hand again, and shook his head, no.

"There is no God in the way you live, Etta. I see you both in church at the occasional mass, and what does that mean? Nothing. You do it out of your guilt toward Minerva who would disapprove. It has to be more, from the heart."

The priest told us to go home and for perhaps the first time, in the silence of our home, get down on our knees and pray for strength and wisdom to make the marriage work, we needed to start there.

In the car as I drove over the causeway, Etta turned to me with a cigarette blowing smoke in the air, and said, "That son of a bitch. Who does he think he's talking to, somebody off the goddamn boat?" With that comment, she looked out the window at the bay in silence until we were out in the countryside and nearing the river.

She added with venom: "Do you plan to get on your knees and pray? I don't think so. You're not even a damn Catholic, a real one, for good Christ."

There came a change over her, a side that I hadn't ever seen before, and her words seemed to have barbs that were all meant to hurt. It was so unlike her to behave that way.

We more or less reverted to silence, which had become the common solution to these difficult moments. I could feel my mouth harden with frustration. I stuffed the emotion, though I had honestly wanted to try.

It was a new replacement behavior we had adopted during the past year it seemed. If we could ignore those emotionally painful things and our reaction to the unpleasantness, it would somehow dissipate. Naturally none of it ever did. The anger and frustration would emerge at another time and for another reason. I started to build a case of what I didn't like, starting with her mother, and with Etta lately as she became exasperating and edgy.

Counseling continued for a few more sessions only because she was a loyal Catholic. The priest seemed to be of the opinion that nobody had to change their behavior, or spend more time listening to the other. Instead, prayer and a review of Christian practices were needed in our lives.

I didn't talk about the temptation I had felt with other women. She didn't criticize the way I approached our lives together. We both were faced with what I used to call in the Navy, that "sing in the choir solution." I heard a Chaplain tell a distressed man that once. He had been concerned with his wife's fidelity while he had been deployed in Vietnam. Did it help? I don't think so. It had seemed the wrong kind of answer, though the Chaplain's spiritual response to the world's problems was that of the Mobile priest.

Later I found out Etta had seen the priest once or twice on her own, and whatever was said in those private conversations would stay hidden in the realm of the so-called confessional. Why wasn't it out in the open? I never understood.

This was a sophisticated Catholic cathedral and the pews were filled with doctors, lawyers, and corporation heads. It wasn't the coal town church where everyone was a rough hard rock miner, unaware of conciliation and counseling skills. It was the same 'God is in the details' sort of mentality that the priest had, and it wasn't enough for us.

Etta had used her own clinical background to circumvent half of these sessions with psychobabble for some of the questions we needed to answer. She might even throw out three or four bookish terms during the conversation. She could ease out of anything that reflected back upon her. The priest was useless, and as I looked across the study at his complacent half smile, I could only see the same look on Minerva's face sitting in some judgment of me.

Perhaps I wasn't enough for Etta. Minerva believed that at least. It had gone too far and there was no exit as divorce was a thing that her Episcopal friends practiced with surprising regularity, but she eschewed that. We would stay married, and Etta had to make the most of it as Minerva had done with the doctor.

Her father hadn't been an ideal life companion. Minerva had spent a good part of the years drowning in a sort of boredom, a dispassionate existence with a man of monumental eccentricities. Minerva always believed he had harbored serious psychiatric demons though he looked perfectly functional in medicine and society.

I would sit across from Minerva for years on the terrace, and had this innate feeling that she was looking through you, looking for something better, someone else. Maybe it was the bane of her generation of long suffering and disappointed women in the South. I thought the morbid spin she added with her Catholicism made it even more gothic. She could be hurtful, and her daughter had suffered through that unspoken, or rarely exhibited anger, yet the disapproval was constant.

Minerva's sister was an unorthodox and slightly deranged woman whose husband had come to terms with her madness. He mostly ignored it and did what he wanted.

As the oldest of two female children, Minerva had to do all the thinking for her sister. She had extended that responsibility to her own daughters too.

I called the priest once after I learned that he met separately with Etta, and asked him if there was something I should know. Was there something she had been reluctant to say directly to me? He had answered, no, there was nothing to concern myself about. Look to thoughtful prayer and a Christian community, he added before hanging up. What else could he say? Most anything, I surmised.

Etta's drinking got far worse. She seemed to depend more on the nightly drinks. It was odd in a sense too, because we didn't argue. Etta seemed at least satisfied, if not happy. Perhaps it was the empty phase that all couples face, the middle years, where the excitement has worn thin. Both people are grappling to find compromises and deepen understanding. It was a difficult time because it was so well disguised.

During this time, I'd gotten an offer to go to Washington and work as a senior staff and policy director at the GOP party headquarters, and at the same time, I had been offered a fellowship at Georgetown in its policy institute. When I had discussed it with Etta, she was mute for the longest time during the conversation. At last she got up to light a cigarette then walked toward the window.

She muttered slowly, "You knew when you married me that this is my home. I have no desire to leave. None, and your ambition's only for you, not me. Remember that little detail."

"We could try it for a couple years and come back," I added.

"No, you can try it for a couple years. Count me out."

The seemingly one-sided viewpoint angered me. I thought to myself, how selfish she had become from the young girl I'd met at Mardi Gras. Back then she had thought all the world was one marvelous party with equally wonderful people.

Exasperated I blurted out, "It's for both of us. More opportunities and challenges. It's the big time."

"That's nonsense," she stated, snorting her dismay.

"I'm not moving, period. I'm not going to live in some boring Virginia suburb with stupid dull bureaucrats, or worse, some lame ass apartment complex in Georgetown. Forget it."

It struck me with such force that this wasn't simply a place to live for her, but so much more. It was something more carefully layered in her mind and its hold on us would be permanent, like it or not.

"But wait," I countered.

Then she did the strangest thing. She stood and interrupted me. She put both her hands over her ears and started to hum loudly like someone in a mental hospital pushing away the reality of bathing, or even meals. It was uncanny.

Etta did it for only a moment, then saw that I stopped speaking and was staring at her. She smiled, and walked over to me then bent down to kiss the top of my head.

She said, "Let's not fight over this. We have such a good life. Just look around you," She swung her long arms in a half arc toward the encroaching forest and the water.

"What's the payoff there? You'd be out with the next election, and we'd have to start all over again here. It's too much for us. We're too fragile."

It was at that time that I knew that something was fundamentally wrong. It was something we both hadn't identified that wouldn't go away unless we did something about it.

The next day, with a stony face, I made the call to Washington and told three people the deal was off and that personal issues made it impossible, though the desire was there. I received cordial responses from the disappointed, and we agreed to stay in touch with one another since things do change. Life isn't often predictably linear.

Etta treated the refusal like nothing had happened. She didn't bother mentioning the decision to Minerva, whom it would've pleased even though she didn't expect anything different from her eldest daughter. Be in charge, was her motto, the non-existent sampler in the kitchen.

Still, why do people ignore the obvious and pretend it doesn't exist? It's because a closer examination is too painful, and we turn our backs on it.

Etta was now half way through her doctorate, and now that she was armed with clinical weapons, she grew more successful in compartmentalizing our problems. She had the weapon of absolute rightness, couching it all in psychology terms to convince herself.

Her drinking accelerated and instead of battling over the things that bothered us at home, we chose silence, which was far more convenient and easier to employ. That damning quiet could be interpreted countless ways.

# Chapter 8

Minerva became more erratic. She had always been short with Etta, but the woman took it to new heights. Over dinner one night in Mobile, Minerva started saying things about us and our behavior towards her which could only be regarded as bizarre. It was far beyond the normal in-law sarcasm and disappointment.

It appeared Minerva may have some kind of early senility coming on, and during the next weekend visit right before the Thanksgiving holidays, she didn't make any sense in her conversation fragments. We both looked at each other in astonishment.

We generally celebrated Thanksgiving at Minerva's. We were joined this time by half of the grown children: Etta's brother with his wife and Mary Agnes with her new husband. During some meaningless exchange at the table, Minerva had called Etta vile, excoriating her in the most unusual terms, all while smashing her knife on the fine wooden table like a medieval mead hall.

Eyes began to roll around the table. In the kitchen, Mary Agnes admitted to Etta and me that she thought their mother had Alzheimer's. She noticed the forgetfulness, she had seen it for certain, but more than that, the venomous conversation particularly toward Etta.

Two weeks afterward, Etta convinced her mother that she had a thyroid condition. Minerva agreed to see one of her late husband's friends who was also a doctor. After some testing, he told us that he suspected she would lose her cognitive facilities sooner than later. It was indeed a progressive loss of memory and had already accelerated. It was such a shock to Etta, and to me as well, since Minerva had represented a staunch matriarch to the entire family.

Something had to be done. So, we agreed to move into a spacious colonial down the street in Spring Hill for a while.

Etta would monitor her mother's condition as the last two youngest girls at home finished high school.

The defining incident that really brought home her dementia was a last minute driving trip to Birmingham to see her son. She had been driving in an entirely different direction, but this time it was on the highway to Pensacola. She was driving thirty-three miles an hour while the speed limit was fifty-five and a state trooper had pulled her over. Completely disoriented, the cop had followed her back to Mobile and right into the driveway of the Spring Hill house.

The second youngest daughter, Clara, was going to Auburn the next year, but she moved out of the house for the summer to work at a Dauphin Island marine ecology project that required a residence on the government station. She was also taking art classes at the Museum on a few weekends. Only the youngest daughter, Maggie, was staying at home. It appeared that she did pretty much whatever she wanted, and there was some rebellious behavior that worried Etta. Minerva, of course, was clueless.

Family responsibilities swallowed up whatever soul-searching we needed to do as a couple. It was unfortunately postponed. Etta had to monitor her mother's daily routine, though Minerva was only sixty-eight, and it became frustrating.

Bill paying didn't get done any longer, or school visits for her youngest, or even determining that her daughter was at home for the evening. Maggie often wasn't, showing the unpleasant teenage side of total resistance. When Minerva did pay the bills, like the utilities or insurance premiums, she might pay them several times, if at all. It was difficult to know which.

It put a terrible pressure on us as a couple. Etta took over the everyday activities of her mother, and the strain of the memory dysfunction also inhabited the brain's anger centers.

Minerva started to lash out almost blindly. She fought with her long-time neighbor, calling him horrible names to his absolute astonishment one afternoon as he supervised his yardman's raking of fall leaves. He telephoned Etta perplexed. The judge and his wife had often sat at their table for dinners during holiday celebrations, and clearly recognized the rage as some sort of dysfunction.

Around the same time, Etta received a call from the branch manager of the bank who said that her mother had emptied two accounts and left the bank with several bags of loose cash. The whole uncharacteristic transaction had alarmed him, as had her reasons for the withdrawals. They were almost childish. Etta found forty-three thousand dollars in two shopping bags on one of the shelves in the basement balled up next to the Christmas decorations.

The only thing left to do was to summon a family meeting. Etta did that at our Spring Hill rental with Mary Agnes, her husband and their brother and his new wife. Clara and Maggie didn't attend.

Out of the meeting, we agreed to hire a nurse to live at the house and monitor Minerva's daily behavior, though that only lasted maybe three weeks before the woman was physically attacked. Next, Etta suggested we move in with her mother, at least temporarily. It was a huge house anyway, and we would be in a wing of our own. I was dubious, but went along with the plan anyway. It had become apparent that Minerva was at risk of losing her mental faculties, and soon.

We were in the house a week before she started screaming at Etta. Minerva took to pounding Etta's arm with her fist if she didn't get her own way. When night came, Minerva would be in the back garden before dawn doing something that was inexplicable to either of us. She dug up the plant beds for some unknown reason.

Adding to the current madness, Minerva began to pick up stray cats then bring them into the house. She had visited the local shelter several times, and we ended up returning five kittens she had adopted. The shelter personnel were now aware that the woman appearing at their door didn't have the capacity to care for these animals. Dutifully, they had refused to let her adopt more cats.

The doctor who prescribed some regime of fairly benign drugs, upped the dosages. Unfortunately, they met with limited success. Minerva might sleep longer at night and not roam around the garden any longer, but she became more lethargic with all of it as if she were in some catatonic trance.

Finally, the outrageous surge of anger returned, and became unbearable. The family, with heavy hearts, agreed to put her in a convalescent facility near the airport that offered around the clock care. Minerva was installed in what might have been termed a small villa, with a living room, large elegant bedroom, and screened in porch. Her meals were provided in a rather upscale resident dining room, and a breakfast delivered in the early morning to her inside villa.

Exile to the care facility had always been considered as temporary. The psychiatrists adjusted her medication, hoping for some kind of normalcy, which never arrived. She had a breakdown one night after Etta had left her. She was found wandering around the facility grounds in her nightgown, uncertain of where she was. She began asking for her husband and demanding the staff contact him immediately.

The dementia grew more extreme. It appeared Minerva would not be leaving the facility any time soon. Etta, at last, took on the responsibility for her two youngest sisters, getting one off to college while trying to reason with the youngest who had disappeared into a self-absorbed teenage world. It was tiring and exhausted her physically and emotionally.

Etta remained convinced that her mother should live in her own house. She would bring her to the Mobile family home for the weekend, and we would try to have some degree of home life, or pretend we did. I might sit out on the terrace with Minerva at sunset. She would drink a gin and tonic, and talk sensibly to me as if nothing had been altered in the past year, and we were the same people we were before.

Once the evening had been concluded, she would go off to bed. Later she might wander around the house calling for her dead husband. Also, the nightly visits to the garden would occasionally continue.

Minerva stopped bathing and the once fashionable and stately doctor's wife, started to have a pungent body odor, though apparently unconscious of the smell herself. She refused to change her underwear or her everyday clothing. In the morning, she would put on the same clothes as the evening before. It was all a vicious cycle, and it had been daunting at the care facility.

When Etta attempted in her loving manner to encourage Minerva to change clothes, a string of obscenities directed at her eldest daughter might come out of her mouth. She'd become physical, sometimes slapping or punching Etta, if she tried to help her mother remove her dress, or even a blouse.

The youngest teenage daughter, Maggie, ignored her mother. She treated her like some pariah. Maggie was only concerned with her friends, and we feared, sex and drug usage. She was unlike all the other children in the family who behaved in a conventional and affectionate way toward Minerva. The girl had no use for her mother as she considered Minerva insane.

Money, or I should say its absence, motivated Minerva's youngest child.

Etta bought her a used car with family proceeds, but she needed far more. Maggie talked about getting an apartment with her girlfriends. They were all still in high school, and we speculated whether or not it might be with a young man, someone equally free of his parents' reach. Maybe it was an older boy, but who knew? It was exhausting.

Maggie's lateness at night started to become endemic. The principal at the Catholic girl's academy she attended complained that she showed no interest in school, unlike her other studious siblings. She had developed a rather bad attitude toward the place, and its students and faculty. Maggie had told one of the Catholic sisters that she would not be attending chapel, or even mass. It was her constitutional right, she pronounced.

It all fell on Etta. Mary Agnes might come by occasionally to see her mother or her youngest sister who wasn't home anyway. She had a strange fear of the care facility and would only come to the Mobile house, so her visits with her mother became fewer. Her husband did whatever she told him to do on the subject, always eager to please her, so he stayed away too.

As if Minerva's illness wasn't enough heartache for Etta, Maggie became pregnant. She had never attempted to use any birth control methods, nor had her partner. She finally admitted this to Etta after she determined that she was two months pregnant. That forced Etta to seek out a female gynecologist friend from the city, and once it was confirmed, they both talked to her sister and explained the possible options.

Mostly, I remained silent through the whole episode. I tried to approach the problems we had been encountering with patience and compassion. Still, it sometimes seemed that Etta's and my life had spun out of control.

Maggie announced to us one evening on the terrace that she had intended to keep the child, forgoing an abortion or even adoption. She told us the child's father was a motorcycle mechanic she had taken a fancy to. He had turned boring and was such a low life who was hardly a candidate for a blissful married life.

That started the nightly talks which ended more like arguments as Maggie wavered between abortion and keeping the unborn child. They got loud and vulgar most nights, and once or twice I had started to intervene to ask them both to calm down, but they had turned on me.

Etta had only told Mary Agnes, not her brother. I feared she would bring in the old cathedral dean who had somehow miscounseled us, and her sister's option would be neatly closed off with his convenient theology. Etta and I tossed around all the conventional Catholic rationale. That's what she wanted her sister to do, though it struck me as wrong in this situation.

How could a high school girl with no job, or money of her own, or even training as a mother, take on this lifelong responsibility?

Her sister wasn't even a practicing Catholic anyway. Maybe she had grown up in a Catholic household, but in the end she had simply rejected it.

I told her to call another family council, get them all in here: Mary Agnes and her husband, the doctor and his wife, and even Clara who was trying to plan a backpack adventure in Europe. Etta refused, and we argued about it.

I told her that I'd call her damn brother and tell him what had happened. He can come down and participate in the decision, whatever that was going to be. Mary Agnes could make more than her cursory trips across the causeway and take some responsibility too. It went on and on.

What eventually occurred was that Maggie took herself with a girlfriend one afternoon to a clinic that did unspoken things for the upper middle class of Mobile. She ceased to involve any of us for the present. Etta's family was well known and a bill for this procedure would be sent to them, and it was all done rather clandestinely. It only took a single telephone call.

The abortion slowed her youngest sister down for the best part of a month afterward, and I believe it was more dealing with the physical discomfort than the moral recovery. By the beginning of the next month, her sister Maggie was regularly chirping, "Fuck you," when she was asked to come home before midnight on weekdays.

Maybe there might've been a counterculture spin playing out too, exasperating her already rebellious nature. To that end, Maggie brought a guy home one evening and announced he was spending the night. Furious, Etta told her no, and she grabbed the boy by his bare arm and escorted him forcibly out the front door like some staggering drunk. We suspected with the silly smiles pasted on their teenage faces that they had already smoked several joints and were caught up in their youthful euphoric stupor.

It wasn't long before Etta and Maggie were screaming at each other in the hallway and when I tried to separate them, the sister ran up the staircase.

I put my arm around Etta who moved between sobs and rage, and guided her out onto the terrace where I had prepared a pitcher of sangria. I poured her a glass and patted her on the forearm for some reassurance. What could I add?

She shouted, "Stop fucking placating me," and bolted from her chair into the garden. Etta stood there fuming for maybe a minute as I watched her then slowly started to walk back toward the terrace.

When she reached me, she put her hand and then her head on my arm, "I didn't mean that," she said.

"Of course not," I automatically answered, then embraced her and walked her to the bench swing we usually sat on.

We both remained there as the sun left the sky. We simply sipped our cool wine, as she kept glancing back through the French windows inside the house, looking for what I didn't know.

"This whole thing is making you terribly upset, this responsibility for your mother and your sister. It's too much, honestly."

She almost hissed at me, "Who's going to do it? Mary Agnes? Jackson? Don't make me laugh."

Naturally she was right. They both wanted to get on with their own lives. They didn't want to get dragged down with a demented mother, and a rebellious teenage sister caught up in the newness of sex, and possibly recreational drugs, or perhaps worse.

It all came crashing down around on our heads. It would be impossible to install her mother in her home again, and also somehow transfer back to her what remained of her sister's childhood years. It was a battlefield in so many ways, maybe not insurmountable, but damn difficult to cross.

We were aging long before our time. I told her that, repeatedly to deaf ears, and the marriage suffered. I started to harbor resentments, but kept them all neatly stuffed inside. All we ever did was talk about our problems. If we weren't talking about them then, we would be thinking about them, possible solutions, and what to expect the next time around. It wore us down as surely as a millstone. It ground up our emotions along with our spontaneity and sense of adventure. It was visible. We would only have to look at the mirror, and see the worried lines on our faces with dark shadows under the eyes from lack of rest.

Work didn't go away. I traveled even more during the week. I had no choice because we needed more and more money to be able to balance everything.

Etta took control of the bank accounts and securities. Etta's brother proved to be a reasonable man so he and Mary Agnes were able to move this along, which made life so much easier. Clara was never any trouble as she was always quiet, reticent and agreeable.
Maggie tried to disrupt us with most every stratagem she could.

On Saturday's when Etta shopped and I was doing campaign expenses and paperwork, Maggie would saunter into the den with an open bathrobe, loosely tied, revealing her blossoming figure. I had to lock the door to prevent it from happening.

She thought somehow that if she had seduced me, she might get something she wanted. I was uncertain of exactly what that was: revenge on Etta, or exploiting my weakness, or just some demonstration of her womanly gifts to get money for a new car. I had no idea of what Maggie wanted as I sat mute behind the closed door.

The once or twice she had tried the exhibition I had ignored her and closed the door, but hadn't mentioned anything to Etta. The last time I finally told Etta, and she stormed down the hall to her sister's room who happened to be at home and lolling in her own bed.

A screaming match ensued and I heard Etta uncharacteristically call her sister, "slut," which had made me wince. Maggie returned as much, and the result was only seething anger.

"What did you hope to prove?" I asked Etta who was sitting on the bed, and had nervously lit up a cigarette.

In an instant she turned to me saying, "Maybe you're not getting enough? You'd like some young poontang."

At first I laughed, but saw it simply made things worse, and reached over and hugged her.

"She's a confused child, that's all," I whispered, "One day this will be behind us. You'll see," and Etta nodded with her rightness.

It did change for the better, though it took time. Sort of, if history is a judge.

This awful burden on Etta's shoulders was too heavy. Even when I stepped in to assume some of the responsibility, she would simply wave me away as she was determined to do it all herself.

In the middle of her senior year, Maggie seemed to awaken a little, and started to pay attention to some subjects like English, French, and one of the sciences. Her advantage, if there was one, was that she had inherited the family's intelligence. Although her grades were horrible for a time, she had done well on the standardized college tests. It was the single bright spot throughout the entire time. Etta could call friends, who in turn would make calls to deans, who would talk to their admission officers, and the girl might be admitted somewhere.

Etta leaned on the cathedral dean who beseeched his seminary friend of many years ago at Spring Hill College. The Jesuit school said they would admit her provisionally into their liberal arts curriculum, and hopefully by the end of the first semester, she would fit into co-ed life. After two luncheon meetings with the Cathedral priest and an interview with the Spring Hill dean, it had been accomplished, and Etta finally breathed a sigh of relief.

Around the same time, Maggie distanced herself from the local bar crowd. She started to embrace Eastern religion. She would constantly pester Etta to let her travel to some Ashram in San Francisco. Maggie had heard about it from someone whose sister had left Mobile for Berkeley and its free speech culture, and had sung its praises.

Each night there were arguments about it. During the late spring of that year, Etta drove her youngest sister to another Ashram, this time in Georgia. Etta found the place barely habitable though she let her sister stay there for four or five days among the unwashed gurus and the sitars.

Upon Etta's return, Maggie had changed her name to Lakshmi, and also changed from her jeans into some pastel-colored sari and leather sandals she had bought. Finger bells would now be heard in the evening, calling for meditation.

On the drive home, the arguing continued, but this time for Maggie to spend a year studying with this Indian guru. After that was put to rest, Maggie agreed to go to the Spring Hill campus. That loud discussion continued from the car into the house. Maggie's wardrobe had suddenly changed into something you might see in New Delhi. The miniskirts disappeared overnight.

It was exhausting to absorb all of this. Each time Minerva returned for a weekend, it became even more obvious that she would have to be institutionalized for the balance of her life. None of the children were prepared to give up what lives they had before them to care for Minerva at home.

Maggie became bearable, though it was a gradual process. She also brought home a young man she had met at the Ashram who was a student at Georgia Tech. He told us he remained at school only because of his pious parents. He figured out that his earlier Baptist path was a terrible waste of time, explaining that the belief was totally wrong-headed.

Presently, the Hindu Sutras guided him. He was on the verge of leaving college to pursue that spiritual journey though he hadn't wanted to shock or hurt his family. It was a rather thoughtful thing, really, at a time when so many young people didn't care what the earlier generation thought or felt.

His name was Josh, and he would come every other weekend for an evening and for appearances, we would put him in the guest room. He and Maggie were free to do whatever they wished once we retired, however, and I'm certain that they did.

We discouraged the pot smoking in the house, but mostly ignored it as we had little success. They stayed to themselves, talked and played loud rock music, and chanted various mantras behind closed doors.

Since her sister Maggie had already experienced sex, there was little we could do about that now. Perhaps we might discourage the frequency, and go through the familiar motions of disapproval. The only thing left was for Etta to counsel Maggie on birth control, but her sister was adult enough to find a birth control pill prescription source, so a lot went unsaid.

Etta's other siblings were all disinterested. They preferred to let her take the responsibility and mostly didn't quibble about how the reserves were spent. I imagine everyone believed that the college tuition for the large family and the mother's care would eventually finish all the money anyway.

The role into which Etta was unwillingly thrust into took its toll on us, and we never assessed the damage. Sure, we argued more often, and over the smallest things. We had a life before us, and we'd put that on hold for the present.

Minerva's dementia had progressed much more rapidly than we figured. The efforts made for family dinners always ended in some tragedy and crying from someone at the table. The mother's fits of anger were almost unbearable to every one of the children and their long-suffering spouses.

At a holiday dinner, Minerva had thrown her plate across the table when Etta continued to disagree with her about the placement of the floral centerpiece.

Minerva had stood up and yelled, "You ungrateful bitch," and threw the Limoges plate the length of the long mahogany table.

"Put cotton plants in the centerpiece, you idiot," Minerva had said to her scowling.

That evening I pleaded with Etta to stop these dinners, and let her mother's care rest with the doctors and nurses at the memory care facility.

"That's because you don't care about family. You're a cold unfeeling man," she shot back at me, and I didn't try to respond to her. It seemed futile.

Truthfully I didn't care much for her idea of this family or anyone else's for that matter. This crucible of my own warped childhood maybe was to blame. What else could it be? The chronic depression, the alcoholism, the physical abuse. It all roiled about before me like some psychiatry clinical textbook: one abuse after another.

Etta's obsession with saving her mother worsened. Dinner after dinner, I found myself looking across the table at this demented woman whom I had never really liked. I grew resentful. I loathed this act I had put on as the supportive husband because it was phony. I did this all out of some morbid compromise with Etta. I didn't like it one damn bit. It made me bitter, and after a time I didn't bother to hide it either.

This was just another thing I had to deal with as those supposedly greatest years of my life flew by faster than I'd hoped. Etta didn't do much to shield me. I guess it was because she couldn't protect herself either, and so we limped on to the next phase of our lives. What we continued to do together was all hit or miss. I accepted this as my lot. I'd better make the most of it, deepen the compromises, and simply live with this dysfunction if I could.

The political work increased and I encouraged it. The travel took me away from the unhappiness that I once had tried to fix, though nothing ever changed.
I was in Lexington for a gubernatorial campaign and it had been going well. I stayed a few extra days trying to amuse myself at some of the bluegrass garden parties that had been arranged for large donors and relaxed.

Late Saturday night, Etta called me and said Maggie was in trouble again. This time she was arrested on a drug-related charge and was being held in jail. There had been a police raid at someone's college apartment around Spring Hill. She had been high on LSD with several others when the officers forced the door open.

In total, six students were arrested, and a cache of drugs found. The serious outcome of the drug party was that one of the young women ended up in an ICU unit, and doctors had predicted brain damage, or possible paralysis.

Preliminary questioning by the police had established that Maggie and her male companion supplied the illegal drugs. The young man hadn't been a student, but a local day laborer. He had a short rap sheet with a handful of juvenile offenses like stealing bicycles and shoplifting.

Spring Hill suspended those students involved including Maggie. There was a hearing scheduled on whether to remand the sellers, meaning Maggie, for a criminal trial.

I flew back at noon the next day, and Etta met me at the airport with more news, and not good. The hospitalized girl had suffered brain damage from overdoses of the so-called party packs made with some ridiculous amphetamine mixtures. Worse, the student was new to drug use. She had helped herself to several doses, encouraged by others with little more knowledge of what they were doing themselves.

The girl was in the care of several Birmingham neurologists, and had been permanently hospitalized. They blamed Maggie and the boy. It was a serious criminal charge. The family lawyer warned Etta of the prosecution's appetite for quick justice, which also had the faint odor of political ambition.

It was the end of Maggie's career at Spring Hill. She would be expelled for criminal activities alone. The Jesuits wouldn't need to dredge up any additional moral arguments for the expulsion. Etta had driven to Spring Hill and pleaded with her priest president friend, and had enlisted the dean of the cathedral, though to no avail. Other family friends had later joined in, blaming youthful indiscretion without any results.

Etta and I sat around and tried to reason about what to do next. Maggie was staying at home, boarded up in her room upstairs and barely speaking to either of us.

The rest of the family, notably her brother, distanced themselves from the tumult. Mary Agnes occasionally visited the house, though only for ten or fifteen minutes, and then she would hastily retreat home.

There were news articles in the paper. Half a page of sordid features detailed how the drug epidemic was gripping the country and had found its way to tranquil Mobile. There were also police precinct line-up photos of Maggie and her boyfriend. They had been named as the drug kingpins, which was sensational, yet it sold newspapers. One article followed another and a third, and a network affiliate television station sent its so-called investigative reporter to talk to Maggie. Etta slammed the door in the woman's face.

The hearing was set with Maggie alongside a criminal lawyer hired by the family barrister, and a punitive jail term of a month was assessed. There was a brief appeal of the sentence by Maggie's attorney, though in the end Maggie went to the state correctional facility in Bay Minette.

It was sordid, and totally unnecessary, though it caught the attention of our social circle. Etta knew that it was discussed at every cocktail party her friends threw, and on every tennis court, and probably on the way down the steps at the cathedral after mass on Sundays.

Coming from a prominent family that could hardly utter her name any longer except behind closed doors, Maggie vanished. The embarrassment and later the shame had taken its toll on our dinner party invitations, and even the holiday gatherings. Etta hardly left the house anymore. Mary Agnes and her new husband kept their own counsel, reluctantly joining his extended family in attendance during the trial and later for a visit to the Bay Minette jail.

Upon release, Maggie had been considerably changed. It was hard to know exactly how though, because after two weeks' upstairs, she announced that she was moving to New Orleans. She found a childhood friend living there who would take her in, and she left early one morning in her beater car.

It was difficult to know how this change in her would unfold. I had tried optimism, though I couldn't help but think it might become worse. She would eventually become her own worst enemy.

In New Orleans, she merely let go of things, everything, and became a part of the counterculture edginess that had affected that generation. It made her wilder, first with more drug involvement and then with a string of unsavory lovers and friends, most of whom were worthless parasites.

Etta and I trumped up some excuse to finally drive there. We asked her to join us for dinner at some low-key restaurant Etta knew in the Quarter. Maggie showed up with a guy who was so high on some drug concoction he could barely speak. He kept drinking glass after glass of water for his terminal dehydration.

Maggie had tattooed her long beautiful white arms. She tried her best to be pleasant at the table though Etta made it difficult.

Then the sarcasm took over and the sisters openly quarreled. I finally slammed my hand down on the table, and said, "You two stop, please."

Etta went to the restaurant bathroom and I asked Maggie to level with me. "Are you OK, really?" I asked her.

She shrugged her shoulders, and added, "Yeah."

"We want to help you. Etta doesn't know how. She can't get past things but I can," I said meaning it. "You can talk to me. Tell me anything. I won't throw the past in your face. Believe me."

I reached over and put my hand on hers, and shook my head to get her acknowledgement of what I had said, and she slowly nodded.

"Call me anytime, and I'll help you. It doesn't matter with what or where, or the circumstances. Etta wants to do that too, but she can't."

Her boyfriend, or whatever he was, kept staring at his large hands, or maybe a fly, and had shown no interest in the exchange.

Another few months passed, and I started to work on a senate race in Louisiana. The candidate was a state senator and ex-state attorney from New Orleans where the campaign was headquartered.

With Etta's agreement, I tried to keep in contact with Maggie. Gradually, after every third or fourth telephone call, she would call back and we would meet somewhere for dinner and talk.

She told me she really didn't use as many drugs as most people blamed her for, particularly Etta, and it was mostly on weekends. The earlier boyfriend had left, and she wasn't seeing anyone.

The more or less quiet evenings were fine. I reported back to Etta that I thought she might have turned the corner with the earlier madness. She had been looking into Loyola University part-time and maybe working in retail, or as a cocktail waitress in the Quarter.

Etta arranged for the bank to pay for her tuition expenses at the school, and Maggie enrolled in two courses with the fledgling Walker Percy writing program launched by the renowned New Orleans novelist. She did well, and made poetry her focus.

Into the late summer and the beginning of the fall campaign season, we continued our dinners as well as our friendship, and she seemed fine, or at least better than she had been. I met her one evening at Jackson Square Café following a campaign strategy meeting, and she asked me to come back with her to her small studio for a moment to show me some of her poetry. I was flattered.

The studio was charming, and that surprised me. It was a large room overlooking a courtyard. Maggie had draped it with Hindu fabrics and had futon furniture. It felt rather like what I suspected an ashram might.

"Maggie, this is a wonderful little place. Its charming," I said, "I can see why you like it, and on the porch too in the evening."

"I write out there at sunset. It's when the thoughts come to me," she said, and gave me the first warm smile she had for such a long while.

We sat on the makeshift couch, and she brought out a journal. She sat down next to me, crossing her bare legs guru-style below the denim skirt.

She read four or five pages of very lyrical poetry, much of it about the heavens, animals and spirits, perhaps more metaphysical than not, but with rich language and understanding. After she finished, she leaned against me with her head on my shoulder and said, "Let's be silent for a few minutes and watch the sunset."

"Sure," I said, and tried to be quiet inside for a few moments, even if it seemed impossible.

156

We must've been frozen for almost thirty or forty minutes, and then she stood up and said, "C'mon inside. I'll make a special tea. It will soften your thoughts."

"Of course," I said, and looked at my watch. "I can stay a few more minutes, then I need to get back to the hotel to get ready for tomorrow."

Inside she pulled out a metal tea ball, filled it from a jar, and made the herbal brew, which smelled of cinnamon and cloves. She was right. It did seem to relax my mind more than my muscles, and I felt this deep pleasant sensation.

We were sitting on her futon. I was also cross-legged holding the small bowl when she took it from my warmed hands and put in on a small table nearby. She leaned over and took my head into her hands, and she kissed me deeply on the mouth. I didn't resist her, instead gave myself over to what was happening without much thought.

Before I realized it, she was standing naked over me. She bent down to remove my clothes, while smiling and humming as she did, but still I did nothing but watch her unashamed movements. With both of us nude, she slid into my arms and this euphoria seemed to overtake me, something I can barely describe from memory but so fraught with sensation that I let it take me over as I surrendered.

I slept soundly until almost dawn, then I stole out of the apartment after waking her first and telling her I must return to the hotel. She simply smiled and squeezed my hand.

In the taxi, my mind raced to explain to myself what I had just done, but I couldn't find the words of reason. There was no excuse, nor justification for it.

"My God," I uttered in a half whisper, and tried to find some solution to this agony. There was none. Both of us were responsible for doing this, and perhaps I had been the worst. I clearly knew better and had so much more to lose.

Half in a daze during the meeting, I nodded knowingly to affirmations of things already in place. I returned to Mobile upset that night, a day earlier than I had planned, wracked with guilt and self-doubt. As I drove through Biloxi, I created various scenarios I might use to explain it to myself, though none could ever hope to work.

Why had I done it? I couldn't explain, but for desire and the obvious opportunity, there was no other real reason. Had I subconsciously wanted this to happen all along, and my reaching out to Maggie in the first place had been some precursor? What did I want from her? I didn't believe I loved her.

That seemed impossible, yet I did what I did and created the circumstance for it to occur. She had been weak and troubled, and I had taken advantage of that need. I couldn't believe I had been that calculating and insensitive, though perhaps I had been. All those thoughts continued as I drove across the causeway toward Magnolia Springs. Would she tell Etta? I had no idea. We hadn't discussed anything of the night or what she felt. I'd simply left, fearful.

I stopped in Fairhope at a café and nursed a coffee before using the pay phone booth at the garage next door. It took four rings before she answered, and Maggie uttered a sleepy hello into the receiver. After a moment of awkward silence, I told her that I was sorry that I had left so abruptly without talking, and that we had a few things to discuss.

"Don't use the telephone. It's too anonymous," she insisted, "I want to see your mouth move and your eyes when you talk to me. It can wait."

"I need to tell you, I'm sorry. I didn't…" and my words dried up and I started again with the lack of enthusiasm, that was more like fear.

"Stop," she ordered me, "I'm not going to tell Etta anything. You needn't worry. It simply happened as it was meant to."

"But…" I stressed.

"There are no buts. We wanted intimacy. We made it happen. Forget the apologies, please. It was simply what it was. No more, no less," And she started to gently laugh into the receiver.

"When you come back, we can talk all you want, or not. Let it wait," she said. "I thought it was exquisite, and long overdue."

"It wasn't like me to do this," I pleaded further with her.

She talked more about the spontaneity of the night. It was something I had clearly wanted for some time and planned for, and not to overthink it.

"Most of all, don't burden Etta with this, please," she said. "It'll become what it's meant to, period."

I went on with some explanation of my poor judgment that night. I didn't want to add to the hurt Maggie had already experienced. I had gone on too long in the self-debasing rant.

She simply said: "You and I should be honest with each other, that's the first thing we need to do. I'm telling you I wanted it to happen. I made it easy and you wanted it as much as I did."

Finally, my pleas started to make little sense to me on the telephone. I told her that I would be in New Orleans that following Monday for three days, and that we should talk then.

"We'll have dinner or walk, and it becomes what it becomes," she said. "I'm comfortable with all that. If you want to stay with me for some of the time, that's great. But we'll talk."

With reluctance, I agreed we'd meet. I hung up the phone with trepidation on what I'd done and how to deal with it. This was my wife's youngest sister. The way I had behaved in the past two days couldn't stand scrutiny from anyone, even myself. Surprisingly, she had seemed calm on the telephone. I was the one who appeared to be coming apart, and the whole episode appeared uncanny.

Was this a one-time thing meant to be forgotten and kept secret between us? That was possible, and as I turned on the car ignition I thought that was how I'll treat it. Push it away and ignore it as if it were some aberration, some blurb of consciousness.

I wasn't that kind of man; the sort of men I'd seen on the campaign trail with the young volunteers in the back of the bar at the Sheraton with their room keys in sweaty palms waiting for the right minute to ask, to make sure enough liquor had passed the table. I had witnessed it in every campaign I worked in; from the staff to operatives from the national committee who would find one of the women staffers attractive and try to interest her in a little taste of power.

In Kentucky, my aide on the trail who had just finished law school warned me away from a campaign donor. A recently divorced heiress of some bluegrass fortune was available. She had pointedly said to me, "I know her and the family. She'll use you once, or maybe twice, and throw you away. Don't do it."

I hadn't thought about it much at the time. I had laughed at her dogged insistence, and it didn't matter to me that the woman disappeared from the campaign scene after a time. I had acted as if I'd missed all her seductive signals, but mostly I did.

At home, Etta was fuming about something connected with work. Her practice in counseling had grown to the point she had added two additional therapists, and had leased a small classic home off Government Street for an office. She was talking about opening another office in Fairhope. Etta had heard from maybe a dozen Mobile friends who had moved to the Eastern Shore where their class of people increasingly might be found.

Etta's strategy, as she explained it to my disinterested mind across the table, was for her to staff the Fairhope office, spend four days a week there with a day in Mobile and possibly a Saturday here and there. She would make a success of it. There was no doubt that she had the contacts, the clinical experience, and she knew how to charm people. It was that

160

wonderful part of her. The Minerva legacy that would get people to do her bidding and the need to dominate. I told her to do it.

It meant floating thirty or forty thousand dollars, and I thought we could do it ourselves. Etta could pull it out of the family reserves as trustee, and replace it when the Fairhope office showed a profit. She typically did what she wanted anyway, and this was no different.

Etta had already signed a lease for an old dentist's office across from the Eastern Shore Art Center, and by the end of the next week she would have it furnished. A friend's daughter, who had taken a semester off from college, would act as the receptionist. It would have the feel of an authentic clinical practice right away.

In reality, I had little to add, and gradually the guilt that had constricted me earlier seemed to dissipate. I sipped my drink and agreed with the plans explained to me. They obviously didn't really require my approval to move forward, and I told her with some enthusiasm to move ahead. It sounded like a splendid idea.

What was I going to do about Maggie? I didn't know, though I thought it was important I talk with her next week. I would try to explain to her that it had been a mistake, and that I regretted the whole thing. But I honestly didn't, when I thought about it, after the fear was absent.

Maggie was soft and excited me with her girlish hippie ways. I found myself attracted to her as a woman, and starting thinking that I wanted more, wanted to see her whenever I could. I thought to myself aloud with almost dread, "You've crossed the line, and it won't be pretty."

Had I fallen into the trap so many men had? Or was it that this marriage with Etta had become empty? We moved through the motions of the polite society we inhabited, no better or less than any of the others.

On Tuesday I checked into The Hilton Hotel, and met with the campaign staff, finalizing the newspaper advertising for the race. I had begged off the dinner which generally followed. I told everyone I needed to work more on position papers since the national committee speechwriters were scheduled to join the campaign next week. They had laughingly waved me out the door.

I called and left a message on Maggie's answering machine. She had called my hotel leaving a message to meet her at a café around the corner from her studio on Royale. Rushing out the door, I got there ten minutes early and sat nervously looking out the tall windows over my coffee while tapping my fingers on the wood plank table.

In an instant, I got a glimpse of Maggie's long dark hair moving in the breeze as she crossed the narrow street. She waved to me from the sidewalk as I stared out the café window. She was dressed in a poncho, skirt and cowboy boots. She looked like some flower child fashion model, but that was pretty much what she was.

She kissed my cheek and called to the counterman who brought her a coffee and cream, then took a long drink before speaking. You could smell the rich coffee aroma in the air, like an exotic perfume.

"You look so tense, don't be. I won't bite, I promise," and she made her teeth chatter with a click. Her face broadened into a wide smile, and she reached across to put her hand on top of mine, which was deadly still.

"They have the best coffee in the Quarter. Far better than that chicory swill down at the French Market, and they're nice people too. Andre, behind the counter, owns it," she said matter-of-factly finishing her coffee while standing.

"C'mon, let's go to a better place to talk," she continued and pulled me to my feet.

I gave no resistance to her insistence nor did I push away her arm as it encircled my waist as we walked down the shadowy street of overhanging trellises toward her cramped studio. Inside, we made the smallest of small talk when she said she was going to brew us some tea, then laughed out loud.

"You don't know there's coca leaves in this blend do you? That's why you must feel like you're floating through mid-air," she said jokingly looking into my bleary eyes. "It's not addictive, so don't worry. Just pure pleasure."

"So that's what I felt. The lightness before," I answered, more amused than irritated at the last episode. "Let's try some more. I don't have to meet anyone until noon tomorrow."

For some reason, the natural euphoria in me seemed to erupt, and a hard laughter filled my body then brought tears to my eyes. I imagine with that feeling I pretty much sanctified what we were doing and accepted my role without guilt. If I had any, I had simply pushed it aside.

She slowly brewed the aromatic tea, and we talked about her poetry. Maggie told me she saw herself becoming an important writer, a chronicler of perhaps this chaotic time, but more likely her family and its shaky history.

"We're all messed up. Everyone in the family, even mister perfect doctor. With parents like that, my God," she explained in her musical voice.

"You've met my aunt, who's absolutely crazy. I don't need to tell you much about mother. You've seen that up close. Her need to run your life."

With the steaming tea in our cups, we walked out onto the balcony and got comfortable on the futon chaise overlooking the small courtyard garden facing the other apartments. Maggie had changed into a t-shirt with harem pants ballooned at the legs. She was naked underneath and her nipples seemed to harden under the colored fabric.

The result with the tea made me anxious and more amorous. I saw her through my bleary eyes as a goddess, a sea siren, whose dark hair and white skin bade me to come hither. It felt as if I were losing all my bearings, and whatever propriety I had convinced myself of, gradually disappeared into the ether. I slowly reached over and pulled her to me. She came willingly. With that embrace, I had set the present course of my life. What was this woman to me?

I was in love with my wife's youngest sister, and perhaps it was time to admit it to myself, though how could I justify this? It was wrong of me to sit next to Maggie alone in this New Orleans apartment. I was ready to spend the night and a few others with this beautiful woman. Maggie put her arms around me, and rested her head on my chest. She hummed some soft melody and looked out at the changing orange sky.

"What are we going to do about this?" I finally blurted out, and moved her away from me to look at her face.

She smiled in response, "Whatever we want," and began kissing my neck with her tongue.

I felt like a prisoner who built his own jail cell. I sighed with resignation, and gave myself to this night. After the noon meeting with the campaign the next day, I was obligated to a dinner with half of the participants. I told her I'd come to her late, maybe ten or eleven. She had answered willingly, "I'll be waiting."

So I did, creeping around the Quarter like a criminal and slipping into her courtyard and up the wrought iron stairs with furtive footsteps. It was now out of control. I had no longer any command over my emotions with her and my only thoughts were of the time I would be with her.

Each evening I called Etta and made false comments: The complaints about long campaign hours, the heavy drinking. We mouthed the automatic endearments as we hung up the phone. This life would become duplicitous, and dishonest. It had already, though I didn't care enough to change anything.

Back in Magnolia Springs, I thought obsessively about Maggie and when I would next see her. It was hard to play the role of the dutiful husband, though I managed. It would be a half-hearted performance at best with Etta. Every time we were with each other, I thought that she could see through me and my transparent thoughts.

She asked me if I had seen Maggie, and I said briefly in passing for a quick coffee. I reported that she seemed to have her life together. I told Etta that she seemed to have a new seriousness and direction from her writing. Loyola and its creative writing program had been the right decision. It might indeed make the difference for Maggie.

I felt that I would be protected in the lie since Etta and Maggie rarely spoke on the telephone anymore. Maggie would certainly be discrete and maybe refer to a quick catch up in a café with me if she were asked.

Maggie was out of Etta's consciousness. She had thrown herself into her clinical therapy business and the prospect of a large multi-office enterprise had excited her. Etta had put all her energy into finding counseling clients for the Fairhope start-up. She was routinely having lunch and coffee with her myriad friends living on the Eastern Shore, while putting out the word.

Obviously there would be marriages in trouble as there always had been, but there were also children with behavior issues, and occasionally siblings and aging parents thrown into the mix, each who might benefit from intelligent and sensitive therapy.

The referrals came, and with them the customers. Within a week and a half, Etta had four couples seeking counseling, all of whom she knew from childhood, and several teenagers with unpleasant and destructive behavior patterns.

In addition, the new female mayor of Fairhope, the first in its history, had asked Etta to head the mental health week initiative as chairman. Despite its low-sounding name, it included politicians and the leading business people living on the burgeoning Eastern Shore, which had a concentration of the area's increasing wealth. It all came together.

Etta convinced the president of the Point Clear Polo Club and another longtime childhood friend to host its first fund-raiser at the hotly contested annual match between Point Clear and the New Orleans polo club. Because New Orleans was the better party town, the match was traditionally played in that city. But this season, it would be moved to the Eastern Shore and turned into a social event with tailgate parties, and a tented sit-down dinner for the largest donors. That would be five hundred dollars a plate for cold chicken salad and white wine, with an auction tent alongside.

Etta was able to convince the area's most famous artist, who had been an apprentice to Dali years ago, to do a special limited edition print of the hard-fought match for collectors. Twenty signed and numbered prints would be available to art collectors for a thousand dollars, all tax deductible. I saw the earliest drawing in the series and it was exquisite with flawless rendered lines. The flamboyant artist would be housed in his own small painting kiosk at mid-field where the donors might drift over and admire a brush stroke. It was certain to bring out a large crowd to the polo field and the event would most likely raise a great deal of money for charity.

Etta was garrulous as she listed thing after thing on her to-do list. I listened patiently with a smile on my face, my mind stuck in the French Quarter.

It seemed that Maggie had been true to her word, and there were no late night confessional calls to Etta about what had happened. I assumed she wanted it to continue as I had.

For me, the affair took on an obsessive quality, and perhaps that's true for most couples during the white-heat stage. Each day I needed to hear Maggie's voice, even if I were working at home. I had to drive down to the gas station, or to a convenience store with a public telephone. We would talk for maybe five minutes, sometimes ten minutes at most. I didn't want to remain on the telephone for too long, or at the same place, in case someone we knew might remark that it was peculiar. My route was usually some ridiculous invention of errands, and spontaneous stops, filling up with five dollars' worth of gas at a handful of stations. It was always so surreptitious.

This paranoia about detection became heightened. It reminded me of those first tense hours in an airplane during naval flight training. That was long before I gained any confidence that I might actually fly the damn thing and land on a shifting aircraft carrier deck in the South China seas.

When I traveled to New Orleans, I kept the same hotel as always, The Hilton just inside the Quarter, where I was known and afforded some degree of discretion by the management and staff. If I didn't come in until morning, no one at the desk or any of the bellmen, would make any comment, or even notice. I had once mentioned to the hotel director that I worked in politics and required a sort of anonymity. He clearly understood my meaning. He put his fingertips to his lips and smiled knowingly.

If Etta called, they were likely to say I was with campaign people, or at a late dinner, or they thought I might be in my room asleep. An early evening perhaps.

I never stayed at the hotel for the night. I would always be at Maggie's studio and return to the Hilton in the morning. That was the usual routine. I absented myself from all but the most important campaign dinners and strategy sessions. Thankfully, because I was such an experienced operative and the veteran of a dozen large scale campaigns, nobody gave a second thought to my absence at a staff late-night drinking bout.

This woman consumed my thoughts. She didn't ask anything of me outside our time together in cafes, restaurants, or at her apartment. Maggie didn't ask me to leave Etta, or even make some kind of declaration to her with some tangible words of commitment. Maggie was silent on the subject and lived in the present as far as I was concerned.

The fact I continued to lie to Etta bothered me. Somehow I never asked myself those deeper questions of why I had done this and what would eventually happen to all of us in this unwieldy triangle. I did it. The lies became more ambitious and outrageous with time. Once I broached the painful topic with Maggie about my guilt as a married man. She shook her head, and put her finger to my lips.

"We do this because we have to. It's something we can't stop. It's a force stronger than both of us. How it ends isn't important."

The way she wove this metaphysical meaning into our romantic involvement served only to confuse me. I wasn't a child of this flowered philosophy. I was the culpable one with both of these women.

Maggie insisted she was not a vulnerable, youthful woman, full of innocent ideas who had been ensnared by her sister's husband, and became a victim of his lustful behavior.

"Put that nonsense out of your mind, right now," she told me, "It was me who wanted this from that first night but I knew all along that you wanted me as well. A woman knows this."

I couldn't figure out what to do next as my mind was in a perpetual fog. Fortunately, the campaign was the candidate's to lose, because I hardly thought about the outcome. I pulled strategies out of a hat. As a last minute tactic, I thought his so-called freshness might propel us to victory on election night. I had no earthly idea where we stood, although the few polls we had commissioned had shown that the senator was fifteen or more percentage points ahead. That was at least reassuring as I sat musing about the other things in my campaign office on Canal.

Like the earlier tidal wave of Minerva, her eldest daughter moved along with the moon's gravitational pull. I could only guess that her success with the clinics somehow made her happy.

I asked her on the telephone, "Are you happy with how the clinics have done? It sounds like everything is coming together."

Her answer was almost maudlin, "I don't like to get too excited until things play out."

None of Etta's latest accomplishments would mean anything to Minerva who was caught in her dementia. It was tragic. Minerva had been such a vibrant woman, and she ran that large family with her matriarchal iron fist, wrapped up in a glove. The price her children paid was the price they eventually paid, for better or worse.

Maggie was almost out of college now, and Etta had done her best as the replacement matriarch. Etta's brother moved into a large colonial house in Meadowbrook with a hundred-thousand-dollar loan from his father-in-law. The pediatric resident washed his hands of Mobile. He sent Christmas gifts, and there might be the occasional afternoon visit, though that was it. He had moved on.

Mary Agnes had a little boy with her new husband and his family was beaming with elation all over town. They had the dean himself do the christening at the Cathedral. I was there with Etta. We had been chosen as the reluctant godparents over the husband's first cousin who had been a football star under Shug Jordan at Auburn. He now had the head coaching job at the University of Central Florida, a perennial loser in the sport. He enjoyed living in Orlando and his children adored Disney World where he had season passes courtesy of a school booster. He still walked with a limp from a late hit in the Cotton Bowl.

Maggie thought it best to stay in New Orleans, keeping her distance from Mobile. I would need an excuse to see her once the campaign finished. I wracked my brain for what to do, and eventually came up with a possible solution. I would have the candidate, once he was elected, pressure the present Governor who was a personal friend, to find me a long-term consulting contract within New Orleans.

Over coffee one afternoon when the candidate asked me what I would be doing after we won, I said that I would like his help in getting me a consulting contract with the mayor. I didn't want anything big, though. Just something that would allow me to spend more time in the city. He smiled broadly at me, and shook his head up and down.

"Consider it done," he said. "I'll be with the mayor next week at a dinner, and I'll broach the subject. He owes me, don't worry."

He was true to his word. We won the election in a landslide because the opponent was such a terrible campaigner. He had only raised a pittance from his fundraising efforts.

I was provided a handsome contract for eighty thousand dollars to assist the mayor with federal legislative program analysis, which was a new position created, but I would be available to consult on most any question he might have. It was real and time-consuming as it was detail-oriented work, actually.

To do the job, I might spend as much or as little time as I chose in New Orleans. That was my ticket to be with Maggie safe from prying eyes.

We went on week after week and month after month, and still she made few demands on me for permanence or even commitment.

She became consumed with her poetry and had one lovely chapbook published by the Loyola Press. It was rich and beautiful in its language. I was so proud of what she had done, and told her that much.

"I wanted to dedicate it to you, to our love like Oscar Wilde. It's a love that dare not speak its name," she whispered to me one evening.

She was a full time student now. Etta had arranged for the family trust to pay the entire tuition, and also provide her with six hundred dollars a month for living expenses. Maggie charged into her poetry studies, and was considered a rising star in the English department.

As we continued, I always had this ominous feeling that I would be replaced by some handsome young bearded poet and become a footnote in her young life. That didn't seem to happen, though I always questioned why. On an evening together at the apartment, I brought up the painful subject and she merely laughed, rubbing her fingers through my hair.

She said seriously this time: "Do you think I'm that shallow? Treat what we have with such contempt?"

"You have your life ahead of you, Maggie," I added saddened, thinking that perhaps I'd predicted the future too accurately.

"As do you," she countered. "We don't need to change anything. Why look for something that isn't there?"

Still, I couldn't manage a smile.

Maggie added, "I see this as a gift we've been given, something we can treasure. Please don't complicate things."

I wanted to explain these fears and say more, and receive reassurance from her that it wouldn't end. Instead, I simply sighed and took what she had told me at face value. We were all right for the moment, and we didn't know how long that moment might last, so why worry? Though I did.

With some small confidence, we ventured out more often in the city: to the symphony, to plays, and restaurants where we might be seen by someone from Mobile. After all, it was only two hours away and a lot of the people we knew came with some frequency particularly for the nightlife in the French Quarter.

It was inevitable that we would at least see someone we knew. Maybe it might be on the street, or worse in a restaurant, though both of us felt confident it would appear as some extended family visit to the onlooker, but people talk, especially in the South. Maybe if they had bumped into us twice, or we looked intimate, which we never did publicly, it would be obvious. We were both careful about that. It couldn't happen. Maggie wasn't foolish. She had a checkered past, but she was intelligent and wanted to avoid a scandal. I did as well. At least that's what I believed, and she gave me no reason to doubt her. But of course it happened, and with the wrong person.

For some reason we had gone to the late night bar on the terrace above the French Market. No one was there at that hour, and we drifted out to the end of the terrace with our drinks. Maggie pulled close to me as we watched the river move in the Louisiana darkness. Her arm was on my shoulder.

"Well, it looks like some old friends, it does," a voice behind us said. We turned to see a Mobile lawyer acquaintance and obliquely a friend of their family. He was standing there along with his wife, who had this serious look on her pinched face that she had quickly tried to hide, though unsuccessfully. They moved closer into the orange halogen light. He reached out to shake my hand, looking over into Maggie's face with some surprise.

He said loudly, "Maggie, my goodness. I haven't seen you since you were in grade school. How are you, darling?"

With that, he leaned over to kiss her flushed cheek, and his wife edged closer, and added, "Good evening, y'all." It was probably all she could manage in the awkward situation.

There was something sinister and menacing in the way this man held himself. I had this immediate sensation he would do us harm. His smile signaled the complicit evil he had hidden in the false words he was speaking.

I interrupted and offered, "Doing my part to see all the family when I'm in town."

He lowered his eyes and peered at Maggie's young shapely body, a look that made me feel dirty. His crooked smile meant, "I know what you're doing."

It felt to me similar to a Western gunfighter moment when you look into a man's eyes, trying to read what he'll do next. Your sweaty hand ready to reach for your pistol to kill him. I felt the sweat bead on the back of my now damp neck. The smile on his fat face lingered there far too long, and I didn't quite know what to do. Maggie remained silent and fearful.

I broke the silence on that humid New Orleans rooftop by speaking first.

"Did you know Maggie is a budding poet?" I said out of nowhere. "She's at Loyola."

He didn't immediately answer me, but looked around to catch the eyes of his wife who stood behind him, perhaps seeking her opinion though she said nothing.

Finally, there was a motion in his body suggesting he knew what to do next, and he spoke. He proceeded first with a loud chuckle yet with a tight mouth.

"Is that so?" the man said in a disingenuous manner over the rim of his drink glass. His wife remained uncomfortably perched next to him with pressed lips.

"A great city to be a poet in, I'd think," he said, "Lots of distractions, and of course, romance." With that remark, he started to laugh again though no one else joined him in the reverie.

"Wouldn't you agree, sugar"" he asked his wife though not really expecting any kind of answer. She mumbled something unintelligible.

He sat down at the table closest to us, motioning for his apprehensive wife to join him who moved sheepishly toward us. She stood still. He reached backed with his meaty paw and urged her forward next to him. At first she did nothing but he continued the hand motion and then with his head. In an instant she obeyed and was standing inches away from him.

"It's always good to run into hometown folks, an unexpected pleasure," he roared. "Let me buy you both a drink?

He turned around toward the narrow bar. "Hey barkeep, bring this lovely couple two more of the same." He snapped his fingers in the air.

The bartender nodded in the other room and grabbed two clean glasses off the shelf behind him.

"No, please. There's no need, really," I uttered halfheartedly to him, but he shook his head back and forth, saying, "We insist, don't we, baby?"

His clearly uncomfortable wife again said something inaudible.

Maggie at last spoke with her broad smile: "Richard, it's wonderful to see you again, and your lovely bride. But honestly, this isn't necessary. I was just leaving after saying hello to my favorite brother-in-law. It's late for me to be out. A school night."

It all sounded contrived to me, though it was something to thwart what could otherwise be an unpleasant encounter. I lauded Maggie for her quick thinking and hoped that it had perhaps neutralized the earlier damage.

The stocky man wasn't hearing anything of it, and leaned over and said to her, "I'll bet you fit into this wide open place like a glove, sweetie. It's maybe too edgy for old folks like us." With that comment, he leaned back rather pleased with himself and emitted a loud guffaw like some hippo.

"It's late, and we're holding up these people," his wife besieged him, pulling on his sport jacket sleeve though to no avail.

"Oh no, that would be too rude. We can't ignore friends because of the lateness of the hour. People expect some evening conversation in this town, don't they, Maggie?' he said with this sadistic grin on his porcine face.

The brute was well aware he had trapped us in this painfully embarrassing moment, and he intended to milk it for all it was worth. His wife prolonged her silence but he pushed onward.

"We like to come to The Quarter. Have for years, because anything goes here. People do whatever they damn well please. Don't bother hiding a thing. We like that spirit, don't we?" He glanced at his mousy wife for an instant.

She at last said, "Maggie, I saw Mary Agnes last week at a Junior League thing. It had been ages. We didn't have much time to visit. She's a chairman of something there. What a whirlwind, that girl. I'll tell you."

He added, "Always was, that Mary Agnes. A little dervish."

"I never see Etta, ever, but we hear she's got this huge medical practice now. Everybody's talking about what a marvelous thing she's done."

I finally added something to the inane banter of the two. "I'm so proud of her. That's one superwoman, I'll tell you."

After I had said it, I thought that the hollow words hung in the air, and everyone could sense the falseness of what I had attempted to do.

There was nothing more to be said by any of us. The quiet filled the night except for some bar music waffling through the air from a side street tavern.

The stillness became broken by the conversation of what sounded like a couple of drunken tourists who were trying to get into the French Market for a coffee, though it had been closed for five hours.

One of them was yelling, "I want a goddamn creole coffee. I came a thousand miles for it, and the fucking place is closed. Open up." The drunk was pulling on the metal gate over the front door, and his friend finally talked some sense into him. The bars made a clanging noise.

The calmer guy downstairs said, "If you keep this up, the cops are going to throw us in jail. You think they put up with shit like this?" In a moment they both had started up the street singing something in a half intelligible manner. There were laughs and singing in the distance.

"Lots of texture in this place," the fat man suggested, referring to the two drunks, and by then he had finished his own drink. Slowly he stood up ready to leave.

"We'll let you get back to your chat. We just wanted to be neighborly," he added, "It's way past our bedtime too anyway, isn't it, Marlene? Got to go home tomorrow morning at the crack of dawn. Bye."

He insisted on kissing Maggie's cheek, and he shook my hand with this stadium enthusiasm. "Good to see you, partner," he said as he turned to walk out.

In an instant they were gone, and I breathed a sigh of relief. I had the feeling that the incident wouldn't bode well for us, though reluctant to mention it.

Maggie turned to me shaking her head. "They won't keep quiet about this, you know. Not him. She's a mouse and won't want trouble. But he'll tell people, count on it."

"They didn't see anything, really," I stated, trying to disarm the fear we both felt from the encounter.

"You hugged me leaning against the wall. There's nothing in that, c'mon," I pointed out to her, unconvinced myself.

"Look, it's late. We're together on some bar rooftop," she explained. "What would you think if it were you? And where's your wife? Nowhere to be found."

"That's the worst case scenario," I stressed. "They didn't see a damn thing."

She said sadly, "They saw enough. We're standing close to each other. My hand was on your back. That's not a sisterly act, not to them. Probably not to anyone."

With that, Maggie reached into her purse on her shoulder and pulled out a pack of cigarettes, and quickly lit one. She had never smoked around me before, and it shocked me. I thought of her as this completely holistic woman, though there had been the drug-infused years.

"I can tell you this," she said blowing a cloud of smoke into the air. "They won't talk about anything else on the drive back. They'll agree, both of those pathetic people, that we're having an affair."

"Look, you're guessing," I said, trying to get around the sense of foreboding.

She said too forcefully: "Goddammit, I'm not. They run into somebody's husband and his wife's sister at midnight hidden away in the dark, playing kissy face. They're both congratulating themselves they caught us."

Her otherwise calm demeanor left her, and she began to pace around with the cigarette in her hand. At the far end near the wall, she began to shout, "Shit, shit." She kicked the low wall several times hard.

"We'll get through it. I'll tell Etta you only had time for a drink while studying and I met you late, then we ran into her friends."

Maggie said, "You'd tell her that after the fact. Because he's going to tell someone like Mary Agnes, or shit, someone who'll mention it to Etta." She walked to the far edge of the terrace and looked out at the rolling black Mississippi.

"Maybe when I talk to Etta tomorrow, I'll say you only had time to meet me for a drink late since you had exams, and we saw one of her old friends who had been in town. Innocent enough."

She laughed softly to herself, and said, "Oh, he won't tell Etta. That's not the way it works. What he'll do is tell somebody tomorrow or the next day at lunch at the country club. They'll mention it to somebody else at some dinner, and maybe that last person might say something to Etta."

"I'll be careful how I do it. Downplay everything," I stressed.

"Just pretend you're writing some dumb speech. You'll figure it out," she stated with a sigh. "Anyway, let's go home, and drift off somewhere else."

Maggie pulled away from me. She started to dance this adagio dance around the terrace, singing lyrics from some psychedelic tune, and motioned for me to join her. Oblivious to the world around us, or the one we had perhaps set into motion that night, we danced in the New Orleans moonlight, the only couple at the rooftop bar.

That night was probably the turning point. I couldn't help but think as we moved to some unheard rhythm. I was uncertain how I could save it, and it would all come crashing down around my head, and hers. It was the beginning of the reckoning we would face, but could we survive it? I didn't know, and I guessed neither did she.

The couple wouldn't hold their tongues. It was too much to expect of normal human beings. The taste of gossip and blood was far more delectable than the two unfinished whiskeys they had left on the wet table. Their appetite wouldn't be sated until they had whispered this scandal to some conspirator. It all had come as a shock.

What could they do, but behave as they had? Pretend that they hadn't seen anything? Hadn't noticed the husband of a dear woman friend embracing her college-age sister in the New Orleans moonlight, hidden from the unsuspecting eyes of family and friends? This clandestine rendezvous away from home. Who would dispute what they had seen? Nobody would.

I had another evening in New Orleans after a meeting with the mayor who had seemed to take a liking to me beyond what he owed the senator. He had laid out a long-term proposal for me. Its payoff was me possibly moving permanently to the city.

This was his last term in office, as it was his second. He saw himself as the next governor, and he knew I could get him close to achieving that dream. So our discussion at the lunch in the Quarter was about his considerable ambition. He had the grassroots political organization ready to deliver the crucial big city vote. He had black support, and we would work together on developing popularity upstate, which I knew I could do for him.

Why was I doing this? It was pure madness. I was putting together some escape from Etta, ready to spend my life with her younger sister. Is that something I had really thought through? Would it even work? Did I really want it?

We had been seeing each other sporadically, and it had all that excitement of newness about it, but could it stand the light of day? I had no earthly idea. I loved her, though did she feel the same? Truthfully we had never discussed any sort of future; maybe she had always assumed that there wasn't one.

When I got back to Magnolia Springs, Etta was out at the clinic seeing some evening clients. When she did come back, there was the hug and the requisite peck on the cheek, then she got ready for bed, exhausted.

She asked about the mayor. I told her what he wanted, and she said, "That means more work. You like being a gunslinger. You're an outlaw at heart, aren't you?"

"An outlaw, how?" I asked her, perplexed.

"I think if we lived a hundred years ago, you'd be with the James Gang, robbing banks, and shooting bank tellers. You're that kind of man, ruthless."

"Wait a minute," I exclaimed sitting up in bed, "My life is pretty ordinary. Maybe I don't go to the bank every day, but really."

"Please, half the people you get elected should be in jail," she said with this wide sinister look on her face.

"That's not true," I answered confused at her sarcasm.

"Isn't it?" she added. "I sometimes don't think I have any idea of what you value. You're like a stranger half the time, closed mouth."

"That's my way," I said defensively.

"Oh forget it," she said, and added, "We're booked in Fairhope solid for the next two months. It's working."

"I'm pleased," I said, and leaned over and gave her a hard hug but her body seemed unresponsive and limp to me.

Something had changed within her. She knows, I thought to myself, but how? That fat clown hasn't had enough time to do his damage yet, or his serpentine wife either. It's my imagination. She's behaving like she always does, a kind of passive aggressive flip flop that has gone on with her for years.

179

My mind started to race: She knows I occasionally see Maggie when I'm in New Orleans, she expects it. That wouldn't be odd that we would have a drink somewhere. I've got to put the panic that we've been discovered right out of my head, or I'm going to become a nervous wreck.

The two of us continued to act like we had always acted. She was busy building her clinical empire, and even her visits to Minerva had been reduced too.

There was still a little lucid pleasure to be found in her mother's company where she would actually participate in some normal back and forth conversation, but that was between the absolute forgetfulness that had her asking you the same question every five minutes.

Mary Agnes was safely consumed within her new married life, and her husband's extended family. Their brother had his medical practice and Meadowbrook, and the second youngest was absorbed with university life and art.

We had each other and our circle of friends, and had settled into a predictable routine that was probably common with many couples. Everything was the same. Then, Minerva fell and broke her hip at the assisted living center in the bathroom during the early morning. She hadn't pressed the nurse call button, and fell off the commode, an unfortunate accident but not uncommon in dementia care.

She was rushed to Thomas Hospital for emergency surgery to repair the hip, but that put her in a seriously weakened state. The doctor had warned Etta that about half of the elderly patients don't survive a year afterwards, or may die on the operating table as it happens too frequently. One thing was certain and that was she probably wouldn't walk again, despite the planned physical therapy. Etta was trying to come to grips with that.

Minerva refused therapy during the next few weeks of her rehabilitation and Etta had become haggard spending every night at her mother's side. Mary Agnes was there about once or twice for a visit, and everyone else might blow in once during the visitation half hour. Their brother attempted to supervise the care long distance, talking at length with the hospital medical staff. He, too, was pessimistic about the chances of recovery and after a while, he halted his calls to Etta.

On a windy evening, both Etta and I were at her bedside, and Minerva was more vocal than she had been.

"It looks like I'm going to the great beyond," she said, and had a coughing fit that followed what I reckoned was some kind of a laugh. "I'm going to die, Etta," she said.

"Oh hush, momma," Etta said, "you're still a strong woman."

Minerva looked over at me with a sad smile, and she said, "Go ahead, tell her, boy. I'm not long for this world. Tell her."

"You'll outlive us all, Minerva," I said to the supine woman. From the bed came a distinctive shriek followed by a painful cough.

As we walked out of the rehabilitation wing to the parking lot, Etta turned to me and said, "I don't think she's going to survive this. She'd rather die than not walk. She doesn't like who she's become, and it's too much for her."

The only thing I could say was, "It's hard to know."

Driving home in the car, neither one of us felt much like talking but Etta tried. She wanted to find some sense in her mother's condition, though she couldn't.

"A cruel end for what was a spirited woman. Poised and confident her whole life. An awful end."

I sighed because I knew she was right, and I could only add, "It came earlier to your mother, that's all. To both of them. I'm sorry. They were extraordinary people, head and shoulders above so many of their friends."

"She was such a beautiful woman. You'd see her in all those Mardi Gras pictures as the Queen, or the life of somebody's party. She never doubted who she was for a moment."

"No, she never did," I agreed as we pulled into the gravel driveway of the river house, exhausted.

I made her a drink and myself as well, and sitting there she looked off into space as I made a fire, lighting the kindling.

"I'd better call Maggie tomorrow and tell her to come right away. She needs to spend some time with her mother. She can stay with us and use my car."

Without looking at Etta, I added, "Sure, you take my car this week. I'm working at home anyway. I don't need it. Be great to have her here."

How that would play out I had no idea, though I had assumed that everyone would act detached, play at being a close-knit family somehow. We would go through some painful charade.

"I'll call her tomorrow morning when I can talk. I can't now," Etta confessed, swirling the ice cubes around inside her glass. She kicked her shoes off and they dropped to the wooden floor with a thud.

"There's little to say, but I think she'll die sooner than later," Etta went on, "She doesn't want to live."

"We could all be fooled. Talking during her worst moments. Each day she easily might gain back her strength," I added.

"You don't believe what you're saying, do you?" Etta pronounced.

"No, I don't, but I might be wrong," I answered.

Etta rose from the chair, and took her drink into the bedroom then stretched out on the bed in her street clothes.

"All this seems other worldly to me. I can't believe the whole thing with Daddy and now her." With that, she put her arm over her eyes, hiding her face, and became quiet.

I sat in the living room for a few minutes and watched the roaring fire. I gradually downed my own drink, then at last rose and trudged into the bedroom for the night. She got up and stayed in the living room caught up in her own thoughts for another hour.

In the morning she called Maggie who planned to take the train to Mobile that next afternoon. I said that I'd pick her up at the station while Etta was at the office with several clients.

Naturally, the train was delayed. It was over an hour late, though it hardly mattered. I saw a hippie-looking young woman bound out of the compartment door with a small suitcase, and waved to her from the platform. She had the look of absolute freshness with her alabaster skin and shoulder length dark locks. I gave her a hard hug as she came to me.

In the car while driving across the causeway, she started to talk, and said, "I imagine this is probably the end for mother. I know I'd rather be dead than be crazy in some wheelchair."

"Half of them survive the hip surgery, and she might be one of them," I noted. "She's always been in charge of her life. At least from what I've seen over the years."

"Hers and everyone else's," Maggie sputtered with a sneer. "She'd meddle in everybody's, trying to rule them. It was awful, the sick way she behaved."

"At her worst, it wasn't pretty, Maggie," I added, "Some might call it a sickness, that control."

Maggie looked out the window at the passing bay for a moment, and turned. "With Etta, it was the worst. She orchestrated every move Etta ever made because she was the first. She never let her have a damn thought of her own."

"It wasn't quite that overboard," I answered.

"Bullshit," Maggie said, shaking her head.

There was a dead silence as we drove through Fairhope and out onto the country roads toward Magnolia Springs.

"I hope I'm not going to have to hear you screw Etta every night I'm here," Maggie spit out.

"Jesus Christ," I said, "Things are crazy enough here without hearing that."

She added, "I don't think I could take that. It would drive me over the edge. I'd throw myself in the fucking river."

"It's about Minerva. That's all this thing is, OK?" I pleaded, "You and I can talk about the other later. I'll be back next week."

"Well, Mr. Perfect, if you think that's fine, I guess it is," Maggie stated with a little girl pout on her face that turned into a slow smile.

As I stopped the car at the empty Magnolia Springs house, she reached over and gave me a deep kiss on the mouth.

As she left the car in the driveway she said, "It's far from over. You coming?"

I put my hand on her soft shoulder next to me as I put the key into the lock and opened the door.

I told Maggie to take the car into Fairhope and do what she wanted. Perhaps she could stop at Etta's office and make an appearance. Compliment her on the whole enterprise she had built from nothing. She agreed, and with her own brand of cheerful demeanor sped out of the driveway.

Later that night, Etta came home first and told me that Maggie had stopped by and was running a few errands in Fairhope. She had driven over to Thomas Hospital to see Minerva and we could expect her back at seven thirty.

Because I felt I had to do something, I pulled out some frozen triggerfish fillets we had bought from a local fisherman, and made a fish Veracruz dish with the vegetables we had in the refrigerator. I tried to piece together the great grilled fish dishes I'd had on fishing trips to Mazatlan years ago.

"Maggie seemed alright to me," I said to Etta as she settled in at home, throwing her burgeoning soft leather briefcase on the empty desktop in the living room alcove. As she slung the briefcase, a few files fell onto the floor, and I heard her say, "Shit."

Must be a family trait that word, I thought to myself with a grin and finished the final steps for dinner.

"Well, how nice," Etta said looking over the efforts in the kitchen, "Is there anything I can do?"

"Set the table," I said and finished the wild rice I had on the stove.

"There's a bottle of Chardonnay in the fridge. I'll wait till Maggie gets here before I open it."

Etta was standing in the kitchen doorway watching me, and added, "We won't want to disappoint the princess by drinking without her."

"It's for dinner. I'll make you a scotch."

"Better make it a double scotch. It was a long day." Etta said and went into the bedroom to change from her business suit attire into something more casual.

I suspected that Maggie wouldn't say anything that might make Etta suspicious. Of course, there would be no reason for her to do that. She wasn't the uncontrollable and rebellious drug-addled teenager of those high school years that had vanished long ago. It had been replaced by this sensitive and intelligent woman, in complete command of her own life. Headstrong and passionate perhaps, but stupid, never.

I heard the car come into the driveway as I finished mixing the drinks. She pushed open the door with resolve, looking over at me silently mouthing an endearment as Etta finished in the bathroom.

"Maggie's here," I called out to Etta through the bathroom door.

"Be out in a second," Etta shouted from inside, and I could hear the water running in the sink.

Dinner went well. It was cool enough so we had it outside at a picnic table riverside, and we all sipped our second glass of wine as the sun began to set. A deep pink color filled the Alabama sky in front of us with horizontal bands of the deepest dark blue. It stayed illuminated for an hour or more.

"Mother looks half dead," Maggie reported during a lull in the conversation, "I can't imagine she's going to get over that surgery, and her mind's worse too. She repeats everything like some parrot."

"You never know. She could surprise everyone," I suggested.

"There's nothing I can do for her. I'll see her tomorrow and leave the next day if that's fine with all concerned," Maggie announced to no objections.

"I'm going back to New Orleans for a meeting with the mayor, so I'll just leave early and drive you back. Save you train delays."

"Great if it works for you," she said. "Do you mind, Etta?"

"Oh me, why should I mind? It's his bread and butter. The honorable mayor whom you may or may not know will be running for governor in maybe eight more months. And guess who his campaign strategist is going to be? That's right, golden boy."

I shook my head at the reference. "It's work, and gets you in the public eye, which doesn't hurt."

The race for governor didn't interest either woman, and they started to talk about childhood friends, their successes and naturally their foibles.

One man whom Etta had dated in college had a nervous breakdown and he had accidentally rammed his car into the back of a state police cruiser. He had been charged with a felonious assault against a police officer.

The poor soul had been convicted with a later plea bargain that had him serve four months instead of the possible fifteen-year maximum. He was such a nice man Etta offered, though he had bouts of odd behavior that had doomed him in both the workforce and with his short-lived marriage.

One afternoon he had started breaking dishes in his Spring Hill kitchen and his panicked wife had called the police who had found him stretched on his front lawn. When they had asked him to get up to talk with them, he had grabbed one police officer by the leg. They fought with him, cuffed him, then booked him for assault and resisting arrest. It was a rather sad case. He had joined us at a holiday open house, and appeared to be a reticent and rather shy man. He had a degree in forestry from Auburn, and had briefly worked for Georgia Pacific as a salesman. Now his family helped him with his rent and living expenses.

Also, there were several girlfriends with unpleasant divorces. One in particular had a long trial where the focus had been on her adultery with her father-in-law, a prominent Mobile attorney and a deacon at the cathedral.

The next morning the mayor called me from New Orleans. He said he had good news on two fronts. The first was the largest developer in the French Quarter had agreed to become his campaign finance chairman, and secondly, he had also offered a furnished one-bedroom coach house to the campaign. The mayor was making it my permanent city residence. It was inside a courtyard just off Royale Street, and everything inside it was new.

This would end the in-and-out traffic with hotels, and I could spend as much time in the city as needed. It also included a rare garage at the rear which had been some type of nineteenth century tool shed.

"We're off to the races," the mayor sang into the telephone, and we set the next week's schedule for committee nominees to discuss.

"I suspect we can start raising some real money in a month, maybe two, and you can spend as much time as you need up in Shreveport getting things organized for the Red River," he noted.

Unlike the previous two mayors who had been ward-heeling politicians brought up on spoils, this particular mayor had made his mark as a prosecutor and had been particularly active in his organized crime roundups. The mayor was a new wave politician for a state where the Longs had ruled for a generation. He believed his time had arrived. No Huey Long connection. Rumors of competition in the primary uncovered a few lackluster party hacks. His biggest task would be to bring together several disparate voting blocs with high enough numbers to thwart the old party machinery.

I thought it best to keep the news of the New Orleans apartment to myself until I had returned from the city and had actually taken residence. This part-time life had its uncertainties.

The time together with Maggie and Etta was pleasant enough. No one had much more to say than conversations of nostalgic chit chat between the two sisters. It appeared that nobody had gotten to Etta after the obnoxious couple surprised us in the French Market.

I decided to get back to New Orleans a day early and chauffeur Maggie. We packed up and said our goodbyes. We didn't talk much in the car until we got near Pascagoula, and I told her about the apartment offer.

She laughed, and turned to me and in a slight whisper said, "Oh goody, musical beds. One night in mine and the next in yours."

Most people could easily criticize the way I was living my life, the duplicity and lying and the seeming absence of gut-wrenching guilt. Maybe at the deepest level, I really loathed what I'd become. It wasn't something I was proud of, yet it didn't stop me from doing it. Of course it would have to end as it was, it couldn't continue. Maggie would no doubt demand some permanence, some show of commitment. I'd either have to walk away from her, or from Etta.

As I drove into New Orleans I kept thinking, when will it all collapse? When will Maggie meet me for coffee and tell me she's living with a young bearded poet she met in class, and they're moving to Berkeley? It had to happen, right?

These few years of Etta's obsessiveness had exhausted me. It was the worst of Minerva's personality without the meanness. Though yet, it had me on edge for years. With

Maggie, I could relax, be myself, and not worry where I placed my shoes at night for fear she would object, and continue her incessant onslaught.

After two weeks off and on in the New Orleans apartment, Etta called me late one night to tell me that Minerva had been taken to the ICU at Thomas. The prognosis was grave. She had suffered some sort of aneurysm, and it would probably end her life. She was calling me from the OR waiting room, and would stay there until she talked to the surgeons.

I drove directly to Fairhope, not bothering to call Maggie. I figured that Etta would want to do that. She could come later. Minerva was in a coma, and there would be no bedside exchange of goodbyes. The best we could hope for would be for her to regain consciousness, but it was hard to imagine what cognitive damage had occurred. Could she speak, or move her limbs?

Inside the hospital, I found the elevator and took it to the OR floor. I could see Etta pacing around a small lounge and when she saw me she started crying.

I held her and comforted her the best I could, but I had the feeling this was the end for Minerva, and probably a blessing if she lost most of her faculties. She would want to go before that happened. She had always been a pragmatic and practical woman, on her terms naturally, and she wouldn't want to live with tubes and monitors. Etta told them not to resuscitate her mother. I wasn't certain that she would do it, but Minerva had signed that paper years ago.

She called all the siblings, including Maggie, and told them to come to Thomas because this could very easily be her end. Their brother was driving south, Maggie was taking the morning train from New Orleans, and Mary Agnes and her husband were already in transit. Clara was coming too. She was the most reclusive of the entire family.

Clara was the family member I had the least to do with. She had always been a standoffish and rather withdrawn, self-contained child and then young woman.

She had gotten two graduate degrees in art history as far as I knew. Clara had worked for a time at the Mobile Art Museum as a fine art appraiser. She left two years ago to move to Sarasota where she now worked as a curator for the Ringling Museum. Clara managed their large poster art collection, which I'm told had some national prestige. Otherwise, she lived alone with two or three cats, and didn't seem to socialize much. She didn't seem to be dating men, or women. She was the Mobile family sibling no one ever mentioned in conversation. Etta once said Clara had become an expert on Toulouse-Lautrec, and I can't remember her saying much more over the subsequent years.

I sat on the hospital couch, and held Etta's hand while she rambled on about how full of life and opinionated her mother had been. Certainly Minerva had been formidable when you first met her, intimidating actually. I had never known anyone quite like her. The women in my mother's family were reticent and fearful of any exposure. They hid in their coal town kitchens, waiting for their drunken miner husbands to return from the bars, and maybe bat them around a bit.

Etta had her head in her hands and slowly raised it to speak. "There were a lot of things about mother that weren't good, but she was my mother. She did things to me that she couldn't help, and I'm past that, I think."

"We only get one mother," I told her.

No sooner had I spoken those words, a gown-clad surgeon walked out of the OR and over to us. He knew Etta, as did so many people of a certain circle in Mobile and their families.

"Etta, she's gone. I'm sorry," he said in a sincere drawl. "Her body gave out. Minerva had several minor strokes, one after the other, and the aneurysm made it impossible for her to survive."

I said, "I'll call everybody and tell them quickly."

"Yes," she said. I started to make the calls when we got home. I reached Mary Agnes first and told her, and asked her to telephone the others. She agreed and I helped Etta into the bedroom to lie down for a while.

"Your mother was a product of a distinctive time, and of extraordinary people," I said to her. "What other ten-year-old girl would go to the 1932 World's Fair in New York City with her eight-year-old sister without reservations, parents, or even knowing where New York was but Minerva? Alone, the two of them. That sums up who she was. It baffles the imagination of ordinary people."

"She was one of a kind, yep. I don't know how we survived her, any of us," Etta said looking out the window into the Alabama darkness.

\* \* \* \* \* \*

It was a large funeral and the dean of the cathedral officiated. He was assisted in the rites by the Jesuit president of Spring Hill College and the ever present Father Jelinek. The sanctuary was filled with half of Mobile, and a gifted black soprano from the local opera company sang Amazing Grace which was Minerva's favorite hymn, odd perhaps for a rigid papist though her favorite nevertheless. It was a part of the contradiction that had been the woman.

I noticed Aaron's family in a back pew. As I walked up to the front with Etta, she nodded to his white-haired father who forced a smile in her direction and quickly bowed his head.

The eulogy was heartfelt and quite beautiful. Everyone in the church could easily see how much the dean had loved Minerva. It took all of his Jesuit discipline to hold back his own tears.

A mass was offered in Latin as Minerva would have wanted. The procession left to follow the black hearse to the Civil War cemetery on the outskirts of Mobile by the local Monastery where the notable Catholics of this delta civilization were interred.

At the gravesite, Minerva's son said a few parting words fraught with emotion, and Mary Agnes read several scripture verses before Minerva was lowered into the ground. Maggie was on my left and Etta on my right side. I put my arms around both of them, these important women in my life, and we felt free to grieve each in our own way. Etta started to cry, and Maggie held her tightened lips together while her eyes began to water.

A reception had been scheduled afterward at the Mobile house, and it was more festive than morbid. They were a great family in many ways and it was a fitting departure for the matriarch.

Etta was moving from one group of family friends to the other, thanking them for their condolences and lifelong friendships. I stood in the interior living room with Maggie, and opened the den door and went inside.

She followed me to the old doctor's study, and we looked at all his odd collections of beetles, butterflies, stuffed sea birds, and animal bones.

"Do you remember when I came in here with my open bathrobe to tease you?" she said, laughingly.

"How old was I? Sixteen or seventeen?"

"How could I forget? My heart was in my throat when I saw you," I said. "I couldn't speak."

"We started back then, didn't we? You and I? We knew that somehow something would happen."

"That was so long ago. You were a child, full of an uncontrollable spirit."

"I always wanted you, from the very night that Etta brought you home. You sat out on the terrace, and mother paraded the children one by one to meet you. I was the only one to give you a hug. Do you remember?"

I snorted hard at the thought of the barely adolescent girl with her pigtails and the death grip she had around me.

"They didn't know what to do," I continued, "They couldn't understand you. Like you'd been someone left on the doorstep. No one else was quite like you. The old doctor was strange in his standoffish manner, a half mad introvert of his world, but you were different."

Maggie walked over to her father's butterfly collection, and stared at the glass. She reached over and put an index finger on one of the pinned butterflies.

"I helped him catch three or four in the garden with a small net. There is a unique species of Monarch's in the Delta. Look at those three on the bottom. I caught the big black butterfly myself, there." She moved her fingers in a small arc to show me.

I walked over and looked closely inside the glass, and with a quick glance toward the door, leaned down and kissed her shiny black hair.

You could hear a momentary laugh outside as someone no doubt had told an amusing story about Minerva. There would be many. It wasn't a sad afternoon. There was a French or Irish Catholic spirit of remembrance, and celebration of an earlier life, much more pleasant than the droll Baptist funerals I had attended. I liked that about being a Catholic. It seemed to me the better alternative to crepe hanging coal town ceremonies.

The cathedral dean had a smile on his narrow face as he sipped a decent cabernet in one of Minerva's grandmother's Civil War crystal glasses, carefully blown in a mean garret by hungry immigrant lips in a bustling New Orleans. He was talking with Mary Agnes and her new husband, who was also now a congregant. They were laughing about the day Rachel would be at The Bishop's Academy as a first grader.

As I looked around the room, I saw the present mayor and his pencil thin wife, and most of the people and their aging parents who ran Mobile. There was a black family there too. It had been Etta's nanny and half of the others whom they all called Brown Mama. I slowly smiled. Even now, Etta stood there with her arm around the rotund elderly black woman, talking with her two grown daughters who themselves were also grandmothers.

It wasn't an event for children, so there were none around. As we came into the living room again, I whispered to Maggie that I thought it best if we circulate for a while. She nodded in tacit agreement.

At the bar getting a wine, I turned around and saw the stocky man who had bumped into us on the French Market roof terrace with his wife standing behind him.

"Our condolences. Such a fine, fine woman," he said, and glanced back at his small wife for her concurrence.

"Yes, one of a kind," I answered, and looked around to determine where I would move next, and as I turned, he stepped in front of me, smiling.

"It's refreshing you're all close, like you and Maggie," he uttered with the meaning clear in his vulgar words. "We believe in tight-knit families. It's real nice."

His wife interrupted him with her hand on his arm, showing some discomfort at what he had said, adding, "We're sorry for your loss. Such a wonderful woman."

Smiling a false smile at them and thanking her, I excused myself and left them at the bar.

It would happen soon. They had no intention of keeping quiet about the French Market night and what they had seen. I needed to prepare for the slander.
I had wanted badly to slam my fist in his fat face, and my whole body tensed as I walked over to where Etta stood with the president of Spring Hill College. There had been earlier talk about a scholarship for religious studies for women in

Minerva's name. They were discussing the possibilities as I strolled over to them.

Maggie had joined her sister and her husband. Mary Agnes was telling them some story that had a humorous spin and her husband was already laughing.

I glanced back at the bar and the obnoxious couple had departed. In a second I noticed them out on the terrace in a tight circle with two other couples. That conversation had a hushed feeling I somehow imagined and quickly looked away.

Maybe out of some misguided loyalty to Etta's family, the fat man and his wife might remain silent after all, it sometimes happened. People held their tongues for decades. Upset and distracted, I hardly heard the learned Jesuit's conversation about the latest Vatican initiative, which had him concerned. Etta's attention was rapt as he laid out his somewhat dissenting position on the recent Papal letter.

"We need to serve the times. This isn't the middle ages," I heard him say and Etta's head went up and down in agreement.

As we talked, I felt a hand touch my back, and as I looked, I saw Maggie pass by me into the kitchen to tell the caterers that enough food was already on the tables and only half of it eaten. She was smart and observant too.

I finished my wine as the Jesuit president told Etta he had wanted Spring Hill to eventually become a smaller Georgetown, or a rigorous southern liberal arts institution similar to secular Davidson.

A breathy sigh came to me as I began to believe I had become my own worst enemy with these fears of detection. I looked from Etta to Maggie, and they both seemed relaxed and serene.

In another hour and a half all the guests had left, and we got ready to return to Magnolia Springs along with Maggie. All the other siblings would spend the night in the Mobile house.

Going across the causeway, Etta broke the silence, and said, "It all went well. I think mother would've been pleased."

In the backseat Maggie laughed and said, "She was never happy with anything. It wouldn't be any different with this."

"She could be difficult," Etta admitted, to which Maggie retorted with a loud snort. "You think?"

I interjected by saying, "She was extraordinary. I've never met anyone quite like her, ever."

"Well, she managed to fuck up five lives, that I know. Six if you count Daddy and maybe even poor Aaron too."

"Maggie, that's mean, and it isn't true," Etta threw back over her shoulder.

"We grew up in different families then," Maggie said finally, and changed the subject to the boat traffic on the bay.

Was I some crazy man, I thought to myself? Tearing myself apart emotionally with these two women, sisters for heaven's sake. I'd acted like a lunatic determined on self-destruction. Yet I couldn't seem to stop myself.

Etta had started to tell stories from their Catholic girl's school, and Maggie chimed in with her own, and they both began to laugh hysterically. Maggie recounted that during one year, it might have been seventh or eighth grade, she had been suspended a day each week for almost a month. Minerva had gone apoplectic, roaming around the house muttering aloud, "That little bitch, that bitch."

Sitting in the living room after dinner, Etta and Maggie talked non-stop about the amazing family they'd been a part of, one anecdote after the other.

"For years, all of us thought you had been adopted. Maggie, you were so different from the rest of us," Etta recounted.

Maggie could only laugh at that. It brought back those difficult years when Minerva became ill, and Etta more or less had to take over the family responsibilities. The other children went along with this natural progression from Minerva to the

196

oldest daughter, but not Maggie. She resented Minerva's heavy-handed methods, and felt the same way about Etta in those turbulent days that followed.

Honestly I don't know how Etta did it. I was some help in the rearing I imagine, but not a lot. I was too passive on how I imagined children should be treated.

Since I loathed my own father and his barbarity at home, I wanted this live and let live atmosphere where everyone took whatever journey they had chosen without interference, or too much authority.

With Maggie, that simply hadn't worked, and actually I don't think anything would've worked, short of having Minerva around. Even then, Maggie had become too much for her mother to monitor, let alone control. It was a raucous adolescence, though a wonderfully intelligent woman had come out the other end unscathed.

We all talked and laughed well into the dawn hours, sharing one and then a second wine bottle, until we all fell asleep half drunk.

In the morning I was up first, and having drunk the least was probably the best person of the three to attempt breakfast. In the kitchen I found what I needed and made French-style runny omelets with the aged cheddar I had picked up somewhere for holidays and hidden away in some crock. There were fresh shallots in the crisper and it was a joy to cook. It was something I hadn't done for a while except for the occasional dinner. I made some fresh ground coffee as well.

Once I set the table, I put the eggs in the oven, and woke them both, giving each a minute or two to dress and throw some water on their faces.

Everyone had a hangover, including me, but we had a lively breakfast conversation. Afterward, Maggie and I made plans to leave for New Orleans around four that evening, giving everyone sufficient time to recalibrate.

Breakfast over, I had some errands to run in Fairhope. I left Etta and Maggie down on the riverbank skimming stones and talking.

In my absence I didn't expect any sort of spontaneous confession from Maggie about our involvement. She seemed to want it to remain as it was, and the fat man's slander probably hadn't yet started. It might take weeks, or even months, or longer. He would have to go out on a limb in his accusations, and the circumstances of what he had seen were dubious anyway.

In the early evening, I packed and readied for the trip, which was becoming a weekly occurrence. Etta knew that I had been the one chosen to run the mayor's campaign for governor, and he was the favorite. It would fuel all of my, or even our, ambitions in this part of the world. We were considered a sort of power couple, though that term hadn't really come into vogue.

On the drive back to New Orleans, Maggie was mute for a fair distance. I assumed it all had to do with the grief over Minerva, and re-living the bittersweet moments of life in that Mobile home.

"I want to tell you something," she said to me with some seriousness, "and I want the truth about how you feel. Not how you'd like to feel but don't. No, give me your raw honesty."

"What's this about?" I asked, perplexed.

"Do you promise complete honesty, no matter what happens?" she insisted.

"Of course," I said, "yeah."

She took in a deep breath, and let it out, "Here goes. You remember I had that abortion in high school?"

I was uncomfortable with the subject she had chosen to talk about, but I said, "Yes, you talked it over with Etta. She told me later you would consider it."

"I went and did it myself, and they sent the bill to the house," Maggie continued in a low voice.

"Sure, I knew all about it, Maggie, after the fact," I answered. "Look I would never judge you for that, please."

"That child would've been black. The man was a blues musician and gang banger who dealt drugs to the twenty-something's in Mobile."

"Alright."

"If that kid had been born, it could've been as black as the ace of spades," she told me with almost some relish I thought.

"What do you think of me now?' she asked, and I could see her eyes filling up. "How trashy am I? Tell me, go ahead."

"Why would I care either way? It's you that matters to me. That's the past, and there's nothing to be ashamed of. Maggie, stop this," I insisted. "None of that means a damn thing to me."

She leaned into me on the car seat, and whispered, "I wanted you to know everything. Nothing kept secret."

We spent the night at her studio, and I told her that she might want to try one of the two nights in the new apartment.

The next morning the mayor was glad to see me, and we had coffee behind closed doors in an anteroom off his main office. He asked me about the apartment. I had dropped my clothes there, and I told him it was comfortable and too fashionable for someone like me. He only laughed.

"I have this file on my desk from the FBI," he said, motioning with his head back toward the office. "Your late brother-in-law's name is in it."

"Really?" I answered, surprised that he would even mention it, since it was past history to me, and to all concerned.

"The FBI is convinced Marotta killed the drug trafficker and ex-CIA pilot Barry Sloan. They plan to charge the judge who had refused to put in him protective custody. The indictment after-the-fact also involves Aaron."

"In what way?" I asked.

He told me that Aaron was the only halfway clean man in Marotta's crowd. He could safely visit the judge and became a courier for bribe payments, reaching maybe a quarter of a million dollars, possibly more.

"They let me see this because I worked with them as a prosecutor, and they trust me," the mayor volunteered.

He explained that during the hearing and the final plea arrangement, Sloan was housed in a Baton Rouge motel. Literally everybody knew he lived there at the time. Everybody in New Orleans certainly did and in Chile, too.

The judge refused three requests from federal and state prosecutors to get him out of that place, and ferret him safely into hiding. He set him up to be killed, and that's what happened, the mayor recounted.

"Aaron made three night-time visits to the judge's house off St. Charles. He would visit around midnight, and go through the gate into the back garden. This was, no doubt, arranged by the judge himself. On each visit, he carried a large briefcase."

"The FBI was watching all the time?" I asked him.

After a long pause, the mayor explained: "The FBI had received a court order to wiretap the judge's home telephone; the second line he kept dedicated to so-called legal business in his home office. It recorded several exchanges between the judge and Marotta, couched in code words, though clearly about money he'd receive."

The mayor continued, "He told the judge that a man would come to see him, a young man, a journalist who could be trusted and unrecognized. He would make the cash deliveries. He would leave the briefcase that could be opened later, and the contents verified. This man's name was Aaron, and there would be no need to talk during or after the exchange. He would enter into the back garden gate, ten minutes before midnight on three staggered weekdays."

"How do you know it actually was Aaron?" I prodded.

"That part's simple. We have him on ultraviolent surveillance film from across the street in an agency van that was parked there for each of the deliveries."

"My God, "I uttered.

"So had he lived, he'd be on the indictment you can read on my desk as an accessory to first degree murder."

"What the hell did Mary Agnes think when he left the house at midnight those nights? What did he tell her, Jesus?"

"Maybe she was asleep, I don't know," the mayor stated. "This has nothing to do with us, and the campaign. You're behind the public eye anyway. But it's ongoing, and I thought you should know about it because it involves your family."

"I guess it's best forgotten, the whole Aaron mess," I said, shaking my head.

The indictment would eventually be made public, and as a former prosecutor, the mayor thought that perhaps this time the judge would be caught. He had never liked, or trusted, the jurist over the years he stood before him.

"He came from the same neighborhood and Mafia background as Marotta, and was appointed to the bench with string pulling that probably involved soft money," the mayor went on. "I think he and Marotta are the same age, and went to the same parish elementary school."

He said Aaron might have been forced to do this, be Marotta's bagman for bribes. Aaron was the only supposedly clean one in the crowd, and unknown to police. It was hard to know if he did it willingly, or not. Maybe he did it for a high dollar delivery fee, as he had already taken hundreds of thousands.

"When this comes out, it will be in the Times Picayune, and on the television stations. At least the part the FBI has to put into the public domain. I can't say what will be reported, what so-called players," he laid out. "There is no reason for your name to be any part of this, or mine."

"Do you think they'll mention Aaron by name, and follow a storyline about the suicide or the trafficking flights from Chile?" I inquired of him.

"Well, some enterprising reporter might do all that. But only investigative reporters with the newspaper. The TV people are rip and read off the wire services, and what gets called into the stations."

He told me to read the indictment on his desk. He said he would stay in the anteroom for a few more minutes, maybe ten, and later meet me in his office. I could walk in there. He would call his secretary and tell her that I needed to go over some confidential figures on his desk for a few minutes, and to give me some privacy. Seated at his desk, the folder was right in the middle of his elegant leather encased ink blotter that was some hundred years old, and maybe even of Civil War vintage.

As I read the twenty or so pages, Aaron's name appeared four or more times, and the FBI report clearly involved him as a criminal participant. If it became public, it would be an embarrassment to Etta and her family, and certainly to Mary Agnes. It did not state in the indictment that Aaron had committed suicide.

In a moment, the mayor was at the door, and asked, "Are you finished?"

I told him yes as I got up from his desk, and slowly made my way out of his office and through the alcove where his private secretary sat.

I smiled and spoke to her as I walked past, "How are those two little girls of yours, Joyce? They're so darling."

"Darling and very bad," she answered looking up from her pile of unopened mail and waved at me as I left.

# Chapter 9

As I walked down Canal Street and into the Quarter, I stopped for lunch at Felix's. I had a dozen oysters while leaning against the mahogany and brass bar and sipped a cold beer to wash them down. Not surprisingly, there were a few of the city hall lunch crowd in there. Several people at the tables toward the back of the small restaurant moved their heads in recognition when they saw me.

It was common knowledge that I was the mayor's campaign manager for the governor's race, and the room was full of his supporters anyway. After all, this was his hometown. He was a good Irish Catholic boy who had gone to Loyola then Tulane Law School, and he worked his way up the prosecutor ranks. He had friends on the police force, and among the ward politicians too.

This town, and the whole suburban parish was almost forty percent of the state vote. If he could get bits and pieces of the rural northern and southern Cajun parishes, the election was his. We both thought we could do it, and the early polls seemed to tell us the same, and we weren't wrong either.

He had chosen a popular state senator from Shreveport as a running mate, a devout Baptist with a countrified wife, and two college football player sons. We had cinched the whole deal. No opponent could successfully call us, "Catholic fools in New Orleans," and make it stick. We would buttress that before it would ever take hold. We made two trips to Shreveport to talk to the Baptist senator who was onboard, and ready to announce his candidacy for lieutenant governor.

As I calculated, we needed to pick up eighteen percentage points in the northern parishes to win the election, and it seemed to be easily within our reach.
The mayor was clean. He had no baggage that anyone could use against him, as his record as a prosecutor spoke for itself. There was no love lost between him and the Marotta people. He was unsullied.

At worst, some enterprising reporter might be able to trace Aaron back to me through the Mobile family connection. However, I never had any involvement with him in New Orleans, so it was a dead end. Maybe they could write a story that was embarrassing saying the mayor's campaign manager had a dead brother-in-law who could be tied back to the murders and bribery scandals, but it didn't involve me, really, nor did it compromise the mayor. A story like that might never be written; though one needed to know you might be vulnerable.

The secret to winning was to be above reproach, like Caesar's wife, and be untouchable from scandal. The revelation with Aaron made me cautious. The mayor wasn't concerned, so I shouldn't be either. He had wanted me to know that it could possibly happen, particularly in the heat of the campaign.

He was an ethical man and a damn decent candidate. However, there was the risk that someone might try to use this against him. Maybe suggest a lack of vetting on his part with my hiring, seeking to pull him into the Barry Sloan murder even as an outsider. Elections were about perceptions anyway with a few facts scattered in the mix. Voters made their decisions on what they thought they knew, not what they actually did know. It's that simple.

That night I told Maggie what I had learned about Aaron, and she had a look of absolute horror on her face, "Sweet little Aaron, always trying to please everyone. My God, what a mess."

"I know," I answered, "It may never come out, but we can't count on that. It might find its way into the papers with the FBI indictment. That becomes a public record with the court. They could drag me into it to try to smear the mayor."

"A party to murder, poor Mary Agnes. She never knew anything, nothing about what he did," Maggie lamented. "She wanted it that way, to live in this pretend world. She still does."

I told Maggie that I would continue to manage the mayor's race. If it comes out that Aaron was my late brother-in-law, they'll most likely look for further collusion. They will try to besmirch me with guilt by association. If that happens, I would simply resign. I would make a public statement about having no knowledge, or certainly any involvement with criminal acts, as would the mayor. Then it would be finished.

"But all this may never happen," I stressed, "and we'll continue with this through Election Day. I can be with you more and more, which is what I want."

She kissed me when I finished my little speech and pushed me onto the bed as the evening light began to wane in the Quarter.

"Maybe it's time for us to talk, about this whole thing, and what we really want," I finally managed to get out, preparing myself for a more difficult task.

"No talk," she whispered to me in my ear, "Not now, not ever," as she slid off her Arab house gown.

As Maggie lay sleeping beside me, my mind drifted back to what I'd read on the mayor's desk this morning about Aaron. Was the judge bribed by Marotta to keep Barry Sloan out of protective custody? That made him an easy target for the hired assassins who had murdered him before he could testify in court on drug trafficking.

The FBI moved quickly by employing the resources of several federal agencies, including the Central Intelligence Agency. They obliquely tapped some powers of the State Department to pressure the Chilean government to make some shady deal with their illegal drug cartels. Two suspects were found. They were interrogated with subsequent confessions, and then extradited to the U.S., bound in chains on a Chilean air force plane that landed in New Orleans. The men were ferried off to some federal compound unknown except to its jailers.

There was a federal hearing in front of a judge, not the one named in the indictment obviously. They were remanded over for trial along with the eight or nine others named in the legal papers the mayor had on his desk that morning. It had all moved much quicker than I had imagined.

There were several New Orleans officials named in the indictment, a court bailiff and two high-ranking precinct commanders in the New Orleans city police force. It would be a high visibility and messy criminal trial.

The mayor had been above the fray, and had wanted long prison sentences for Marotta and his lieutenants for years. He claimed they were personally responsible for at least fifty unsolved murders in the city. How he knew that I never learned, but he had mentioned it to me on several occasions.

The drama around the case got more convoluted when one of the Chilean suspects had been found hung in his cell. They had wisely been separated in the holding facility and everything was supposedly monitored on surveillance camera feeds. How it had happened was a mystery. That same day the surviving Chilean was moved undercover to a more secure and dedicated facility that the FBI operated somewhere else.

Thus far, the newspapers and several of the city television stations had been caught up in the excitement following the capture of the Chilean cartel assassins. They had supposedly gunned Sloan down getting out of his car one night at the motel while he was awaiting transfer to a different location. He had been at the same location almost a month when the killing occurred.

The indictment said that the judge had delayed putting the endangered witness in protective custody long enough to allow Marotta to arrange for his murder. Naturally, this had been done for money the judge had received in illegal payments from the mobster. The cash was delivered on three occasions by a New Orleans journalist working for Marotta and unknown to city police. That journalist had been Aaron who was also a trafficker. It all was a seedy story.

No one at this point had used Aaron's name, although that would come out as the wheels of investigative journalism turned, however slowly. When it did, if it somehow led back to me, I would deny any knowledge of Aaron's activities, particularly since I had lived in Mobile for the entire time it was underway except for the two visits there with Etta.

The mayor asked me to be patient, and put the anxiety to rest. We would cross that bridge when we came to it. I appreciated his clear thinking.

The days passed by slowly. A trial of this magnitude takes months and sometimes a year or more of preparation. There were many disparate players involved, and so much physical evidence to sift through: reams of bank statements, telephone records, and flight manifests. The election would be over long before Marotta would ever be sitting in the dock.

No enterprising reporter had tied Aaron to the mayor's campaign director, and I set about the task of electing the new governor with a relieved enthusiasm. Everything we had planned fell nicely into place. The state senator from Shreveport was a marvelous stump campaigner. He had endeared himself with his own coalition of ministers who unofficially advised him on the role of spiritual values for governance. There were almost weekly news photographs of him at church socials with root beer and a chicken drumstick with his arm around the elderly ladies who had prepared the marvelous feast, smiling and sincere.

In New Orleans itself, the mayor knew what he had to do to get the necessary votes and he did it. Every weekend he walked each neighborhood of the city in shirtsleeves, and sat and talked with everyone who would listen. He was a natural that way.

When I was with Maggie I often lamented to her that news about Aaron's criminal past couldn't remain secret forever. At some point the world would find out.

"You did nothing wrong. Stop," she'd scold me. "The mayor's going to be the next governor, then you're finished."

"It could happen the week before the election," I continued morosely. For some reason, I believed this scenario would actually occur. The world would know in time to vote against the mayor and his disgraced campaign people.

"That's such nonsense," Maggie constantly warned, "What do I have to do to get you to stop. Do you tell Etta this nonsense? Well, do you?"

I admitted to her that I hadn't told Etta about the whole Aaron mess. I didn't want her to stir up Mary Agnes and everyone else.

"Then leave it!" Maggie shouted at me one night.

As things would have it, nothing ever came from Aaron's name in the indictment. The press never tied it back to me in the governor's campaign. He handily won based on increased returns from the northern parishes. The lieutenant governor did his job and drummed up support for the ticket. It represented twenty percent of our total.

The governor offered me a position as his press secretary and though flattered, living in Baton Rouge had little appeal. After all, I had been a hired political gun for some years now and had gotten used to the life.

What the governor finally did as his gesture of thanks was to arrange with his developer friend to give me a low cost lease for the French Quarter apartment for two years. He told me that there would be consulting contracts coming from state agencies and both of his campaign promises came to pass.

He also arranged for the next mayor, who he had helped into office, to throw me city consulting business on the same basis. Everybody likes a winner, and the new mayor was well aware that I had been the governor's chief campaign strategist. He was more than eager to have me around in some advisory capacity.

All this served to keep me in New Orleans and close to Maggie who had graduated from Loyola. She would take two years off to write and maybe later get a graduate degree from Tulane, while working part time.

Etta had gotten comfortable with the New Orleans connection as it provided us significant income. We had a great deal of flexibility in our lives because of it. Her clinical practice had taken off quickly, but had flattened out, particularly on the Eastern Shore. This had brought her great consternation though my income allowed her not to worry and nothing changed in the way we lived. Money wasn't a real problem. We increased our entertainment. On most weekends, we had at least one dinner party or a barbecue. We had convinced ourselves it was necessary and continued to do it without much thought.

Most weeks I made certain that at least two days were in New Orleans with Maggie. It struck me as strange that she never complained, or asked for more. Perhaps this life suited her view of the world, I don't know. I never had the courage to make a stand, as I was always afraid that I'd lose her.

One night after a creole dinner and a walk around the Quarter finished with late night coffee, I told her on the street that I wanted to divorce Etta and marry her. Even if she didn't want to marry me, we could live together permanently. I'd leave Etta, I told her.

At first, she didn't say anything and we walked a block and a half in silence, then she turned to me, and said, "Alright," And we continued to walk.

"Alright, what?" I asked, undone. "What do you want me to do? Which one?"

"You choose," she said with some seriousness, "That's fine with me."

I stopped on the street: "Maggie, talk to me," and she kept going, finally coming back and pulled my arm to come along, "We can talk at home, silly."

What the hell did she mean? I thought to myself nervously. Did she want me to divorce Etta, and marry her or simply do nothing? What?

The uncertainty was draining as we walked along though elation moved through me like a river. Maggie had admitted that she wanted some kind of life together with me, a sort of permanence. The excitement was more than I could contend with, and I yelled out on the street, "Yes, sweet Jesus."

"What was that outburst?" Maggie asked.

Within the next minute, we were at the entrance to my coach house apartment, and opened the double wooden doors on the street.

Inside was a courtyard of plantings and a terrace in front of the coach house window. As I opened the front door, I turned to her and said, "Let's get a wine bottle out of the fridge and sit out here and drink it. Take in the night."

"Sure," she answered, "But let me get out of these clothes." She rushed in the door to change.

In the kitchen I found a good Chardonnay that I had been saving from the campaign, and opened it, then grabbed two wine glasses on my way out.

With the moon shining overhead in the Quarter courtyard, she came out wearing a flowing purple robe that I had never seen before. The moment left me speechless. She came over to me and kissed me on the forehead. She picked up one of the wine glasses I had filled for us, then sat down and put her sandaled feet on the table.

"I like my life," Maggie announced with a breathlessness, "and being with you, and that won't change. When this comes out, people are going to blame you. Everybody thinks I'm half-crazy from the prison thing. But not you, a church-going successful family man, and the nicest of people, really. That's what everybody in Mobile will whisper if you leave her. Can you live with that?"

"Yes," I answered. "I can live with whatever they say about me. It doesn't matter, even now."

She said if I did what I wanted, then Mobile was finished for me. There would be no reason for me to continue living there.

I said, "There's nothing there now, Maggie. We have people over most weekends in Magnolia Springs that neither of us care about. We sit there and smile like fucking robots. I make some small talk, and then it's Etta's turn. It's all bullshit."

Maggie laughed. "We're misfits, and somehow we're together. The world won't be kind to us for that." She talked slowly, measuring her words. "Do you care?"

I finished the drink of wine I was sipping and put my glass down on the wooden table. I looked at her for a split second before saying a single word, "No."

When I was back in Mobile for the balance of the week, I noticed that Etta had become self-absorbed with the absence of new patients for the Fairhope office. She seemed to be pushing too hard to fill the empty waiting room.

It's difficult to recruit people standing in line around you each morning at the Coffee Loft for a half dozen therapy sessions. It's particularly hard when the prevailing feeling among most people was you didn't talk about family or unpleasant issues with strangers. You only did that if you were a lunatic, or maybe, if your husband beat you up a couple nights a week.

Etta became depressed over the downturn at the clinic, yet the Mobile office seemed to do all right. When she would get home from work in the evening, she would immediately go to the bar and have two drinks, downing them in quick succession. With that, she would then find a reason to argue easily and with my life as duplicitous as it was, I rarely engaged her in any angry exchanges.

I would let her rant, or just inventory my failings as a husband and a human being. I would sit immoveable across the room absorbing the verbal taunts. She started to sound like Minerva at her worst, before she lost her faculties of reason.

Minerva could never have been called kind, though she could be charming and even personable. She was a passive-aggressive woman, and required total control in her life. Her family was an extension of that. She didn't trust people to make a decision, any decision. She felt compelled to manipulate them to her own ends.

Etta was a more generous woman than her mother. I imagine it was this particular softness toward the world where her father had influenced her. He had innate kindness and acceptability, though his self-contained manner kept him far removed from family life.

By the time Maggie came along, there were too many children for Minerva to dominate. But with her eldest, she had full rein to make Etta emotionally unfit to live her own life.

True, those in the psychological sciences seek to fix the most troubled among us, and they are themselves admittedly broken. They need the same remedies they endeavor to provide others. It seems such a vicious, and unequal paradigm of belief, all somehow strung together with ready formulas.

Reluctantly, I went with Etta to counseling as her own emotional life became bumpy. We saw a psychologist in Fairhope who had been practicing for forty years. As a young man, he had been an apprentice to the great Adler in the Chicago school of psychological thought who had studied with Freud and later Jung in Europe. He was a gaunt man whose office looked like he had moved it from 1937 Vienna, replete with a cracked burgundy colored leather couch, dim lighting, and busts from Greek and Roman mythology.

His second wife, recently deceased, had been from Montrose. They returned home when she became ill. Almost as a diversion now, he saw a few selected patients. Etta had pleaded with him to accept her as one of the few he would consent to treat.

He had a slight German accent when he spoke, but provided no description of his own background during the introductions, or conversation meant to make us more comfortable. It appeared in the first session to be all Freudian method where he said little, and the onus of conversation and explanation fell completely on the patient. He had more of a take it or leave it attitude.

This wasn't marriage counseling; it was something else. During that first session, Etta talked mostly about Minerva. The analyst didn't seem to notice my presence in the dimly lit room for the entire hour we sat there.

The only thing he seemed to say, and not to me, was, "How do you feel about that?" Etta would answer him with her elaborate and perhaps too detailed answer. It sounded to me like she had been defending a university thesis, refuting what she had felt or was feeling at the moment, almost point by point.

He finally asked her toward the end of the session after she told him that she had begun to drink too much, "Do you think you're an alcoholic?"

That flustered her, and she blurted out, "Oh my, no, but it seems to calm me down. That's all."

He turned to me, and gave me a half grin, and added, "And your husband joins you in this drinking?"

I answered him, "We have several drinks at night, before dinner, and maybe one before bed. Never any other time."

The bearded analyst uncrossed his spindly legs and crossed them again with the opposite leg on top.

"I don't think that drinking is your greatest issue," he pronounced, "There may be other factors to your unhappiness that are far more important."

"What do you think they are?" Etta said automatically to him in response.

"We don't know those answers quite yet," he answered calmly. "Only further analysis can provide that window."

With that he stood up, consulted his wristwatch, and looked first at Etta smiling and then at me, saying, "I fear our first session has come to an end, but we've already made progress."

As I stood with Etta in his office ready to leave, I asked him, "Do you think it would be better for you to work with Etta alone?"

She turned to me incredulous, although the entire session had directed nothing to me to answer or attempt to explain anything.

Quite calmly the psychologist answered, "That's rather astute, and perhaps you're right, though for the time being, I believe if the three of us meet we'll make better progress toward what we want to achieve."

At the door he turned to Etta, announcing quite matter-of-factly, "If you feel you may want some anti-depressants, I'm an MD, so that isn't a problem. I'd recommend against them, but…" he didn't finish.

As we walked out of his home onto tree-lined Fairhope Avenue, I could see the bay in the afternoon haze and wondered exactly what we hoped to achieve with this visit. I guessed at the most fundamental level that it was an elusive happiness: waking up in the morning with perpetual smiles, and unbridled optimism. Good luck, with both our chaotic childhoods. We would have to deal with my double life. Still, there were other things too.

A poetry workshop at Sewanee would occupy Maggie the next week. She was one of the younger poets to read their work with southern luminary James Dickey. It would be three days, and travel. She had rented a newer car and was overwhelmed with enthusiasm. I decided to stay in Mobile.

Etta had asked the Freudian, or whatever school of psychoanalysis he claimed allegiance to, for back-to-back therapy sessions. The second session would be the following Tuesday afternoon.

As the day rolled around and we seated ourselves in his dank office, I asked him again if he thought that I should be present. It seemed more an investigation for Etta, who did all the talking anyway. Etta was irritated that I brought it up, and turned to me for explanation.

He emitted what sounded like a throat-clearing cough, turning to me, making the predictable Freudian response, "Is that what you feel we should do?"

214

I told him that the analysis seemed more directed to Etta's needs and issues, and I couldn't speak to what had happened during her childhood. After I had finished, I thought I had made myself clear to them. The objections I had to being a passive participant seemed legitimate.

"May I ask you if you're threatened with having your behavior examined, which we won't do, certainly? But are you more upset about showing your vulnerability to Etta?"

What he said took me off guard momentarily because it rang true. I was concerned with this inner and outer life of duplicity I had adopted.

"No, that's not it," I finally answered with difficulty.

He smiled, and it seemed this German shrink, or whatever he was, could look right through me. I was exposed to his awful grey eyes that penetrated my soul. At least, it felt that way, and I began to perspire.

"Tell us more: What is it? If I may inquire," he continued with a deadly calm demeanor. He stared into my increasingly sweaty and wet face, noticing any false muscle movement I feared I would make, calculating the slightest tick, which might signal to him that I was lying.

# Chapter 10

He could sense my obvious discomfort, and held up his hand as a gentle reminder, "Please relax, this isn't an interrogation. It's meant to help, not harm. You have done nothing wrong here." To him I suspected we were all broken toys.

"I'm new to this, that's all," I offered to defuse the exchange, and I could see the consternation on Etta's face.

He smiled again, adding, "We'll let Etta talk a bit, and you can join in after she's finished with whatever you care to. There are no right or wrong answers. It's a process of self-discovery."

Quite pleased with his Freudian or Adlerian explanation of psychoanalysis, he began to inquire about Etta's feelings concerning her mother, and what she saw as dominance for a great part of her life.

Etta wasn't reticent about speaking. She talked almost non-stop about Minerva during her childhood and well into her life as an adolescent young woman. The German physician didn't comment on what she had said, except to interject once or twice into Etta's story,

"Well, how did you feel about that?"

Following his question, Etta would explain to him exactly what she believed she had felt at that moment, and how she felt now which was the same. I found it disconcerting.

Once, I tried to interrupt and give him my interpretation of some past event, and he had held up his hand to stop me with a gentle scolding, "No, this is something Etta must investigate on her own." Again, that condescending smile to be silent.

Minerva had been the sole topic of conversation for most of the hour, and except for setting the ground rules for the analysis procedure, he hadn't spoken directly to me.

There was no cross talking he asked for, and that meant Etta and I couldn't discuss between us how Minerva might have behaved at some past garden party, or if I'd overhead an argument between mother and daughter.

I thought the whole Freudian thing had become awfully tedious. I couldn't see how I might fit into the puzzle of what Etta had wanted to solve within her past. Mostly I lived in fear of having my own duplicity exposed, and being forced to confess what I had done, the violation of our marriage vows and adulterous behavior.

Etta's Catholic world would no doubt condemn me harshly. I thought that the Freudian might not judge what I'd done on such a cut and dried moral basis, pointing instead to the disintegrating marriage we had endured.

A hurried third session was arranged right before I was scheduled to return to New Orleans with a project from the governor's office. Maggie would be back from Tennessee tonight.

The Freudian turned to me and he asked a few fundamental questions about Etta and me that were easy to answer. Then he paused for a moment and tried to get me to talk about the relationship I had with my own mother.

Finally, he explained: "You spent your entire life feeling guilty about your own mother. The fact that you couldn't protect her and save her from your abusive father."

To that officious remark, I laughed out loud.

"Is there humor in that?" he asked me with a rather straight face.

"None at all. That was a laugh of irony."


"That's suppressed anger you harbor," he continued. All the while Etta was transfixed in the room, and didn't move a muscle.

I shook my head no, and stated to him carefully in rather measured words, "I don't believe that. I'm not angry with my dead mother. I pitied her instead."

217

"You may think you're not angry at her, but you remain focused on that particular anger. It influences the way you deal with all women. You may indeed love them; yet you hate what you see as their weakness. Like your mother's. All women become your mother."

"That's absurd. I don't believe you," I told him heatedly. "I don't want to insult your many years of training, but you're wrong."

"Think about what I said for a while. You don't have to explain anything to me," he added, falling back into his disinterested doctor mode.

I told him I'd give what he had said more thought, and he smiled back at me.

"I don't think the world revolves around this Freudian sex formula, this Oedipal thing," I continued uncertain of myself.

"It's far more complicated than what you describe," he offered in explanation, "yet in truth, it really isn't."

By that time most of the session had expired, and he asked Etta a quick question about her relationship with Minerva. Etta answered it briefly from what she had heard over the years, and he shook his head in affirmation. That concluded his questions.

Outside his office as we walked up a block and half to Section Street where the car was parked, Etta turned to me and she seemed angry.

"You embarrassed me in there, arguing with him, as if you had any real knowledge about how the mind works."

That pushed me over the edge, and I raised my voice and shouted at her, "Don't start your half-assed analysis on me. You're the damn patient."

By this time, we were standing in the middle of the sidewalk, and she shouted right back at me. The argument escalated and went back and forth until people had stopped on the sidewalk and across the street, and were staring in disbelief. There was a couple standing silently across the street

218

that we both knew listening. When I spotted them, this only served to increase my anger.

Here was this seemingly educated and supposedly well-adjusted upper middle class couple screaming as if we were drunkards inside some trailer park.

What people noticed were these two attractive late-thirties people behaving like spoiled fifteen year olds, or maybe even worse. I had begun to curse loudly, and the word fuck seemed to preface my answers to her. It had honestly gotten out of control.

At last Etta put her hands over her ears, and yelled this earsplitting, "Stop," and that immediately calmed me. Already a half dozen people stood on the sidewalk looking at us.

"OK, I've stopped. See?" I whispered to her, "We can go. Let's get into the car before everyone in Fairhope sees us." I put my hand on my chest and attempted to put this false smile of conciliation on my face. "Calm down, please."

Her fiery black eyes were wide with heightened emotion. She turned on her heel to cross the street at a diagonal in front of the Page and Palette bookstore and into the grocery store lot where the car had been parked.

As she walked quickly in the street about ten steps ahead of me, I thought to myself, how can she be this unbalanced in an instant? Is she on the verge of some mental breakdown? With that, I conveniently absolved myself of responsibility for any of the tantrums as she had been the one to initiate it.

Etta was waiting at the car door since I had the keys, and when I opened the door she slid inside, and slammed the door hard.

Behind the wheel, I turned toward her and said, "Etta, I'm sorry. That was my fault. I'm the one who blew up, I apologize."

She was looking straight ahead, and turned toward me. She nodded her head too, saying, "I was wrong too. Let's just forget this ever happened."

I held up both hands in the air: "You have my word, it won't happen again, I promise."

"I want to go home and have a drink," she said, "Let's be decent to each other, and put this behind us."

As I started the car and drove out of the parking lot, I had readily agreed, "It won't happen again."

"Maybe that man can help both of us. It won't hurt you to be open to that," she continued as we entered the main highway.

I told her I was ready to work with him in any way that might help us, and I said I realized these things are never easy. How could I continue to be such a liar?

Etta leaned into me gently as we got onto the country roads to take us to Magnolia Springs. I feared my lies would drown me as much as if I had been abandoned by a destroyer in the North Atlantic. I would drown. What had she done to have all this in her life? It was inexplicable, really.

Had my mother made me distrust women yet love them all the same? But never completely trust them to do what I wanted, the thing that might satisfy me and make me content? I thought that Maggie may have succeeded, though the damn Freudian had made me doubt myself.

I had become more comfortable with Maggie somehow. She could take over the apartment, and we would cease to behave like half-wacked bohemians. She would be a college professor one day, and I'd continue to run campaigns. We could have some children in the house. All that could happen.

When was I going to break the news to Etta this charade was finished? That we both had found little solace together. It was this life sentence of being a miserable couple like a thousand others who hadn't the courage to leave.

What was the Freudian going to tell us anyway? That we had dysfunctional parents, or we had been sexually repressed all our lives. Was he going to suggest sex surrogates, or shock treatments? It was a farce, the whole thing.

Well, Etta was a psychologist; she needed to believe mental manipulation might somehow solve her emotional problem. What did we need to do anyway, destroy the ego? Wasn't that the prescribed cure? Or pick up one of those trashy self-help manuals for couples, and join a group? Then we might switch partners if the therapy appeared to be too slow. Isn't that what you did?

Freudians take years; we had been there a couple of times. I was already looking for the exit. How could I persist for years? How many times could I listen to this Goethe ask me, "How do you feel?"

"'It's raining, and how do I feel about that? Well, I fucking love it, if you must know the truth, doctor."

As I drove along the country lane toward home, it was getting pitch dark, and I flicked on the headlights. Up ahead in the headlights, it was almost as if I could see a grey bearded face in front of me like I was hallucinating. I was the one who needed a drink, not Etta.

When we got home, I played the answering machine and there was one work related message from the New Orleans mayor's office, asking for a confirmation that I would be in a staff meeting on federal funding next Tuesday.

Etta heard the message, and she didn't comment. It was rather normal after all.

She said in her preachy voice, "It was better when you worked here. The constant travel is awful. It's so destructive."

I laughed. "It's money. We do it for the money, don't we?" I added, "It allows some breathing room, and you can finance your clinics."

"Oh now, I'm the reason you have to get on the road like a trucker. It's me," she continued. "It has nothing to do with your ambition?"

"Of course, it does," I answered, and felt wherever we went with this conversation I was going to remain calm, and pleasant.

"It has brought me cash, and given us more flexibility than other couples we know so maybe it's worth a little sacrifice."

"What if I told you that if this doesn't change, I'm going to leave. That I want some permanence in my life. What would you say to that? I'm curious."

"Come on, Etta, didn't we have enough anxiety with the Freud lookalike?" I reminded her. "I've chosen this because it's challenging. It pays better than anything I can possibly do here, and until now, it was alright with you."

"People and circumstances change. Don't you get that?"

I threw up my hands in frustration, and asked, "Are you telling me I have to change the way we live, or you're leaving? Is that the ultimatum you're giving me?"

"Stop it," she said, "You always jump to the wrong conclusion. Normal people talk about things without anger."

The conversation went on and on like this, taking twists and turns, and always spoken in some future tense. At last she tired of it all, announcing she was going to bed.

"Are you coming?" she asked as she rose from the wicker living room chair, and I told her I'd follow her in two minutes, no more.

I poured myself another neat whiskey and downed it right away though she had already disappeared into the bathroom. In bed she was affectionate though not particularly amorous. It relieved me when she easily drifted to sleep.

Once I knew she wouldn't wake, I left the bed and went into the living room. I poured myself another whiskey and walked out onto the patio facing the river.

It was a bright moonlit night. As I peered into the heavens, I could see a yellowed harvest half-moon to my far left in the darkness, while above me Libra occupied the starry sky.

Taking a few more hesitant steps, I found the wooden gate in the dark and stepped onto the small dock in the river. The moon's reflection shone on the surface like a mirror, and as I looked at the dark water, I noticed the white orb in its magnificence.

Sitting on the hard dock, the boards rough on my cotton pajama bottoms, I glanced again into the darkness, maybe hoping for some celestial sign: a shooting star to appear, an Orion of good fortune. I only saw the monumental vastness and void above me, and thought of my insignificance.

I thought about that long ago coal town, and the wretched life of drunkenness and abuse from my army sergeant father, and the debris of what could never be truly fixed.

In my last year of college as I was about to receive a Navy commission, I had visited my mother and younger sister who were living together. I had driven my sister to a local dairy with a retail store for ice cream.

What was odd at the time was my sister, a former high school cheerleader, had gained maybe forty pounds. The miserable life in that town would do that, I figured. It was one of the reasons I preferred to take my chances flying jets off aircraft carrier decks because it was better than rotting there.

Later, her weight increased, and I asked my cousin who was a nurse in a nearby town to look in on her to see if she might have a stomach ailment she had ignored. My cousin called me late one night at the barracks in Pensacola, and told me that my sister was pregnant, probably almost five months into term.

What was worse than that news, was that she was pretending she didn't have this child inside her. She said it was simple weight gain from junk foods she usually ate. The whole experience became a horror for her. The baby's father disappeared when he learned of the pregnancy. The guilt my mother foisted upon her at every moment left her life in ruins. I felt brokenhearted about it all, mostly for her.

I became angry at how she had allowed this misery to find her. Although it broke my heart to see her suffer, as it had with my mother, I blamed both of these women for their weakness. I hated myself, perhaps again, for failing to save them from the encroaching hostile world around them, and from themselves. It was a legacy of bad choices for them, and in a sense, they became all women for me.

On the dock the memories flooded back. Maybe the Freudian had been correct in what he saw with me. I was smarter than allowing this ridiculous belief to take over who I'd become, but later I would succumb anyway.

Had I chosen Etta because she would never be right, and then gone to her wounded sister to reap perhaps the same heartbreak? It chilled me to think I was so broken, unable to pretend I could live a normal life.

Finally, as the night wore on, it appeared there was no clear path for me to take. Exhausted, I slowly found my way back into the house. The crickets and cicadas serenaded me, almost like some chorus in a Greek tragedy.

I wanted another go at the Freudian, and I planned to put off the meeting with the mayor's council and plead the flu. It was a rather routine budgeting anyway and only informational for me, about how much would eventually come from federal funds into the city coffers.

The next morning, I told Etta that truthfully I had gotten a lot from the session with the analyst, and it had made me think. I asked her if she might call him to schedule another meeting this week. I said the New Orleans budget meetings could go on without me there. I would spend an additional day during the following week's visit. She merely shrugged her shoulders at the breakfast table, and scheduled an appointment for late Wednesday afternoon.

Once in his office, he greeted us cordially. He said that Etta told him that I had found his early comments of interest as I pondered their meaning. With an immediate response, he asked me, "How do you feel about that?"

"It's strictly about feelings, right? Nothing about whether or not you did or didn't do something, and why?" I presented to him, far more animated than usual waving my hands in the stale air.

His office had a dusty funeral appearance, and perhaps he tried hard to make it seem more like Austria and less of Alabama.

"Those are simple facts, events you're referring to," he calmly explained, "Our concern is what you feel about them, that specific interpretation, and the obvious why's."

From what he had said earlier, I had an unhealthy relationship with my own mother. Gradually that dysfunction had found its way into other relationships with women.

He said, again with a low clinical voice, the German accent ever so slight underneath his English words, that my understanding had been correct. What had occurred in childhood and adolescence with my own mother, what he termed as a maternal dysfunction, had indeed contaminated every relationship I had since with women.

"Do you think Etta and I have a dysfunctional relationship?" I asked him, point blank, and again watching that confident, knowing smile.

"What I think doesn't matter. Rather it's what you feel," he continued. "Do you feel you and Etta have an unsatisfactory marriage?"

I let out a deep sigh, and didn't answer him immediately. Instead glancing over at Etta for some sign of what she believed, but her face looked blank, with empty eyes.

"I think we have some problems to work through, yes," I confessed, and leaned back into the leather chair, awaiting his criticism of what I'd said.

He nodded as if he agreed with what I said, though he didn't comment, but rather he turned to Etta and asked her, "Do you agree with him?"

Unsmiling she gave him a rapid single word answer in response, "Yes."

I wanted him to give me some insight into what he saw in my behavior with women that had become dysfunction, and how it was manifested. He avoided giving me any assessment of how he saw this unhealthy behavior of mine.

Finally, he chuckled at my dogged persistence for some clarity, and said, "If I were to give you my observation on how this unhealthy behavior you've adopted shows itself, I'd simply say that it appears in chronic passive-aggressive patterns."

"What's that mean? I don't get it," I blurted out.

Etta was transfixed, and she looked from me to the doctor, and back to me as I sought these reluctant answers from him. Yet he did speak:

"You want to avoid conflict at all costs, as your mother probably may have. Instead you tried vainly to persuade her to avoid these fights with your father, and she wouldn't do it. So you resented her for making your own, and her life, miserable. You may have hated your father though your feelings for your mother were in classic imbalance too, that love and hate seesaw. From this unhealthy childhood, you may well have developed passive-aggressive behavior with women. In the end, none of them ever truly fulfill your needs. No one can."

After the Freudian had finished, I leaned my head back on the leather chair and closed my eyes for a brief moment. The room was quiet.

Straightening up in the chair, I stared at the elderly German, and added, "That's an interesting theory, doctor, but it's only a theory."

"It's a cursory observation, nothing more," he answered again with this unruffled psychiatrist demeanor, and gave his narrow shoulders this momentary shrug, his body language dismissing what I'd said.

"The other pattern in what I described is that you may be fully capable of doing unorthodox or distasteful acts. Call them amoral even. However, this damaged ego requires whatever exit you might choose from this conflict or

226

relationship, it must always depart as the blameless party. Whatever you did. You want to be thought of as the nice guy, regardless of what you do."

With that, he turned his attention to Etta for a few moments, pretty much ending our conversation, and after another five minutes the session was finished.

In the car as we drove out of Fairhope Etta turned to me, and said with a slight hardness in her voice, "That was the truth back there, the passive-aggressive thing. It's insidious."

"I don't know if I agree with all that," I answered, "but I'll think about it."

She added pointedly: "If you don't attempt to change, this will get worse. You know that, don't you?"

I didn't respond right away to what she said except to add, "Yeah, I get it."

We drove in silence for most of the way back to Magnolia Springs. The only topic encouraging further conversation were the friends she expected for dinner tomorrow evening. At least that was safe ground.

I liked the couple. The man was a longtime childhood and college friend of hers, and his wife had her amusing moments too. They were decent dinner company, loquacious and often humorous in a self-deprecating way.

Maybe a child for us would have made a difference, though after the first year's stream of doctors it was determined that there was evidence of possible sterility and a malfunction in Etta's normal egg production. A second year followed with more inconclusive diagnosis, and after, discussion simply stopped. The third year brought what doctors called a hysterical pregnancy. There were definite signs Etta had conceived though, it was psychosomatic, and she suffered through that painful experience. I felt so badly for her.

Gradually we somehow moved on to other things. Her father died and Minerva's dementia crept in, and then came Maggie's craziness and the drug involvement. Children became a subject we never addressed. Maybe she thought about it, though Etta never brought it up again. She had the responsibility of holding her broken family together, and set herself to that task.

At the house when we had eaten and relaxed and moved outside to look at the stars on the warm night, she mentioned again what the German had said.

"What he told you sounded right," Etta admitted, "You want this failure, to not get what you want, unconsciously maybe. But you search for it all the same. It's your childhood. You expect it, you want it to happen."

"That's insane," I stated, "You can't believe this psychobabble."

She stood up and walked toward the dock, not speaking, and turned slowly back toward the house. The sky had blackened and stars appeared.

"I believe what he said, and so do you," she told me without hesitation, "I could see it in your eyes. They said he was absolutely right."

"My eyes said that?" I responded, showing irritation.

"They did." With that, I started to argue with her but she stopped me cold, and said there was really nothing to argue about. It was the psychiatrist who had said what he said, and she had agreed with him.

"He couldn't be wrong; you're saying?" I persisted.

She turned to me as she opened the sliding terrace door, and answered, "You can argue that he may have misinterpreted what he saw, but he's been at this for almost fifty years. He's seen and heard it all, every denial you can imagine."

There was little I could add, and I didn't bother to continue the uncomfortable conversation and just admitted that it had me thinking at least.

"Good," she said walking through the living room.

What this Austrian, or whatever he was, had said clearly upset me, though what upset me most was I believed

228

he was right. For so many years, this passive-aggressive stance ruled me, especially with women. I expected them to betray me, and when they didn't, I was disappointed. It took me some hours to find sleep; I tossed and turned in the bed, and eventually went into the living room until sleep started to overtake me.

In the middle of the morning, I started for New Orleans and had set a late afternoon meeting at city hall with several staffers who would brief me on the budget discussions. I would meet with the mayor the following day.

It was shaping up to be a routine week, and probably half of the proposed civic appropriations would be made. That meant I would continue as a paid consultant. I needed two hefty contracts for the year, and they had been proposed by the people who delivered on these promises. I believed I was safe. Maggie said she would meet me tonight at my apartment, and we could have a cold dinner. I would pick up some chicken dishes at a gourmet grocery, along with some decent white wine. I'd learn all about James Dickey and the mystery of southern poetry.

When I saw her at the door, she looked so fresh and youthful in a blood orange Mexican poncho and cowboy boots, like some hippie goddess back from a Love-In. A smile slowly began to inhabit my anxious face.

She talked non-stop during dinner on the small courtyard terrace hidden among the giant Australian ferns and palms. The entire workshop had been engrossing, surrounded by wonderful poets not only from the South itself, but from other areas as well. One of the university seminar speakers who ran her particular workshop, was an esteemed Irish bard now almost eighty. He had known Beckett, as they traveled in the same Parisian crowd, and the man had become a well-known literati of the Fifties. He had found her poetry fetching.

Sewanee was the mountaintop preserve of the playwright Tennessee Williams who had loved New Orleans and wrote about it often. Williams had endowed the poetry conference in memory of his late Episcopal priest grandfather who once taught there. Royalties from the continuous Broadway run of his play Streetcar and later from the Hollywood movie had provided for the endowment.

I still feared she might encounter some bearded bohemian nearer her own age, more interesting perhaps and certainly more literary than me. I had been trained as a journalist, though in truth, I'd read little fiction beyond the standard college classics, and almost no poetry outside of the lecture hall.

"Tell me who I should read." I volunteered as we sat in the fading sunlight, "What poets do you think?" Her face became outlined in an orange halo, almost as if she were seated in a Dutch Master's painting. She looked like a Vermeer.

She said, "Poetry isn't for everyone, don't worry," and reached across the table to fill her wine glass once again.

"No," I insisted, "I need some direction. I'm a writer under this disguise, honestly."

"Start with the Beats," she suggested, "I'll get you a couple of books."

"Perfect," I said, "it'll take me away from the backroom deals. That never changes." I added, "Etta has been going to this German shrink, and she wanted me along. He's this old guy with a grey beard and a Freudian. His Fairhope office smells like a cheap Vienna apartment. We should get this out in the open. I should leave."

She fired back, "I told you, you make the decision. I don't care. We can continue like this, that's fine. Don't be stupid, be sure of yourself. You don't know what you want."

The fact was that I didn't know what I wanted. I took the easiest path, and did nothing. Maybe I figured I had known, but the truth was I really didn't.

The guilt I felt about Etta had almost paralyzed me, and with Maggie I wasn't forced into making painful and unpleasant decisions. This served to buy me time, and the duplicity continued with all of us, like some kind of vicious charade.

The second Marotta's trial was about to begin, the government had air tight cases against all the drug traffickers they had rounded up. They tried him as an accomplice in absentia, as the agreement for his deportation to Sicily was already in effect. Aaron's name did finally surface because the trial had been about convicting the federal judge for corruption and complicit murder. It left the CIA and White House weapons for drugs scheme untouched.

During that first week of testimony, Aaron's name and role were presented in prosecution evidence. It established that he had physically delivered these cash bribes, and they had been accepted. Surveillance cameras had shown him with the briefcase and in conversation late at night with the judge in his Garden District garden. This took place on three separate occasions, and it was all part of the prosecution record. It was impossible for the seated court judge to deny these meetings had taken place.

The prosecution claimed that the tainted judge had refused on two occasions to honor the federal law enforcement agency's continued requests to put the admitted drug trafficker, Sloan, who had turned state's evidence into protective custody. This had been done to encourage his assassination by cartel criminals. His whereabouts during the indictment and court hearings was known, and considered common knowledge, and as such, had hastened his murder. Everyone knew exactly where Sloan had lived while at the suburban Ramada Inn.

The trial lasted almost two months. To no one's surprise, it ended in a mistrial because Marotta had gotten to one of the jurors either with bribes, or death threats. A second trial had been scheduled for the spring. It usually took a subsequent trial to get criminal convictions to stick.

Around this time, a Washington journalist friend called me and told me a story, which sounded so strange that I thought it might actually have some truth. The Washington Post where he worked as a reporter had tabled a long feature article on the Contras indefinitely for additional fact checking.

The Post reporter said Langley had anonymously whispered Marotta was playing all sides in the Central American conflict. He had been selling arms to both the Contras and Daniel Ortega's Sandinista government. He bilked everyone at the same time, but he was found out and that's when the real mystery occurred in the tale.

Marotta and two of his lieutenants had been flown to Nicaragua on an Air Force plane to meet with the top Contra commanders. They discussed increasing the arms shipments and using larger and longer-range aircraft with American government money. That would also mean building larger, more modern, jungle runways.

At this secret Contra conference, Marotta was fingered as a collaborator with Ortega and imprisoned in some primitive jungle cage for about a month. Marotta somehow had paid off his captors, and returned unscathed to New Orleans. The two men with him weren't as fortunate and had been shot. It was hard to know what exactly to believe about Marotta, though he clearly wasn't a man to underestimate, or foolishly try to intimidate.

In the trial, Aaron's name came up and the physical evidence examined showed his participation. His suicide had been mentioned, and nothing, certainly nothing from the press, connected him back to me through his Mobile in-laws.

My role within the political arena was no longer front shelf. I had simply become a trusted consultant serving a mayor, and someone who also had state contracts through the present governor.

A lengthy Times Picayune article on the trial appeared that mentioned Aaron as its former reporter, that's all. It stated that he had committed these criminal acts without the paper's knowledge. None of what he had done was connected directly to the newspaper itself or its editorial staff or the publisher.

The man acted on his own. That was the end of this saga, and Aaron's memory would disappear.

* * * * * *

It drove me to distraction that Maggie wouldn't push me to leave Etta. Whenever I tried to manipulate her, she simply refused to push back. She repeatedly told me she was perfectly happy with the way things stood between us. It made me wonder if after all this time together, now almost a year, she had some exit strategy.

Since I had been duplicitous, I started to become obsessed with Maggie's betrayal of me. Increasingly, I would suspect her of things where nothing before had existed. I became anxious when she received telephone calls from people I didn't know, especially strange men.

I thought as I drove back to Magnolia Springs that I couldn't survive another session with the Freudian. I would blurt out some sort of confession, and come unglued under his clinical prodding techniques. For the next half hour, the empty highway unfolded before me on the coast road like a mirage.

Was I a madman? I feverishly searched my own chaotic mind for excuses to cancel future therapy sessions with the German, blaming recurrent migraines that I'd been suffering from the unrelenting pressure of work and uncertainty.

Leaving the Biloxi city limits behind, I reckoned what I would do was to tell Etta that she wasn't receiving his true psychiatric benefits with me sitting in the room. It had robbed her of finding solutions to her problems.

It was best if I saw him independently. I planned to tell her that, and began to rehearse the speech I would make when the time seemed right to broach the subject. Maybe in conversation after dinner, gazing up at the stars from the terrace when she was most relaxed. Then I'd speak up. I was afraid this cunning German would surely break me at the next meeting, or the one after that.

It would become this psychological cat and mouse game with him, one that he's played at before and won. I couldn't continue to successfully oppose him; he would find my Achilles heel, and pounce.

There was no doubt that I would eventually confess to the relationship with Maggie in that foul smelling room. I'd blame Etta for her cruelty and indifference, and the emotionless and controlling behavior she had learned at the feet of Minerva.

Our life together had become a never-ending journey to fill this bottomless pit of her neediness, whatever the hell that need was. She didn't know herself. This marriage, our supposed life together that we had created had been obliterated. It had been doomed from the very beginning, from that first moment on her parent's terrace in Mobile.

When I arrived home, I put the scampi I had picked up at a stand in a steam pot we had outside, and made a quick lettuce salad for dinner. Later, Etta came home bedraggled from the depressing stories her troubled clients had told her all day, and she welcomed the quick feast.

Afterward we sat outside as it got dark, and in casual talk about nothing particular, I told her I thought it best that she continue alone with the German psychiatrist. I'd continue as well as soon as these consulting contracts were finished. Etta looked at me not really shocked, though probably surprised it had taken so long for me to back out.

She simply said, "Sure, if that's what you want." And that was the end of that particular roadblock I faced.

When she informed the German on the telephone the next day, he acted Teutonic and rather curt in his reply.

"He's afraid of what he might say. I understand. You and I will continue."

With that out of the way, I returned to New Orleans. At noon, I met with the deputy mayor at the French Market for coffee and beignets to discuss routine matters. It all went well. He was a quintessential Crescent city politico who had come up through the ranks, each step a little higher on the totem.

Later he went on his way, and I thought I would walk the four blocks back to the apartment and maybe stop along the way at a vintage bookstore.

Inside the bookstore, I scanned the political section of biographies for a minute but moved over to the poetry section and found one of James Dickey's books.

As I went over to sit down for a few minutes in a leather chair in the front window to peruse it, a man in a long trench coat with a hat bumped into me, knocking the slim volume out of my hand.

I instinctively uttered, "Excuse me, sorry, I got engrossed," and pointed to the slim poetry book. He stared at me with dark beady eyes under his felt fedora hat.

He leaned toward my face as if to tell me something in confidence, and whispered, "Le Pavilion. The answer's there."

With that comment, he hurried out of the bookstore and continued at a half sprint disappearing from sight around the corner.

"Pavilion?" I repeated aloud to myself, "The hotel? What had that man meant about the hotel?" He was a bizarre-looking creature. I assumed he was just another of those deranged souls roaming these Quarter sidewalks, harmless for the most part, who usually panhandled for food, or cheap wine. How odd, I thought.

I bought the poetry book then started back to the apartment at a slow pace. The late fall afternoon was warm, and the sun felt refreshing on my face as I trudged the narrow Quarter streets. It was a part of the city I had come to cherish, vastly different from the older sections of Mobile that had a decrepit appearance.

Part of the budget for the city was to renovate a small portion of the Quarter, piece-by-piece reclamation. There would be a confluence of Landmark funds from Washington, and likewise state money. The governor had already earmarked an appropriation.

Later that day, the former mayor called me from Baton Rouge, saying he planned to host the first Southern Governor's Conference in New Orleans in two weeks. He would be the inaugural chairman and it would include the governors from the twelve states of the Confederacy. Everyone would be housed at Le Pavilion Hotel.

He had blocked off rooms for his staff, and wanted me to stay with them to oversee the operation. The governor confessed I was the only person whom he could trust to see it was done right. I thought the coincidence of Le Pavilion was uncanny.

This was more than a conference. There had been talk in Washington of placing his name on the vice presidential short-list this upcoming election. Powerful people had wanted to move ahead quickly. This would garner needed national attention for his candidacy.

I told Maggie about the conference that night, her fingers twirling her raven hair as she listened.

"God, Le Pavilion of all places," she finally said with a suppressed laugh.

"What do you mean?" I asked, curious why she had said that.

"Oh, you know, the natives think there's something otherworldly about the place."

"It's a twenty story French Quarter hotel. What's strange about that?" I pressed on, expecting some tale in return from her.

"Supposedly the hotel was originally built by the French, and the creole priests claim it's built on a slave graveyard, which is this portal to the other side. Voodoo."

I laughed, "You're telling me it's some kind of door, that the dead come back and forth? That's the portal thing?"

"Pretty much," she said, and shrugged her shoulders.

It was a colorful tale indeed, vintage New Orleans lore, and it left my consciousness as quickly as it had entered.

The night was one of the more amorous ones we had ever spent together, and afterward I promised myself that I had to move ahead and leave Etta. This on and off duplicity with two women, sisters, simply had to end, or I'd be destroyed, or go insane.

I had wanted Maggie to demand I leave Etta and make a new life with her. But she wouldn't do it, saying all the while she didn't care if we continued as we were. It was maddening. I desperately needed that final push from her, because my own courage had been lacking. In my mind, I had become an emotional coward consumed with guilt over what I had wrought.

No amount of subtle prodding had worked with Maggie, and she had been close-mouthed over the clandestine life we lived together. I couldn't understand why she had accepted these terms, yet she did uncomplainingly. Somehow this all fulfilled her needs, and maybe it was nothing more than a dance of two dysfunctional people, riding out some inexplicable fantasy of theirs. We went on as before.

At Le Pavilion, most of the southern governors came late the evening before the opening ceremony. I greeted the Tennessee governor as an old friend since I had been his campaign manager two years earlier. I introduced him to his Louisiana host, and my present benefactor. Everything was cordial and friendly, and I could see that my acumen with these political leaders had impressed him.

On one particular occasion at lunch, he had given me a ceremonial wink after a bon mot of mine had gotten laughs from the assembled governors.

The second night was uneventful, and I left the group early to retire, tired from running around from caucus to caucus, and unofficially talking up the Louisiana governor's vice presidential run. Nothing formal had been said on the subject, mind you, only a few well-placed words over drinks.

In the room, I opened the mini-bar and took a scotch bottle out. I cracked the top and poured it into a water glass, taking a long drink while still wondering about the strange man's comment from the bookstore. But nothing had happened. After putting the empty glass on the bedside table, I dropped off into a deep sleep.

# Chapter 11

Half way into the night I heard a sound and it awakened me. I sat up in the bed, leaning against the massive wooden headboard and looked out into the room. There was only a little moonlight from the window, but I could clearly see what looked like the figure of a man in the shadows, sitting in the leather chair facing the bed.

It frightened me, and I called out, "Who the hell are you?" I got ready to jump out of the bed and confront this thief or assailant.

"Get the hell out of here," I yelled at the apparition not fully visible to me in the grey light.

The man in the shadows leaned forward, and I could see his face clearly in the light, and recognized him.

An icy chill came over me as I looked at the pasty white face. It was Aaron. He was staring out into the room, and seemed alive. He had that stocky full face he had always had, though something was wrong with his eyes. They seemed to have a fiery luminosity to them like they were burning. The whole experience terrified me, and I sat frozen on the bed.

He spoke to me in his own voice, and I was so upset I could only make out some of the words he had said, not the meaning. The sound was familiar.

"You're alive?" I said questioningly to him, and put my feet on the floor ready to walk over toward him in the chair. "But how?"

Uncertain of what to do next, I remained where I was and leaned back again against the headboard.

He spoke once more, and this time he seemed to hear what I had said to him, and he uttered, "It was murder. I murdered myself. As you will."

I watched him move his right hand which had the same ring his father had given him when he graduated from Tulane, that had been his grandfather's in Russia. I could see its gold in the moonlight.

It occurred to me I must be dreaming all this. The confidence that I had made this all up in my mind came to me. I arose from the bed but as I did, Aaron's hand with the ring forced me back onto it. It had such a tremendous strength I couldn't fight against it though I tried.

Aaron was sitting on the bed now, and his iron hand gripped my wrist as my back became pinned against the headboard. When he spoke to me his breath became an arctic wind on my face. It literally froze the skin of my cheeks and a feeling of terror overcame me.

I feared he might murder me and I was ready to lash out to save my life. As I prepared myself to leap at him in self-defense, I closed my eyes for a split second and threw myself forward with my elbow flailing in the air.

With a thud I landed on the hotel room floor. In a moment, I was on my hands and knees, and I could see him standing at the doorway looking back at me, and in another second he had disappeared. In a panic and trembling, I turned on the overhead light.

There was no one in the room. I stood up in my rumpled sport coat and tie from the long day, and the bedspread was twisted on the floor at my feet. The heavy leather chair had been moved from when I first came in. It had been placed next to the bed where I had seen Aaron sitting and where he had gripped my arm. I looked at my wrist, and there was a bluish bruise as if a blood vessel had been ruptured in some violent confrontation.

I tried to pick up the chair and carry it back to the desk where it had been earlier, but it was too heavy for me to move by myself. It would take two men to return it to where it had been when I first came into the room.

I had not moved it, I remembered that quite clearly. It was impossible for me to climb comfortably into the bed where it now sat. I would literally have to vault over it to get onto the large bed.

It was confusing. Perhaps I had a nightmare with Aaron in it. Perhaps in a somnolent trance, I had pushed the leather chair next to the bed and hurt my wrist with that effort. That was the only explanation I could muster.

I opened the mini-bar again taking out a second scotch bottle, and walked over to the desk to take a fresh water glass off the tray. In the middle of the wooden desk rested Aaron's ruby ring, probably eighty years old in its jewelry style. Examining it closer, I noticed an inscription inside the worn band in Cyrillic script. The engraved date next to the foreign words was 1915.

This ring had been on Aaron's finger when he was buried. I saw him in the casket. I served as one of the pallbearers. I watched the casket being closed with this ring on his right hand. I know that he had been buried with it. In fact, I had thrown a shovel full of dirt on the casket as it lay in the uncovered grave.

I waited for morning to arrive, numb with questions.

Routinely, the conference's final breakfast was a time for friendliness and humor, as the more serious political themes had already been discussed. The Tennessee governor shared a campaign anecdote with me as the butt of the joke, a rather harmless story, and it drew laughs and applause from the governors.

The Louisiana governor was delighted with the outcome. He had shaken my hand vigorously for what seemed like forever whispering that 'we' were on our way and the sky was the limit.

As I left the hotel I looked up at the window of the room that I had been in. The discomfort I felt seemed to stay with me as my fingers touched the cold metal of the ring in my front trouser pocket. I could show it to Mary Agnes and ask her if she thought it was Aaron's, but should I dare?

Before I turned the corner onto Poydras, I glanced back once more at the white portico entrance and vaguely remembered that it had been Huey Long's headquarters in

New Orleans for many years when it was the Desoto Hotel. The Garden District doctor who had murdered him at the Capitol often sat alone in the ornate hotel lobby with an espresso reading the Times Picayune. He had been quite friendly with the governor, all the time planning to kill him.

When I saw Maggie that night, I couldn't bring myself to tell her what had happened in the hotel room. Instead I rambled about the governor's plans to be named the next vice presidential candidate, and how he had set the groundwork for support with his fellow Southern governors. She had greeted the news about the governor's ambition with complete indifference, and to be honest, I felt the same way.

What kept burning inside me was the eerie sight of Aaron. I fingered the ring continuously in my pocket as we talked. There was no reasonable circumstance that could explain what had happened. Aaron wasn't alive. I had helped bury this man and I had slowly watched him lowered for all eternity into an empty grave. It was Aaron's face that I clearly saw in the open casket during the wake with Mary Agnes and Etta beside me. I had noticed his grandfather's gold ring on his finger.

"You seem a little distracted," Maggie said, and touched my face with her long white fingers, rubbing it gently with the back of her hand. "What is it?"

I laughed uncomfortably. "Oh the governor and the election nonsense. It's always the bigger chest of gold they want."

"That surprises you after all these years?" Maggie said in her nonchalant manner.

"No, I really don't think about it much. Why would I?" I said half meaning the words.

"Did you like Le Pavilion?" she asked mischievously with ever the slightest smile on her face.

"A different experience," I told her, though I couldn't bring myself to confess more. It was too upsetting to recount. I had experienced such a genuine horror that night.

As I kept silent, I looked down at my wrist half hidden with my linen sport coat sleeve and saw the raw bruise. It had been as painful as if I had sprained it, and hurt to lift anything heavier than an empty dinner plate.

Lying in bed with Maggie fast asleep next to me, I saw Aaron's white face in the darkness, and thought maybe he's alive. His suicide had somehow been faked, the doctors paid to lie, and a coroner's report forged. All this might be possible in the world of criminal masterminds like Carlos Marotta.

But we had seen Aaron in that casket, all of us standing there around Mary Agnes. Maggie stood right next to me along with Etta. She said a final prayer for his spirit's journey. I remembered something from Robert Frost about immortality.

With my thoughts swirling, sleep finally came and when I awoke Maggie had already made coffee and heated some pastries we had gotten from the French Market.

After sipping a little coffee, I said to her, "What poetry did you recite at Aaron's funeral?"

"What makes you think of that?" she asked with some astonishment showing on her face. "Robert Frost, if you must know."

"Oh, I just remembered it was poetry, that's all. It was nice, about the soul's flight, I think."

"Good memory."

"For some reason I was thinking about him. It must've been the trial, and his name getting dragged into it, and all that in the papers," I said to her I thought convincingly. "Do you remember that gold ring he wore? It had belonged to his Russian grandfather."

She nodded, "I remember it alright. He had it on in the casket, but not a wedding ring. Nobody ever said anything about that."

"His family asked to prepare the body, that's why. It was some sort of Jewish thing. Mary Agnes went along with it all, but she was shell shocked."

"Could you describe the ring?" I asked her with anxiety.

"What a strange request!" she answered. "But alright, it was heavy gold, a square ring with a shiny ruby. There was a Russian inscription inside. He showed it to me once. There was a date inside the band too. 1915."

What Maggie said chilled my blood. I put on my best performance of disinterest, and added that most of us have these odd things we recall in our minds, it's the human condition. Quirky things we can't quite let go of.

"Aaron fooled me," she continued, "I never thought he could be that much of a criminal. The man was so mild-mannered, he never argued, or raised his voice. He never fought once with Mary Agnes, and God knows that would take a saint."

She remembered one or two other things about Aaron. As she talked, I turned the ring inside my pocket over and over again with sweaty fingers. Maggie started to tell me about the poetry workshops she would be doing. I listened, though her words meant nothing.

I thought out a possible scenario: Marotta might have had a sinister doctor administer some drug to Aaron to stop his normal body function. Afterward, the coroner would claim he was dead. He would be put into a drug-induced coma inside the casket. There was a time when all the pallbearers left the viewing parlor where a switch could have been made.

It was the task of the undertaker and his assistant to seal the casket by hammering several metal stays shut with a wooden mallet. It had taken maybe ten minutes, and the pallbearers had gone outside for a smoke.

The funeral party was already in the limousines ready to follow the hearse to the cemetery. The back door of the hearse had been opened wide and the uniformed driver was standing there waiting for the casket. When the pallbearers went inside to retrieve the casket, it had been hammered shut. They carried it out of the parlor down a half dozen steps and slid it into the back of the hearse. The driver closed the hearse door and got behind the wheel to start the funeral cortege.

We had only seen Aaron in this open casket. He looked dead, but was he? There are drugs available that simulate this deathly stillness, and they reduce breathing to the point it's barely discernible. Only someone trained in medical forensics could know that person was still alive.

Marotta could make that happen. He was manipulative and unscrupulous, and had murdered some as yet unknown number of people. He could certainly arrange a staged death; it was eminently possible to a man of his sinister talents.

Why would he care if Aaron lived? He was one more witness who might testify against him. Barry Sloan had already been murdered. With Aaron dead, there were no more pilots left to implicate Marotta. It made little sense to save him, and this honor among thieves? Unlikely, right?

I thought more about it all. Was that Aaron at the bookstore? He was about the same size as the man I had seen with a stocky frame whose face could've been hidden between the upturned trench coat collar and his pulled down fedora hat. There was a strong possibility I wouldn't recognize him anyway in such a quick encounter.

After all, Aaron was supposed to be dead, why expect to see him on the street? Had he been trying to tell me he would be at Le Pavilion, and that he would meet me later? It could have easily been him. He might've even disguised his voice. It had been low pitched. It all had happened so fast that I didn't get a good look. I had spoken out of embarrassment after bumping into him.

How could that explain what he said and did inside the hotel room? Had he disappeared into thin air, or simply walked out the door when I wasn't looking? Maybe he squeezed my arm hard, trying to tell me something while I was half asleep. Somehow, I wanted to believe Aaron was alive. He might've been followed by the FBI, and had to be careful. It was dangerous to be on the run. The man was wanted for his part in a murder.

Maggie remarked again on my distraction the next evening, and she said, "Hey, what's going on with you? And don't tell me nothing, I can see something's wrong."

I lied again, and said that the mayor was becoming a problem, and she just shook her head in disbelief.

"Look, that guy eats out of your hand. Tell me the truth, what's up?"

I finally told her everything that had happened, starting with the bookstore, and the night at Le Pavilion.

"Good Christ," was all she could say and got up and walked around the room in circles for a few moments, her hands on her head. "I can't believe any of this."

"I'm telling you exactly how it happened. Nothing's been left out," I continued. I handed her the gold ring, and she balanced it in the palm of her hand speechless, then held it up to the light so she could see the inside inscription.

"This is beginning to make me crazy," she added, "Nothing is making sense here, nothing." She put the ring back on the table quickly as if it had been burning her hand, and turned to me with her face ashen.

I told her I thought someone might have faked Aaron's death, but he was more convenient dead than alive, one less incriminating witness. Marotta didn't care if he killed anybody.

Why, if Aaron were alive, would he not try to see Mary Agnes or his daughter? That was unlike the man that I had known who had been so devoted to his young family. Yet I didn't believe him capable of criminal behavior either; smuggling cocaine to sell to schoolchildren. Aaron had known where the drugs would end up when he took the money.

Maggie, at last, said what she was thinking, and told me to listen quietly until she had finished speaking, and then say whatever I wanted. She said she believed in the spirit world, and what had happened was that Aaron had a mission.

His spirit had resumed its earlier human form so that I might recognize him and listen to what he had come to say. After she had finished, she crossed her arms, and looked quite serious, waiting for my response.

"Whoa," I said to her, "This is going to require some more thinking. I had never thought it possible, you know…"

"You need to think about it, and what's next," Maggie added.

"What if it's all in my mind, some kind of sickness, and I'm losing my marbles, going over the edge," I said with some real concern. "People get delusional. It's screwed up brain chemistry, right?"

She added I wasn't the first doubter of apparitions. It would be up to me to interpret what had happened in Le Pavilion. Maybe Aaron would come to me again. Only time would tell.

What Maggie said gave me some small solace that I wasn't crazy. That night I held her tightly like some anchor until I saw the dawn breaking in the French Quarter sky.

Aaron couldn't be alive. It was against all odds that such a scheme had been concocted and had been successful, and he now walked the streets with a different identity. It was easier to believe he had returned from the other side, and that some spirit world might exist. Though in truth, I doubted both.

Reason suggested maybe I had made up this entire incident, imagined it all, a delusion on my part. The man in the bookstore was a random customer, not Aaron disguised, and I had dreamt what took place in the hotel room. But his ring, how do you explain that? Had Aaron given it to me some time before he died, and I had forgotten exactly where or why? It was bizarre.

He had always worn it, and once at dinner in the Garden District, he talked about his Russian grandfather and the persecution of the Jews. His grandfather had fought for the Tsar. He had been captured by the Kaiser's troops and imprisoned early in the war, escaping only to be later conscripted into the disintegrating White Army.

The man had never been a Bolshevik like many Jews at the time, but remained loyal to the crown. Even as an old man, he always thought of himself as more Russian than a Jew. He had started the furniture store during the Depression while his family lived in a few rooms hidden in the back. With the Second World War and afterward, the store prospered and he moved to a fine suburban home in West Mobile where Aaron's father, Morris, had lived.

\* \* \* \* \* \*

The second New Orleans criminal trial produced convictions and all of the defendants received stiff prison sentences. The court decided against bringing Marotta back from Sicily to stand trial. He was dying of cancer, and had been confined to a hospice that was monitored by the Italian police and Interpol. His doctors had predicted he wouldn't live more than six months.

The Chilean who had killed Barry Sloan never spoke during the trial, and he was given a life sentence. The other accomplices were also closed mouthed though the evidence had been overwhelming as to their guilt. There had been obvious jury tampering in the earlier trial, but this one produced the damning verdicts.

Meanwhile at home, Etta's depression worsened, and the clinics suffered a prolonged lull that had made her despondent most days. The ancient Freudian hadn't done much to assuage her doubt and oncoming depression. He eventually prescribed a low dose of Prozac to get her through the days.

I gladly wrote most of the household checks, and put more money into the clinic cash reserves. I made payments to bring down the burgeoning bank advances. Etta's family trust had been exhausted with the last children's university

248

expenses, and most everybody had become independent anyway.

The decline with Etta seemed to accelerate. I suggested she close the Fairhope clinic and concentrate on Mobile where she was better known and knew everyone in town.

Her reaction was blind rage. She started screaming that I didn't give a shit what happened to her. She went off like a madwoman, and ended up throwing dishes against the wall in the kitchen, breaking two or three plates before she calmed down.
I tried to sit her down and explain this was only work, and sometimes a great idea took time to fully blossom.

People often acted fickle, reluctant to embrace the unfamiliar. None of what I told her had any impact. At one point, she charged out the door and drove somewhere to get lost in her own thoughts. Maybe the inability to have children had taken its toll too, particularly in Mobile where the youngest women sought to have one or perhaps all of their children before they reached thirty.

I forced myself to return to the Freudian, thinking my presence at her side might buttress the obvious breakdown I saw coming. Unfortunately, little had changed with him and his methods. He uttered the same hackneyed questions, and offered her nothing concrete she might grasp onto.

He treated me as if I weren't in the room at all, and for him, I really wasn't. He persisted to rest the awful burden of interpretation of what was happening to her on her own head. He flung everything she said right back at her. She rambled on and on, confused in her meager explanations, and increasingly fearful. This was not the confident well-informed woman who started this psychotherapy. She resembled a wayward child, a troubled adolescent.

"How do you feel about that and that and that?" This artificial litany of his metallic voice filled the musty chamber.

At the end of the psychotherapy, he said to Etta, "I think it's better if your husband doesn't join us for our work together anymore." He saw no further need to address my dismissal. Etta simply agreed without issue.

As far as I was concerned, his treatment had been inconclusive, and I hadn't detected any relief for Etta from these meetings. I wanted Etta to be whole, and even though I believed our marriage had turned irretrievably bad with both of us suffering, I certainly took no pleasure from her continuing agony. Part of it had to do with the horrible legacy of Minerva. The emotional turmoil that had followed left her vulnerable and damaged.

She now drank more than I had ever remembered, and this medicating, if that was what it was, becoming near suicidal. It wouldn't end well unless it stopped and soon.

Miraculously within the next week, there had been an upturn in the Fairhope clinic. During a three-day period, Etta had five new patients, all of whom enrolled in a multi-month therapy regime. These were Eastern Shore teenagers with adjustment problems at home and school. She had proved masterful in reaching these troubled young women in the past. Her skills at bringing them back from the brink of despair were effective. She brought her own heightened brand of compassion to the care that was heartwarming to observe. Etta knew how to save these girls, and she usually did.

This short-term infusion of hope put a ready smile on Etta's face, and the depression seemed thwarted. I only hoped that she would find a path to thread her way through Minerva's emotional carnage. As the oldest child, she had suffered the absolute worst of it, the unparalleled criticism and mean spirited manipulation that went unnoticed for decades.

I had repeatedly beseeched Etta to not believe that "We are what we earn, or what others think," but individuals, pure in this human form. The words may have echoed with hypocrisy coming from my own mouth though they had been sincere.

So there appeared a window of renewed optimism in our Mobile lives, and the earlier self-destruction facing this lovely and decent woman had been somehow shelved, hopefully forever.

Each day, Etta packed a rather complete lunch she shared with her two therapists in Fairhope. I could hear her singing each morning in the small kitchen as she made chicken or egg salad sandwiches and bottled lemon-flavored sweet tea. It was wonderful to hear the joy in her voice.

The mystery of Aaron's ring continued to haunt me. One day I decided to drive over to Mary Agnes' house for a visit since I hadn't seen her for quite a while. She made some tea and finger sandwiches for the occasion. We talked about her parents and all the good times we had as couples, and a little bit about New Orleans since I'd spent so much time in the city.

At last when the time seemed right, I pulled the ring out of my pocket and cupped it in my closed fist. I asked her if she would look at some jewelry I had come upon and see if she recognized it. I slowly dropped the gold ring into her flattened palm.

She stared down at it, and a look of absolute horror crossed her face. "Where in God's name did you get that?" she asked me trembling.

"Is that Aaron's ring?" I asked her with marked determination, "His grandfather's ring? There's a Russian inscription inside on the band."

She slowly turned it in her shaking fingers and looked inside at the inscription.

"He was wearing it when we buried him," I reminded her. In an instant, she got up and walked to the large dining room windows and held it to the light, examining it closely, turning around several times in the sunlight. A look of distress came to her attractive face, and she began to shake her head.

She walked over to the mahogany dining room table and sat down with an almost fall into the chair.

251

"Where did you get that?" she asked, now artificially calm, a forced serenity to prevent a total breakdown on her face.

I told her that someone had put it on the desk in my hotel room at Le Pavilion more than a week ago. There was someone inside my room that I couldn't clearly see, and they left it on the desk for me to find. I lied about the apparition, or whether it was Aaron himself very much alive.

She said: "Do you think that someone stole it, maybe from the funeral parlor, and later felt bad, then wanted to give it back to someone in the family?"

Letting out a deep sigh, I told her that was possible. Thievery must happen all the time with the dying. A mortuary would be the perfect place to steal from while everyone was preoccupied with the deceased. Everyone was wrought with grief.

She agreed, this was the identical ring she and I had remembered Aaron wearing on his finger inside the funeral chapel. I asked her if I might keep it a little longer to find out who had returned this to me, and perhaps something about the circumstances.

She said, "Of course," and we finished the tea with a visit from her youngest who had awoken from his nap. I soon left, glad to be out of her house.

It was indeed Aaron's ring and he had been buried with it, or at least it had gotten as far as the mortuary and the funeral wake with it on his finger. I had certainly noticed, as had Mary Agnes too.

The only logical explanation was that it had been removed by one of the funeral home employees, or the director himself during the few minutes the pallbearers left the chapel as the casket cover had been mechanically sealed for burial. But why give it to me now? Somebody's guilt had perhaps been too much, and I was remembered as a family member.

So maybe I was the most recognizable family member, the most public at least, and the thief had traced my whereabouts to Le Pavilion.

The other possibilities were: Aaron was indeed alive and had been in my room playing the role of a ghost to throw me off. He left the ring behind so I'd know that he lived. The other was that he was in fact dead, and his spirit had returned that night for some unknown purpose.

I needed to know the truth, or it would continue to haunt me. I arranged to check with the police to see if there had been any accusations of theft concerning the mortuary.

The next afternoon, a police lieutenant I knew reported back to me that in forty years of service there had never been a complaint filed against the funeral director, or any of his staff. Most of the employees had been there an average of twenty years and typically included several family members.

I next met with the New Orleans district attorney, another political acquaintance, and he claimed he had never heard of a single case of a staged death in his experience during twenty-five years of prosecution. He had grave doubts that even a criminal as cunning as Marotta could pull it off. It wasn't impossible, though completely improbable.

"You've been reading too many crime novels," he teased me jokingly. "And someone like Aaron would be of far more value dead than alive to Marotta. The deceased's former testimony or confession becomes useless in any criminal indictment. The FBI dumped all they had collected, half of it inadmissible to the Grand Jury."

When I left him, he told me to forget this fantasy of mine. It was a ridiculous theory without any factual basis. Barry Sloan had been murdered, and Aaron's death was a suicide. Those were the facts in this case, which had been undisputed all along, and proven in court. Whatever he had said, I couldn't let it go that easily. I had to find out for myself what had happened.

The next week, back in New Orleans, I told Maggie I had planned to retrace my footsteps starting with a coffee at the French Market and later the walk to the Quarter bookstore. That morning after Maggie had left the apartment for Loyola, I busied myself with paperwork, and I started on my pilgrimage first to the French Market in the early afternoon and then walked to the bookstore.

Inside with the books, I removed another James Dickey poetry volume from the shelf and strolled over with it to the front foyer of the store. I slowly perused the paperback in a brown beaten leather chair, glancing around the store for some untoward sign, or recurrence of the earlier encounter. I sat there for an hour, and the bookstore provided lively foot traffic of mostly out of town tourists.

Back in the apartment again, I confirmed my reservation for the night at Le Pavilion. I had insisted on the same hotel room that luckily was available.

After a drink in the hotel Crystal Room, I went upstairs, and prepared to retire for the night. I cautiously waited for something unusual to happen, some visitation from beyond. I placed the ring in the center of the desk where I had found it.

Lying awake for hours into the night, I saw nothing and could only hear my neighbor in the next room laughing before I drifted off to sleep.

At two in the morning I was awakened by loud noises in the hallway in front of the room, but there was nobody or nothing stirring inside the room except for me. Through the glass peephole in the door, I could see two men who were drunk and trying to unlock the door across the hall with some trouble.

Back in bed, the night passed uneventfully, and at seven I repacked my small overnight bag and left the hotel for a coffee at a nearby café. I had encountered nothing or no one the entire night. The ring had remained on the desk in the same place I had left it. The entire exercise had produced nothing.

I walked back to my place lost in thought. What was going on? Not only was this strange other-worldly mystery happening to me, but also things with Maggie had started to flatten. She seemed less affectionate and playful. I began to fear what I had long expected would happen might in fact be occurring.

She had started to attend poetry workshops at various universities around the South. She had visited Charleston for a second time to read with Dickey and his disciples. That weekend had been extended to almost a week out of town, and I sensed something had gone sorely wrong with us. Upon her return she spent the night with me at the apartment, and was more affectionate than she had been in weeks, and it made me uneasy.

As she was leaving in the morning, she stopped on her way out, then leaned on the doorframe. She looked at me with a strong hint of discomfort on her pretty face and said, "Something's happened. I've been asked to teach at the Citadel, and I'm moving to Charleston."

"Is this temporary?" I asked, already knowing the painful answer.

"No, I'm leaving for good. I think we need to spend time apart. That's the best thing."

"There's another man, isn't there?" I asked, hoping that I was mistaken.

She bit her lip, and tears started to form in her eyes. Instinctively almost like a child, she wiped them with her shirtsleeve.

"Yes, I'm sorry. It just happened. That doesn't mean I don't love you though."

"Oh, I see," I answered with a tight mouth, my insides going numb.

I had put on my bathrobe and was standing in front of her. I walked over to the sink and poured myself a glass of water, drinking it down quickly. Then I walked much closer to where she stood.

"Tell me what it means, Maggie?" I blurted out, and my whole body ached with this intense knotted muscle strain. "It's over, right?"

"I didn't want that. It was always doomed," she said now crying loudly. "I can't talk. I gotta go."

As soon as she had spoken that parting remark, she was gone, running as fast as she could across the terrace. She flung open the heavy street door that slammed back on its hinges with her force. I could see the orange tail of her poncho in the breeze for a split second but that was all.

Sitting alone in the apartment, her scent filled the room. I walked out to the terrace table listening to the French Quarter morning over the brick courtyard wall and stared into the nothingness in front of me. It had ended, but could it have happened any other way? I guess not.

The indecision that had guided my actions with Etta, looking always to Maggie to tell me to leave her sister had kept me in limbo. This way I didn't have to do anything, but continue to balance the deception I was already practicing. It gave me a respite from looking at myself, and judging my actions. Maybe deep down I wouldn't leave Etta. The guilt I'd experience would be too powerful and debilitating, and I was afraid of the unknown. I wanted to leave a safe harbor only to find another, and only then would I take the emotional voyage.

I had been battered in that coal town, so much that I couldn't trust myself alone in the world. I needed to cling to the side of someone, any woman, even if the happiness might only be fleeting. I had expected to be betrayed. I would betray them too before they would do it to me. That's why I did what I did.

I chose Maggie because I knew she would leave me. There could be no other end to it. She was damaged from that troubled Mobile house, and her own terrors. Nothing in what we had attempted could ever survive. It was a relationship built on a foundation of sand, fear and self-absorption, and maybe even a loathing. We desperately clung to each other in the midst of this raging storm of doubt and loneliness and sought the momentary pleasure and newness of that refuge.

My past must have twisted me into some peculiar shape of a man. Whatever affection there was in my family had been hidden in narrow places, and only once can I recall a time when my father ever managed to show me kindness, or even attention.

In elementary school I was a timid student and had waited until the last minute to do a project on ancient Egypt, to draw or sculpt replicas of the pyramids. What I had put on paper had been pathetic. My mother tried to color something that was equally primitive. But that night when everyone was asleep, my half-drunk father had staggered down into the damp basement and found a small plywood board. With all his forgotten army ingenuity born of the American refusal to surrender on the Bastogne battlefield, he had taken my younger sister's colored children's clay and had created a perfect replica eight inches high of pharaoh's great pyramid. Each stone was crafted like slave-ordered limestone, and alongside it rested an even larger scale model of the Sphinx. They were sculpted with such sensitivity and precision, that when I took them to school, my child's heart soared with pride. There never was another time. We were all broken toys.

Mother was a hairdresser, a cosmetologist as she liked to call herself, and he did put up large mirrors in her salon where he had built gilded frames. To make up for this moment of kindness, he beat her sometimes if she argued with him when he was drunk.

As a boy I would lie in bed and think about killing him. Once I had come upon him passed out, face down on the kitchen table. I opened a drawer and held a butcher knife in my child's hand for a moment before returning it silently to its rightful place among the other cutlery.

The single respite we ever had at home was when he was sitting on a barstool, usually at the American Legion, drinking with the other men who had come through the carnage of that war. Like them, he had returned to the dark and dangerous mine shafts of their own father's lives.

Looking back on that misery I understood what had happened to my family, its total destruction, and I had blamed my mother for staying with him. With that single cowardly act, she had betrayed us.

It was irrational thinking certainly, but what choice did she have? Yet betrayal of that trust never left me, and remained in my unconscious mind, that still troubled me.

Why had Maggie slept with me that last night knowing it was finished in her mind? It was a misguided gesture of affectionate send-off. I had deserved one last enthusiastic fuck, and after that, her obligations were over. It wasn't a thing I would do maybe, but she clearly wasn't me. If anything we were worlds apart, always had been.

I thought somehow we could beat those odds, knowing it had been a mistake from the very beginning. Had I the courage to walk away from Etta, it might've succeeded with her, but even then, failure was certain. She would betray me, she was still young, and her life had only started.

Filled with anger and hurt, I hurriedly dressed and walked downtrodden to the French Market for a fortifying espresso before I had to make an appearance with the mayor and his staff. I dreaded the prospect. As I sat in the window with my tepid cup and untouched pastry, I watched the line of morning foot traffic weave its way through the narrow streets, the sun shadowing their faces. Taking a sip of the coffee, I noticed the same man from the bookstore. I knew it was him. He was wearing the same clothes he had on when I bumped into him.

I stood and rushed over to the open window on the street and yelled, "Hey, wait!"

In an instant I was out the door, but he was almost a block ahead of me, and I shouted at him again, "Wait, I need to talk to you."

An older woman walking distractedly ahead of me had turned around, thinking that I had meant her, and I quickly shook my head, dismissing her.

The man had crossed the street, and I dashed across to intercept him, narrowly missing a speeding taxi, which had slammed on its brakes with the driver cursing me from his open window.

In a minute I was ten or twenty paces behind him, and I called out again, but before I realized it, he had turned down an alley disappearing from sight.

Flying around the filthy alley entrance I ran into an overflowing garbage can quickly pushing it away. As I looked down the cobblestone alley, I saw a tall wrought iron fence, and only emptiness. There was nothing or nobody visible. As I frantically looked around for a door he might have taken, I saw none, only red brick walls. He had vanished.

\* \* \* \* \* \*

The political work began to lose its charm in New Orleans. Slowly in my heart I wanted to abandon the city and found excuses to ignore opportunities put on my plate. I found myself reentering the Mobile life I had lived.

Etta's outlook had improved and her clinics were prospering, though I paid scant attention to what she told me about their day-to-day operations. I would listen patiently to her descriptions though I didn't hear a thing, really, all empty words.

Somehow I secured political work in Chicago through Washington friends, and for a time, I began traveling by the lone shuttle United offered mornings every other week from Mobile airport. It was one of those smallish jets that held maybe fifty or sixty passengers, and it was an easy two-hour flight to O'Hare.

One morning I had gotten to the airport two hours before my flight as was my habit from those Navy years in flight school. In my foggy mind maybe I came there that early to inspect the aircraft as the pilot who would fly us to Chicago, doing his routine pre-flight checks. Who knew?

I stood at the window waiting for them to ferry the plane over to the gate, which would be done in maybe fifteen minutes. During my impatience, I watched another similar plane, a passenger jet slightly smaller than most United flew, and it had the metal departure stairs pressed against the fuselage. A uniformed man stepped outside and looked toward the terminal, his face concerned. In the next moment, I could see a stocky young man in an overcoat run across the tarmac carrying a small bag and dart up the rickety steps to the open airplane door. There was something familiar about his movements, the large steps he took, maybe two at a time. As he reached the top of the metal staircase, he stopped.

Looking back toward the terminal building, he had the morning sun lighting his round face and I could see he smiled. His right hand was raised in a half wave and his lips seemed to whisper something into the wind. I could clearly see a gold ruby ring on his finger as the light between passing clouds illuminated his young face. It was Aaron. By God, it was actually him. I recognized him on the boarding stairs, and in the next second, he was inside the plane and an arm encased in a blue uniform sleeve closed the aircraft door.

His body looked as always, although maybe a bit stocky now with some added girth. His thick dark hair came down over his overcoat collar, and he was hatless. It was the identical coat as that brusque man wore in the Quarter bookstore with an oblong stain on the right sleeve. That man who told me to go to Le Pavillon. There was also this slight hint of grey at his temples, a distinguished look you would find with a newspaper columnist who covered national politics

260

in Washington or even maybe New York. But the man who stood on the aircraft stairs was unmistakably Aaron.

In another instant the door reopened, and half of Aaron's body became visible on the stairs. He leaned forward through the doorframe looking piercingly into my eyes. He beckoned me to follow him with his ring hand motioning in the air. He said, "Come," and quickly disappeared.

The aircraft door was still wide open though, and finally the pilot in his sleek airline captain's uniform leaned out to shut it, carefully pulling it toward him as he stood inside. Noticing those shiny four gold stripes on his coat sleeve, I thought too that I recognized his face, the haunting familiarity of his very distinctive features.

And in another moment, I realized it was this kindred spirit, that human form from my childhood who guarded me in my infant's crib. It was the man who sat behind me in the cockpit on the morning that I pushed my F-14 jet trainer far beyond its physical endurance limits. It was clearly him, no one else.

He stared at me and immediately smiled, shaking his head slightly in acknowledgement and perhaps welcome, certain too that it was me at the terminal window. Slowly he raised his left hand almost like a Catholic bishop or a cardinal does with two fingers raised, offering me some kind of absolution before he too was gone.

With the side door at last secured, the United plane began to back up and the pilot gradually moved it toward the two main airport runways and into the bright sunlight which blinded me with its intensity.

261

# Chapter 12

I pinned my face to the terminal window glass and watched a ground maintenance crew remove the L-shaped stairs, and the narrow plane slowly backed away from the terminal gate. Instinctively I ran to the elevator but it was occupied, so I took the exit stairs and rushed down to the bottom level of the terminal. I sprinted the few gates to where I had seen the plane, which had vanished from sight.

There was a United Airlines agent placing a sign on the board at the gate that read Chicago O'Hare and its departure time. He was occupied with sliding the flight time number cards one by one into the metal holder on the wall. This was the gate for my scheduled flight.

Breathless and overly excited, I asked him with this feverish color on my face, "The plane that was here, the one that just left, where was it going?"

He answered with a wrinkled brow of uncertainty at the question: "There was no plane here. Chicago O'Hare is the first flight. It leaves in forty minutes."

"But I saw a plane parked at this gate. I was standing at the window in the main terminal next to the café right above us."

I gestured with my hand in the air above me, index finger pointing upward. He shook his head with increased doubt at what I was saying, and continued his pre-boarding tasks. At last he turned on the desk computer as I remained there, and he finally looked up, adding that I was mistaken.

"Look, I know what I saw. A plane was parked at this gate," and I gestured upward again with my outstretched arm, "I saw it from the upstairs window."

He continued to shake his head, and had begun to print a manifest of Chicago bound passengers from the built-in printer. When the list had been finished, he ripped it out along its glass edge and he put the pages in a neat pile in front of him.

"Sir, I don't mean to be argumentative. I've been down here for almost an hour, and no other plane has departed from this gate. This is the first scheduled flight. You're free to check with the airport authority if you don't believe me."

I walked away from him with disbelief and returned to the café where I had left my carry-on bag at the table along with my coat and half-drunk coffee, still unbothered. With shaking hands, I unzipped the side bag compartment and removed a small Chinese lacquer box I had taken with me from the French Quarter apartment.

Inside the ornate box with its mother of pearl dragon facade, I had carefully placed Aaron's gold ring wrapped in a monogrammed cotton handkerchief. I made certain it never left my sight for very long.

Trembling I pushed the dragon top to one side of the box and saw the neatly folded white handkerchief. I took it out and slowly opened it, but there was no ring inside. I picked up the box and examined it again in a panic, shaking it.

The café attendant had been staring at me as I appeared to be in a frenzy. He said loudly from behind the counter, "Did you lose your ticket?"

I didn't answer, but continued to frantically search all around the café table.

"I lost a ring," I bellowed to the café people.

There had been two men working behind the counter, and in a moment, I was joined by one who with his plastic gloved hand was scouring the floor under the three tables and chairs.

"Can't find a thing," he reported to me, standing and brushing the dust off his pants. "Go to Lost and Found" he suggested, and pointed to the front of the concourse. "It doesn't open until ten. Leave a message. They'll call you back."

I stood there as if I'd seen a ghost, and my head was bobbing in this slight arc of manic distraction. At last he leaned over, peering directly into my flushed face, "Hey, you alright?"

"Yeah," I answered, ignoring him and staring at the open lacquer box in my hand.

"People steal shit. It happens all the time," he said over his shoulder, and he joined the other twenty-something behind the counter who had been brewing a fresh pot of hot coffee for the morning passengers. The man who had helped me started to fill the black container on the counter with milk from a carton he was handed by the other.

I walked back to the gate to board my flight in silence. Onboard the Chicago flight its wheels retracted, the sleek plane started to bank to its starboard side. I saw Mobile Bay below and the seven rivers that fed it like some oversized brown hand.

Impatiently I pulled down the tray table, and reached into the open briefcase on the empty seat beside me. I removed a handful of papers to review, research poll numbers for the upcoming Illinois gubernatorial election. The Chicago vote was considered the candidate's and the party machinery had endorsed his candidacy. It should all fit into place nicely. It would be an effortless race; the numbers were all on our side.

Trying to get comfortable in the narrow seat, a blunt object dug into my backside. I turned uncomfortably with my free hand to remove whatever it was. In my open hand rested Aaron's gold ring. I looked at it closely, examining the inside band for the inscription.

Had I put this in my back pocket, but when? And what about what I had seen from the terminal window, the other plane? This seemed insane. How strange, I thought, and slipped the ring on my right hand much as he had worn it. The ring moved easily onto the bare finger, and I held my hand out flat to examine it for a moment. That would be the safest place for it.

Aaron had escaped this family, and the life here, albeit in a mysterious and gruesome way. When I wore his ring I felt like anything was possible and that freedom was possible for me too. Was this what Aaron had been trying to tell me?

I laughed to myself at the coincidences, and rifled through the poll report as a coffee was put on the table next to me without ever asking. Somehow they had known.

\* \* \* \* \* \*

After the fifth call to the airport a few days later, Etta finally got into her car and drove to Mobile. She left it at short term parking and stormed into the United ticket office inside the main terminal, and asked an agent what the schedule was for the Chicago plane.

Etta told the agent that she had dropped her husband off at the airport three days ago, and he had been ticketed to return yesterday on the late afternoon flight. She hadn't heard from him.

The woman behind the counter smiled with some minor discomfort, and told Etta that perhaps she had been mistaken. Etta explained pointedly that it was the single flight that went from Mobile directly to Chicago. Her husband had taken it several times in the past month.

The middle-aged female agent with the stringy blond bleached hair made a call to Chicago's United Headquarters as her fingers jumped across the computer keyboard. She put on her glasses to examine the grey screen letters and numbers.

"I understand," she said into the telephone receiver balanced between her skinny neck and shoulder, "Yes, thank you."

"Chicago says they cancelled direct flights from Mobile over six months ago. They couldn't fill them."

"Maybe they reinstated it, or something," Etta added to the conversation, exasperated.

The woman seemed confident in what she had heard from United, and she shook her head. "Maybe your husband took another connecting flight from Atlanta or Houston, and forgot to mention it. That might be it."

"No dammit, he didn't. I'll get to the bottom of this," Etta muttered as she charged back out of the double doors to her car, and she sped back to the Eastern Shore, furious.

Christmas came without any real answers, and almost ten months later, it seemed no word would ever come. Then right before Thanksgiving, Etta walked to the mailbox that sat at the river's edge. It was the only post office in the entire country that delivered its mail by boat. This little aluminum fishing skiff stopped at the riverbank houses. It was a forgotten piece of river steamer lore that had been preserved.

Inside the mosaic mailbox was a single piece of mail. It was a Taos ski lodge envelope with a dark blue mountain emblem in the upper left hand corner with the words Broad Mountain underneath in raised block letters.

Scribbled in this uneven, though familiar, hand was a brief message on a single sheet of paper that simply said, "Etta, I'm sorry." Nothing more had been written, not even a signature. She put the stationery and torn envelope in her suit jacket pocket and kept her hand on it, a sort of protective gesture until she was safely back inside the house.

Etta sat down at the dining room table and removed the cryptic note once again, and she wept for a moment, though only a moment. This coming Sunday she would cross the causeway and attend Mass at the Cathedral. It would help her to forgive and forget.

How had time escaped her since her husband left? It had circled around and around and fed upon itself. What part had she played in turning him away? Etta had done nothing wrong but be herself, the same woman she always was, needy when it came to family certainly, though never selfish. But always her, the same woman.

266

She didn't know much about his affair with her youngest sister Maggie. How could she? It all became so shameful when she learned of the betrayal, as it was so unexpected.

The story came to her long after his disappearance, maybe six months after he left her without a word. It came from a conversation with a friend who had heard it from someone else who had seen him with Maggie in New Orleans. They were intimate on some rooftop in the French Quarter. Then the deceit began to fall into place for her, and she remembered the looks, and those hugs that seemed to last too long with her youngest sister. She remembered the countless dinners in New Orleans, and the subtle connection between the two of them. It was there. How could she have missed those obvious signs of their involvement? It was right there within plain sight though she missed the evidence: the constant embraces, the lingering glances, how he rested his fingers on her sister's cheek.

People want to hurt others, that is why these stories were told to her. Did they think that uncovering this incest, if that's the right word, would now make her feel better? Was it to somehow justify her grief for an abandoned marriage? It became a horror for her.

Etta got up from the table and crumpled the note she had received in her strong hand and walked back down to the river dock. Her eyes had been full of salty tears, but she wiped them dry with the sleeve of her coat.

As she trod the path of flagstones to the water, she thought about the night they had met at Mardi Gras. He looked so gallant in his Navy officer's uniform, and his smile was so natural on that handsome face. They had the whole world in front of them, and they shared so much love, drinking from it deeply.

What had happened? How could they ever drift apart when they had so much to keep them together? Why? These weren't really questions to ask herself, no. They were riddles, and something to be calculated, like where you found missing words, and then filled in the blanks like a crossword.

Her sister Maggie had never spoken to her about this thing she had done, even after he left. Nothing was ever said or a single word was uttered. Was it out of fear, or mere shame that she had deceived someone who she supposedly loved her entire life? What a cruel punishment.

Etta stood on the blanched dock and looked at the waves of the muddy brown water slowly lap at the pilings below her feet. Would he ever return? Maybe he had left to simply lick his wounds, hide his great weakness, and would come back to ask her forgiveness. She felt the change of the gentle wind from north to south on the river as it caressed her smooth still girlish face, blowing wisps of dark hair into her eyes.

In her heart, Etta knew he would never return, and with that thought came a pain which seemed to grasp her entire body. She stood rigid on the lonely dock, looking out into the distance to the far shore. She glanced at the surface of the water as if it were some brown desert plateau she could walk across to the other side. Etta thought about how God had parted the Red Sea to save his chosen people from the Pharaoh's army.

She heard thunder in the Gulf skies. A storm was on its way and a bolt of lightning flashed across the sky like a swift sword then there was a second crack. In another few seconds, she felt the lightest of rain touch her face and looked upward into the torrent as the rain increased in earnest.

Soon her hair was wet, but she didn't move from the dock. Instead she held up both her arms and welcomed the rain into her life. She was parting her own sea, and though she wasn't happy there was no frown on her face either.

She said to the dark rainy heavens, "I commend my spirit onto you to do what you will," and expected no answer.

Etta looked again at the note she received from him that she held tightly in her hand. Suddenly like a major league baseball pitcher throwing his fastest pitch to the waiting batter, she heaved it into the anonymous water. Afterward she stood on the dock as the swift current took it away out of sight. As the rain continued to pelt the paper, it grew heavy and soon sank till there was nothing of her past left, nothing.

Slowly, Etta turned and walked up to the house without glancing back. She took off her wet clothes, and in the bathroom prepared a hot bath. Standing in the front doorway in her bathrobe she could see the storm had finished, and the sun began to peak through the clouds.

In a little less than a year, people started to notice her with the Point Clear Episcopal rector at occasional dinners in Fairhope. They were often at the nearby Tin Roof or the Wash House restaurants too, and sometimes at Sunday brunch at The Grand Hotel where they had a table on the waterfront.

There was a rumor she had removed her wedding ring, and Etta had been seen holding his chubby hand following a Sunday service in the church garden.

Naturally, some people she knew disapproved of this because after all, Mobile was a Catholic town. But he was high church, and anyway, those same priests were jokingly called cocktail Catholics. She hadn't even bothered with a divorce, and maybe that might never happen. Etta hadn't given it much thought.

When you're Catholic, you marry once in a lifetime, and perhaps that was enough, really. Her faith was staunch, even now, perhaps more than ever.

Of course, there was her sister Mary Agnes who never had much faith in the church. It was Etta who had arranged for her annulment, even with a young daughter, because of the unusual criminal circumstances with Aaron. The Cathedral dean, now the bishop, had seen to it in Rome, the sweet man.

You could always count on those Jesuits to do the right thing.

## Acknowledgements

I'd like to thank the many friends I've made over the years in Alabama and for the delightful tales they've told me of this magical coast. Graham Timbes and Maggie Mosteller-Timbes together convinced me storytelling is indeed alive.

Bruce Colbert is an actor, filmmaker and author of ten books, most recently the novel, *In the Blood*. A wartime Navy veteran and ocean sailor, he lives on the Alabama gulf coast.

www.ingramcontent.com/pod-product-compliance
Lightning Source LLC
Chambersburg PA
CBHW030655260626
47157CB00007B/2667